The Tamar Black Saga - Book Six

BY NICOLA RHODES

ISBN: 978-0-9561495-6-5

'They'd be bound to notice,' he said.

'Ha!' said Tamar. 'Most humans wouldn't notice if I turned into a hippopotamus right in front of them. They'd make up some explanation for it, or pretend it didn't happen. People have some pretty sophisticated shielding in their heads to stop them from seeing what's really going on around them. It's to stop their tiny brains from imploding – no offence.'

'Bound to notice,' repeated Denny, ignoring this, 'then we'd not only have the police after us, but we'd have reporters camping out on the doorstep twenty four hours a day and government types in big shiny cars with blacked out windows stalking us.'

'It'll never happen, I'm telling you. Never!'

From Tamar Black – Djinnx'd.

"Always consider the possibility that you might be dead wrong."

Source unknown.

~ Chapter One ~

DENNY PEERED ROUND the curtain and sighed. 'Tamar?' he called.

'I'm washing my hair,'

'*Washing her hair*?' thought Denny. 'What next, taking out the rubbish bags?' If this went on, she would be wanting to get a dog next. She might even take up gardening or get a *job*. He would not put anything past her. Ever since she had agreed to marry him, she had been on this "normality" kick. No more magic unless absolutely necessary. And everything Tamar did, she did thoroughly, even obsessively. It was really getting on his nerves.

*

She had discovered the delights of shopping, of taking three and a half hours to get ready to go out (Denny had timed her – it was always exactly this long to the minute) of long hot bubble baths. Denny blamed Cindy; she had started all this. But, as usual, Tamar had taken it to extremes. She was going to be a wife (fittings for the wedding dress were taking up several hours a week) and wives cooked (watching Tamar trying to boil an egg was one of the most painful things Denny had ever witnessed) wives hoovered and dusted and arranged flowers in pretty vases. Besides, Tamar had got the idea from somewhere that Denny wanted a normal lifestyle.

There was just one problem with that.

'They've found us again,' Denny yelled. He banged on the bathroom door.

'What already?' Tamar came out of the bathroom towelling her head. 'They're getting better. It's only taken them a week this time.'

'All the usual suspects,' said Denny. 'News crews, reporters and that blacked out car that just sits there. I don't like that one, could be the government.'

'Don't they park across the road in a telecommunications van disguised as a pizza delivery van or something?' asked Tamar in all seriousness.

'Not pizza,' said Denny. 'Even the densest suspect is going to wonder about a pizza delivery that takes all day. More likely plumbers or electricians or something like that … What am I saying? Who cares? We have to move house again, and I must say, I'm getting pretty sick of … Don't do that without warning me first.'

The house had moved suddenly, leaving Denny's stomach behind it apparently.

'I wonder how they keep finding us,' he said.

Tamar shrugged. 'I'm going to do a face mask,' she said. 'For my skin,' she added.

'But you have perfect skin,' said Denny in exasperation, '*all* the time. You don't *need* a face mask. What's a face mask?'

'And then I might go shopping later,' she said apparently not hearing him.

Denny gave in. She was enjoying this, he realised; it was fun for her. And who was he to stand in her way? She would get fed up with it sooner or later anyway.

He returned his attention to the blacked out car that was apparently stalking them. Perhaps Tamar was right to be acting like an ordinary person; it might allay suspicions. On the other hand … she was so bad at it, who did she think she was fooling?'

* * *

'Target is in The Body Shop,' said the tinny voice over the Directors radio transmitter.

The Director sighed. 'Who does she think she's fooling?' he said.

'Sir?' came the voice.

'Oh – nothing,' said the Director hurriedly.

Special Agent Dawber looked at his partner, puzzled. His partner Special Agent Rook shrugged. The Director was known for his eccentricities; it was a standing joke among veteran agents, but Dawber was new; new and keen. It was the reason he had been given this assignment. He would get used to the Director in time, Rook reasoned.

This assignment, which had been given top priority, was puzzling them both though. What was so damn important about watching some girl going shopping and playing in the garden with what the agents assumed were her nephews. Twin boys aged about two or three – nice little kids, but not any apparent threat to national security.

There were always reporters and TV people around the house too, but the agents had no idea why. Classified apparently, which was ridiculous when you thought about it, they obviously were being kept in the dark about something the whole world probably knew. The agents were not allowed to talk to them even though this might have been of some help in their investigation. Knowing exactly *what* they were investigating would have been a help to their investigation, if it came to that.

There were other people in the house too. A young man, an older man – who came and went, and sometimes was not around for weeks, another two women, one of whom was apparently the mother of the twin boys, and another … man? He *had* to be a man; the children called him Daddy and he was assembled like a man, only… well, it was weird that was all. If it had not been an invitation to ridicule, Dawber would have said he was not human.

Sometimes, he had the feeling that Rook knew a lot more about the occupants of the house than he did. But if he did, he was not saying anything.

In any case, they both agreed that it was an odd set up; them all living together like that, like a commune or a cult (a highly select cult). But it did not seem sinister to Dawber. It all seemed completely pointless actually. He wondered if he was being taught something. And Rook? Perhaps he had been palmed off on this detail as a punishment for something.

'She certainly is good looking,' said Rook as Tamar appeared back on the street. He had said this at least a hundred times, and although Dawber agreed with him (it would be hard not to) he could not really summon up an enthusiastic answer.

He said. 'Mmm, yeah.' And turned back to his notes. She may have been attractive, but, in Dawber's opinion, she was the most boring woman who ever lived. All she ever did was shop and have facials or sit in the garden under an enormous sunshade. A "lady who lunched", that was what she was, a member of a privileged class whose main aim in life was to look good and spend money. Only her eccentric living arrangements made her any different from a thousand others like her. Dawber would not have given her the time of day.

'She's headed for the bridal shop,' said Rook. 'Look sharp.'

'What, *again*?' moaned Dawber. 'How many fittings does one wedding dress need for god's sake?'

'Ah, said Rook (a much married man) knowingly. 'We are mere men you know. We don't understand these things.'

'I understand that if it doesn't fit her by now, it never will,' snapped Dawber.

'She probably just likes trying it on,' said Rook. 'Women are like that you know?'

'Have you seen the groom?' said Dawber. They both laughed. 'Nothing on earth will ever make *him* look well-groomed,' said Dawber. 'He looks like a scarecrow that lives in a dustbin.' He glanced in the mirror at his own immaculate appearance and smiled smugly at himself.

'She'll tidy him up,' said Rook tapping his nose calculatingly. 'You've heard the old saying. "Aisle, altar, hymn"

They both laughed again. They were not particularly nasty men normally, but they were bored beyond endurance and, in those circumstances, people will do *anything* for a laugh.

They waited for an hour outside the bridal shop before they realised that somehow, *again*, they had missed her leaving. This was not good enough. The Director had been pretty understanding about this so far, but even his patience had limits. How was she doing it? They speculated that she was leaving the bridal shop (it was always here that they lost her) by a back entrance, but why? She couldn't *know* they were there, *could* she? They were certain they had not been seen.

Without a word, Rook swung the car around and drove at top speed back to the house, but it was too late, the house, gardens and all, was gone.

Again!

* * *

The man known to his subordinates only as The Director (hence the capital letters) sat in his office. It was not a large office; it was not a plush office; it was a *working* office. Few people had ever seen it, and this was deliberate. He had a fancy office downtown, but he never did any work there.

This office was furnished with a desk; it was made of cheap pine, as was the folding chair that sat behind it. It had five phones on the top and a large mat covered in coffee rings. Nothing else.

Behind the desk was an old fashioned white board. There was a map pinned to it. The map was of an island in the pacific. The Director just liked it. He thought he might go there one day, if he ever had time.

The Director swung the board around to reveal the back, there were names written on it in black. The Director gazed at them in perplexity as he often did when he had nothing else to do.

1 <u>Denis Sanger</u> (Denny) age 28 born Hounslow. One brother, parents dead. Formerly employed "Disc Harmony" record store, currently unemployed.

2 <u>John Andrew Stiles</u> (Jack) age 47 born London. No siblings. Widower. Formerly employed Scotland Yard. Currently – private detective based in London.

3 <u>Cynthia Pittencherry </u>(Cindy) age (probably) 43, formerly self-employed as new age healer/ chiropractor. Currently unemployed.

4 <u>Hecaté</u>. No last name. Age unknown. Background unknown???

5 <u>Finlay Varrens</u>. Age 49? (Estimated) background unknown (possibly of Romany gypsy stock – unverified)

A strange bunch, he often thought; not a man jack of them in a proper job. 'Private detective my ...' {deleted expletive}* and hardly any authenticated background information on any of them.

*[The Director had a problem with curse words in that he did not know any.]

But all this was nothing when you looked at the last entry.

6 <u>Tamar Black</u>. Estimated age – 5000 years.

The Director spent hours at a time just staring at this last entry. There could be no doubt about it; it had been authenticated by... experts. Well one expert anyway. But he was ... specially trained.

No, there was no doubt about it but ... Five thousand *years*? *Five* thousand? Five *thousand*???

And she did not look a day over twenty.

* * *

Special Agent Dawber was trying to sleep. It was not easy. Even if he had been in a normal frame of mind, the motel beds seemed specially designed to be as uncomfortable as possible. He pondered about this for a while; it did not make sense, not if the place wanted any kind of repeat business. But then again, the proprietor had been the kind of hotelier who looks upon guests as a nuisance. Having stayed at a myriad of these places (he had forgotten what his own bed even *looked* like) he had met her type before.

His mind, despite his best efforts, swung back to the events of the day.

He remembered Rook driving like a maniac back to the house and ... and ... he remembered the debriefing in The Director's office. He remembered *telling* The Director how they had followed her back and what she had done for the rest of the day. It was just that he could not remember any of it actually *happening*.

He had a feeling that there was something he had forgotten, something that had happened, something that had happened before, and that, when it happened, he *remembered* that it had happened before. But then, afterwards, he did not.

What's more, he was now certain that Rook *knew*. Knew *what* exactly he could not be sure, he could not remember; but knew anyway, just knew ... *something* in a general way that *he* did not know. Only he *did* know it, or he should, if he could only remember it.

This sort of thing can make a man extremely paranoid, particularly when that man worked for "The Agency".

No wonder he could not sleep.

Rook was on the radio to The Director's office. 'He's getting suspicious sir,' he was saying. 'Perhaps we should let him in on it.'

There was a muffled sound from the other end in a tone of denial.

'Yes sir, but he's a good man, I'm sure that … yes sir, but we can't keep doing it to him is what I'm saying, it's not right sir.

Crackle, crackle, mumble, mumble.

'Yes sir,' said Rook in a resigned tone. 'I understand sir. But he's a bright lad sir, he'll figure it out eventually, he's already… Sir? Sir? *Damn!*

'And goodnight to you too sir … you bastard,' he added once he was sure the connection had been broken.

* * *

Tamar was painting her toenails in the kitchen. Denny watched her in bemusement from behind a magazine about fishing. He was not remotely interested in fishing, but he had needed something to hide behind, and it had been left behind by Finvarra whose interests were wide and varied. In fact, the man seemed fascinated by *everything*. Denny had once caught him reading an enormous tome entitled "Famous Dogs in Brothels in the 19th Century" with every sign of enjoyment. Perhaps there were pictures.

The hiding was to appear as if he was occupied in something other than watching Tamar. He suspected that he was not fooling her, but ever since she had decided to be "normal", he had felt an inexplicable need to "keep an eye on her". In case of what, he had no idea, after all, she was still the same underneath, that is, well able to take care of herself in practicality any situation you could possibly think of and many others that no one (at least no one in a normal frame of mind) would *ever* think of in a million years.

She thrust a toe up under the magazine cover and nearly took his eye out. 'What do you think?' she said, 'passion pink.'

'I don't like it,' said Denny cruelly, 'too bright.'

Tamar pouted. 'Not like you then,' she said acidly. 'I mean who do you think you're kidding? A *fishing* magazine? I don't need a baby sitter you know.

'Or a keeper,' she added after a moment's thought. 'I'm not losing my mind you know.'

'Depends on your point of view,' muttered Denny. 'Who do you think *you're* kidding?' he said louder.

'Oh … shut up,' snapped Tamar and flounced off leaving bright pink stains from her wet toenails on the kitchen floor.

Denny sighed. It was already happening, he thought. No sex and lots more arguments and they were not even married yet.

Stiles poked his head round the kitchen door. 'You shouldn't have criticised the nail polish mate,' he advised.

Denny raised an eyebrow. 'You heard?' he said.

'Yep,' affirmed Stiles.

'God save us from policemen,' said Denny. 'There's no damn privacy around here.' But he did not sound angry, just weary.

Stiles patted him awkwardly on the shoulder. 'It's just cold feet,' he said. 'Best to let her get it out of her system. It'll be all right after the wedding. They all act like this, you know, weird. Things'll settle down, you'll see.'

'*I* haven't got cold feet,' said Denny. 'Why has *she*? I mean we've lived together for five years …'

'Yeah, but you … You're more laid back than she is, you never let anything bother you much. And besides …'

'That's not true,' objected Denny. 'I get wound up too. This whole "being normal" thing is really pissing me off.'

'Have you told *her* that?'

'We-ell, no not exactly. I mean I thought, like you said, that she'd get over it. Anyway, what's that got to do with her having cold feet?'

'It's just her way of dealing with it.' said Stiles. 'I wonder why it bothers you so much,' he added.

Denny shrugged. 'She *isn't* normal, why pretend?'

'You'd have to ask her that,' said Stiles, getting a beer for Denny from the fridge.

'Do you think she's changed her mind, you know, about getting married?' said Denny hesitantly.

'*God* no,' said Stiles emphatically. 'She wouldn't be so damn nervous if she had. She'd just *say* so. You know Tamar.'

'I *thought* I did,' said Denny sadly.

* * *

Tamar was upset too. She did not cry when she was upset – she shouted. Cindy wished she had earplugs; it was not as if she would not still be able to hear her.

'I mean, what's the *matter* with him?' ranted Tamar. 'I thought he *wanted* a normal life, and there was no need for him to be so horrible to me, *was* there?' she demanded, glaring at Cindy, who nodded sympathetically.

'I mean, I never knew he could be such a … maybe I've made a mistake. I should never have said "yes" not if it's going to be like *this*.' she stopped. 'No, I didn't mean that,' she said seriously.

Then she grinned impishly at Cindy, as her sense of humour reasserted itself. 'You can't have him,' she said.

They both laughed. Cindy's laughter sounded a little forced. She sometimes wondered how much Tamar knew about her feelings for Denny. Not that she was not over it now of course. But there had been a time … not now, she thought giving herself a mental shake. She had to help Tamar fix this. If she did not, it would be like admitting that *she* wanted Denny; and she did not, not any more. Definitely not!

Tamar watched the expressions flit over Cindy's face, shrewdly. She knew very well what was going on in Cindy's head. 'I expect you think I should be grateful to have him,' she observed.

'You are I think,' said Cindy, 'really. It's just that … Well, it's not that easy sometimes. If he's acting like a prat, why don't you just tell him?'

Tamar shrugged. 'More arguments,' she said.

'Or possibly less,' suggested Cindy.

Tamar looked thoughtful.

~ Chapter Two ~

THERE WAS A gentle scratching on the bedroom door; both women's heads turned instinctively. Cindy raised her eyebrows; it was not like Denny to knock on his own door, but who else could it be? The same thought had obviously occurred to Tamar; she looked at the door in a puzzled fashion. Cindy shrugged, and Tamar went and opened the door. It was Stiles, looking extremely embarrassed.

He coughed self-consciously. 'Er, sorry,' he began. 'I just thought … never mind eh, I'll come back later.'

'Did Denny send you?' demanded Tamar sharply, but Stiles detected a hint of hope in her voice.

'Not exactly,' he admitted. 'He's pretty upset,' he added. 'I thought maybe … probably not though.' he shrugged helplessly. 'Women are better at this sort of thing,' he ended, looking at Cindy.

Tamar made a decision. 'I think I'll go and talk to him,' she said to the relief of both Stiles and Cindy.

* * *

Agent Dawber shaved carefully in the tiny mirror and stared unwillingly at his own reflection. What he saw, so he believed, was a sucker, a pawn, a pigeon, a fool, a sap and a dupe. But no more, he decided. Today he was going to tackle Rook about what was really going on. He squared his chin and immediately regretted it; it not being a good idea to do this when holding a blade against your face. However, the cut was not deep, and Dawber dealt calmly enough with it then he dressed and stood before the tiny mirror again to straighten his tie and square his shoulders determinedly.

He frowned at his reflection. 'No more mister nice guy,' he asserted and marched from the room stiffly, like a cat when facing a particularly large dog.

Rook was also facing himself in the mirror. He had, if Dawber had only known it, made a decision of his own during the night. He had had enough. Enough of the Agency's underhanded tactics and habitual mistrust of its own recruits. Enough of lying to Agents less senior to himself, and enough of the puzzled look on Agent Dawber's face after every briefing with The Director.

Agent Dawber was not a fool and Agent Rook was sick and tired of treating him like one.

Agent Dawber came into the room at that moment looking determined. Rook had seen that look before. Usually he would have handled this situation differently. He had had years of practice at making a rookie agent calm down and eventually admit that maybe he was getting a little paranoid. That not everybody was cut out for the Agency, the long hours took a toll on the mind and perhaps he *should* take a little holiday, etc. etc.

This time he merely said. 'You want to know what's going on?'

Agent Dawber, who had not even had time to open his mouth, gaped for a second. Then he recovered sufficiently to stammer. 'Y-you're damned right I w-want to know what's going on.'

'Sit down,' commanded Rook, 'and get ready for the weirdest story you ever heard – I guarantee it.'

* * *

The argument could be heard all over the house. Cindy held the boys on her bed, an arm around each of them, they were crying. Finvarra had gone out as soon as it began and Stiles and Hecaté were debating whether or not to interfere before they killed each other.

Tamar had not meant to start a fight. She had descended the stairs calmly, and had been rationally marshalling her thoughts, when she noticed a newspaper on the mat as she passed. Automatically, she picked it up and read the headline. In a normal frame of mind, she would have been amused by it – even now, anger and humour were combating for possession of her features – it was, after all, only a rag sheet, a supermarket gossipy thing. She ought to have wondered who had delivered it, and why. But it never crossed her mind.

Denny was still in the kitchen. Tamar stormed in and slapped the paper down in front of him knocking over his beer. 'Have you seen this?' she demanded.

Denny looked down bemusedly at the paper. His eyes widened as he saw…

THE ENQUIRER

Is Denny Sanger the sexiest man in the world?

'How did they get a picture of you?' snapped Tamar. 'You were supposed to be being careful.'

'I'm not sure they did,' said Denny diffidently, examining the tiny blurry and pixelated image. 'This could be of anyone.'

'It's you all right,' snapped Tamar. Then she conceded. 'Or perhaps David Beckham,'

'Or anyone else with blond hair,' supplied Denny. 'Such is fame.' He grinned. 'I don't look anything like David Beckham,' he added.

'I suppose it could have been worse,' said Tamar not bothering to mention that that had been her point. 'It could have been me.'

'You don't look anything like me either,' said Denny with another grin.

'I never imagined that we would end up practically famous,' said Tamar, ignoring this. Sometimes Denny's sense of humour annoyed her, at least at times like this when she considered it inappropriate.

'Just as long as you don't bring out a fitness video,' said Denny. 'That really would be false advertising. Nobody in the world could ever look like you, no matter how many crunches they did.'

This time Tamar did smile. And it might have all ended peacefully there if Tamar had not walked over to the sink and started rattling dishes.

Denny snapped. He clicked his fingers and the dishes vanished.

'What did you do that for?' Tamar turned on him.

'Because I *can*!' said Denny angrily. 'And so can you. If you must know, I'm bloody sick of all this pretending to be ordinary. You are *anything* but ordinary, and I like you that way.'

'And if I *had* no powers?'

'That'd be different.'

'How exactly?' she asked sardonically.

'You wouldn't be pretending. It's all a game to you, a bloody silly, boring game. I'm getting really fed up with it.'

'Fed up with *me,* you mean?'

That had been half an hour ago and now the fur was really flying. The house was shaking as they threw lightning bolts at the furniture and Tamar screamed. 'How do you like me now? Nothing ordinary about *that* was there?'

'Your aim's bad,' countered Denny sneeringly. 'You haven't hit me once.'

She hit him hard in the chest and flung him across the room. But even in the midst of the raging fury that had taken possession of Denny, he still could not bring himself to retaliate with a like action. He missed her by inches sending her diving for the floor, but she was unhurt.

'STOP IT RIGHT NOW! ARE YOU TRYING TO KILL EACH OTHER?' In the doorway, taking his life into his hands, was Stiles.

There was a silence before Stiles continued in the same bellowing tones. 'YOU'RE FRIGHTNING CINDY'S KIDS AND I HAVE AN ALMIGHTY HEADACHE. OTHER PEOPLE LIVE HERE TOO, YOU KNOW. YOU MIGHT HAVE A BIT OF CONSIDERATION INSTEAD OF ACTING LIKE TWO-YEAR OLDS. SORT IT OUT AND THAT'S AN ORDER.' He stomped out of the room.

'I guess that told us,' said Denny rubbing his head ruefully.

'I've never seen him so angry,' said Tamar, awed. 'I've never seen *you* so angry either actually,' she added.

Denny maintained a tactful silence here. He *had* seen Tamar this angry before, many times, just never with him.

'He's got a pretty loud voice when he wants,' she continued. 'I don't think I've ever heard him shouting before.'

'He had good reason, don't you think?' said Denny. 'We *were* pretty awful. I mean just look at this mess.' He indicated the destroyed kitchen.

'I'll get a dustpan and brush,' said Tamar. But Denny assumed she was joking and held his peace.

He did, however, wave a hand and clear away most of the rubble, just in case she was not.

Tamar sat down on the floor suddenly looking defeated. 'How did it get like this?' she said.

Denny knelt down beside her and took her hands gently. 'Why don't we talk about it and find out.' he suggested.

'I wouldn't have killed you,' she said suddenly.

Denny's eyebrows shot up. 'I know,' he said. But it should not have needed saying, he thought, feeling slightly disturbed. This was worse than he had realised. For the first time since they had met, Tamar felt like a stranger. Would they, he wondered uneasily, ever be able to bridge the gap that had sprung up between them so suddenly?

* * *

A frigid silence had descended over the house. Denny and Tamar had, by tacit agreement, decided to keep away from each other at least for a few days. In a smaller house, he would have been sleeping on the sofa. As it was, he moved his few possessions into a spare room on the same floor. There was a dull ache in his chest that he recognised as a breaking heart. He did not know how to go back, he wished he did. He would have done anything.

Tamar was feeling bad too, but somewhere inside her was the unquestioned assumption that she could somehow fix this. What she was mostly feeling was frustration that she had not yet figured out how. But she did not doubt that she would. It was her unshakable belief that she could fix *anything*.

It was Stiles's contention that nothing would be fixed unless they talked, as he tried to tell them both.

'But every time we try, we end up fighting,' argued Tamar. 'I just can't reason with him.'

'What are you, my dad?' was all that Denny had to say about it.

Cindy, despite her still unresolved feelings about Denny, was distressed by the turn matters had now taken. She tried, unsuccessfully, to ignore the situation as much as possible, feeling that she was neither qualified nor impartial enough to interfere. Hecaté had no such reservations, and was resolving that a month on a desert island was what they both needed when matters suddenly came to a head in an unforeseen and abrupt way.

The atmosphere in the house was nearly normal again, at least on the surface, when they had some unexpected visitors.

The two agents stood rather awkwardly on the front doorstep while Tamar, Denny, Stiles and Cindy appraised them intently.

Tamar was the first to speak. 'Well,' she said, drawing on her experience of Denny's favoured viewing habits. 'If it isn't Mulder and Scully.' she glanced at Denny for confirmation that she had the names correct, but he remained impassive, his eyes flinty and cold.

'He's Scully,' said the older agent pointing at his companion who shrugged bemusedly, he had clearly never heard of the X Files.

A spark of amusement flickered in Denny's eyes for a moment, but only Tamar, who was watching him closely, observed it.

'Agent Dawber,' the younger agent, who had been designated "Scully", introduced himself. He looked as if he was in the middle of a particularly incoherent yet convincing nightmare.

Denny sympathised, but did not show it.

'Rook,' said the older agent curtly. 'Can we come in?'

'What do you want?' said Denny. He sensed a threat here, if not to his person then at least to his peace of mind.

'To come in,' said Rook cagily. He seemed nervous; at least, he kept looking behind him as if he expected to see something unpleasant following him.

'*No!*' said Denny more forcefully than he had intended. Tamar looked curiously at him. 'What can it hurt?' she asked. 'I want to know why they've been following us about.'

'I just don't want them here,' said Denny stubbornly. 'We've got enough trouble as it is, they could be more.' Even as he said it, he knew he was wasting his breath. Tamar never took advice, even from him.

But this time Tamar hesitated. Things were bad enough between Denny and herself at the moment. 'Well,' she began 'if you really think ...'

Agent Dawber bobbed forward. It's important,' he hissed. 'And we need to talk privately.'

'Before all the soddin' press turn up,' said the one called Rook meaningfully. 'We've noticed they always seem to find you too.'

'They're probably following *you*,' said Denny. After all, *we* aren't anybody. Maybe they want to make you a film star,' he added caustically noting the younger agent's immaculate appearance. Behind him, he heard Cindy giggle.

Then Tamar lost patience. 'Oh come in then,' she said and stood back from the door. Denny did not move.

The agents moved forward hesitantly and Denny eventually moved casually aside without taking his eyes off them. The two men shuffled in hastily under his gimlet like gaze; neither of them met his eye. Up close, this apparently scruffy and unimpressive "boy" as they had thought him, was incredibly intimidating.

Agent Dawber, in particular, hoped that he would take his disapproval to the extreme of leaving them alone with Tamar. But Denny had no intention of doing any such thing. He propelled them firmly into a study and ordered them to sit down. 'All right, he said. 'What do you want?'

Tamar stood behind him smiling but saying nothing. She was remembering in exact detail a conversation that had taken place between her and Denny not long after they had first met.

'Always consider the possibility that you might be dead wrong,' she muttered under her breath.

If Denny heard her, he gave no sign of it.

'Well?' he said, as the intimidated agents quailed in their seats.

'We work for a government agency,' said Rook eventually. 'You might say *the* government agency actually, but we can't tell you any more than that at the moment, not unless …'

'Unless what? Denny's voice grated harshly across the agent's.

'We've been sent here to recruit you,' said Dawber. 'All of you really, or as many of you as are willing.' He looked at Tamar.

'What you *mean*,' cut in Stiles. 'Is that you want Tamar, but you'll take the rest of us if you have to.'

'Not at all,' said Rook smoothly. 'We know who you are, who you all are; and we are aware that you all possess remarkable talents that our agency can use.'

'Keep dreaming,' said Denny 'there's no way …'

But Tamar nudged him. And he heard her thoughts clearly in his head, as he had not done for some time. *'Say yes, or at least maybe. We can find out who they are then, what this agency is ...'*

'Who cares?' Denny's thought flashed back.

'I do.'

'You're going to have to tell us more than you have if we're even going to consider it.' Denny temporised, knowing that if he did not say it Tamar would, and a whole lot more besides.

'What *do* you know about us?' asked Cindy with just a tinge of concern in her voice. Denny gave her an approving look, which set Tamar's teeth on edge.

'Everything,' said Rook meaningfully. Which was not entirely true, but they, or rather, The Director, knew enough.

'Are you really five thousand years old?' asked Dawber naïvely.

Tamar gave a start.

'It's not polite to ask a lady her age,' said Cindy, unexpectedly rescuing her from having to answer.

'Sorry,' muttered Dawber looking at his lap. This was all a bit much for him really.

'We *know* she is,' said Rook firmly. 'Really "Scully", don't ask stupid questions.'

'Just like we know that you defeated the Queen of the Sidhe and rescued all those children,' he added.

This was, in a way, common knowledge. At least it had been in all the papers in one form or another. But all the same, it was disquieting to hear in such matter of fact tones.

'We aren't going to get out of here alive are we?' said Agent Dawber looking at the angry, astonished faces surrounding him.

'Don't be silly,' said Denny. 'We don't kill people.'

'Well, *he* doesn't,' said Tamar wickedly. 'I might.'

'I might be persuaded, myself,' put in Stiles, 'given enough provocation.'

'Well, I *wouldn't*,' said Cindy positively. 'But I have no objections to turning them into toads or something.'

'Chickens,' muttered Tamar. 'Or puffins maybe,'

Denny allowed himself a smile.

'Your situation is not a good one,' he told the agents. 'I'd start talking if I were you.'

The agents looked at each other for the first time. Each was thinking the same thing. They had not been told nearly enough about what they would be getting into here. Someone was going to pay for this. But in the meantime …

'We'll talk,' said Rook. 'It's why we came.'

~ Chapter Three ~

CINDY AND STILES were talking in the conservatory. There was a definite air of conspiracy in this, as it was the only part of the house that could be relied upon never to contain either Tamar or Denny. Both were allergic to having glass all around them. Tamar, because it reminded her of living in a bottle, and Denny, because of its reflective qualities. Denny avoided any surface that might contain a reflection as assiduously as any vampire could.

'I don't like it,' said Stiles. 'All that stuff about secret government agencies – secret *world* government agencies – and probing into the supernatural. That's *our* job.'

'I think that was their point,' said Cindy. 'Tamar was far too interested if you ask me,' she added.

'I noticed that too,' said Stiles. 'And with things as they are … you don't think she would …?'

'She *has* been going on lately about getting a *job*,' Cindy said this last word disdainfully. 'In my opinion, that's going *too* far.'

'And she isn't the type to take just *any* job,' said Stiles thoughtfully.

'Time was, she'd have left those two in a dormant volcano somewhere, and that would have been that,' said Cindy. 'But she actually listened to them. *Politely.*' She shook her head.

'I think we need to talk to Denny,' said Stiles.

'What does Hecaté think?' asked Cindy curiously. She thought it was odd that he had chosen to talk to her about this and not his wife.

Stiles shook his head. 'She's not human, like us,' he said. 'She tries, but she really doesn't understand this sort of thing. It's not how gods behave apparently. Besides, you've been talking to Tamar a lot lately. I just wondered what you thought. As it turns out, you think pretty much what I do.'

Cindy sighed. 'It's all such a shame,' she said. 'If two people were ever made for each other ...'

Stiles nodded. 'It's funny really, I mean they've never fallen out like this before,' he said.

'I never thought they would,' said Cindy. 'Not them, not Tamar and Denny. It makes you wonder ...'

'If there's more to it?' said Stiles.

'So many weird things happen around here,' she said. 'You never know.'

'Magic you mean? Can magic do that sort of thing, break people up like that?'

'Ordinary people maybe,' said Cindy, 'but not those two. If someone was using magic on them, they'd know.'

'Oh.' Stiles was disappointed at this stark summation. He had momentarily entertained hopes of a conspiracy that he could unmask and save the day. His life in recent years had prepared him for this type of eventuality. But it seemed that there was no sinister puppet master in this case. Only puppets, being blown this way and that by their own volatile emotions. This was not his area; he doubted that it was anybody's.*

*[Stiles believed that psychiatrists were people who charged you $500 an hour to listen to you talk about your dreams because no one else would listen and then tell you it was all because of your mother anyway.]

'We need to talk to Denny,' he repeated.

'I don't think we'd be telling him anything that he doesn't already know,' said Cindy glumly.

* * *

Denny was reading a note:

Dear Denny,

It's not working is it? I need to get away for a while. I have no doubt that you could find me if you wanted to, but I think it would be a bad idea. Please just give me some time to figure out how to fix this. I'm not giving the ring back – not yet. I haven't given up – I <u>will</u> be back. I love you.

Tamar. X

For the moment, he was more puzzled than upset. It was her handwriting all right, but not written in her usual cryptic shorthand, and this was not like her – *any* of it. She *never* ran away from a problem. She confronted it head on (sometimes with disastrous results). Always! And if she *had* decided to leave, and he still could hardly believe it, it really was not like her to leave a *note*. She would have told him face to face … Wouldn't she? Or was he wrong? Did he not know her as well as he thought? It *was* her writing; he was sure it was.

Then suddenly the reality hit him; she was gone. There could be a dozen reasons for the note; it did not matter. The fact was, she was gone – really gone. The note, he now realised, had been written in a style meant to discourage him from looking for her. The explicit request *not* to look for her for one thing, the promise of return and the last line, meant to convey hope.

On the other hand, if she *said* she was coming back, then she was. He just had to wait.

He picked up the Athame, never very far away from him, and drove it, suddenly and viciously, through the palm of his hand.

* * *

There was an old-fashioned car travelling down a country lane. There was nothing unusual about this, apart from its occupants.

The driver, in a chauffeur's peaked cap and a stained T-shirt bearing the faded legend "Wolves do it doggy style", was lean, gaunt and rangy and extremely hirsute. He wore his hair long, his beard long and his eyebrows bushy, these last, lowering heavily over sharp yellow eyes. He was hunched over the steering wheel, his paws – sorry hands – gripping tightly and his head thrust forward as he continually swung it from side to side like a wary animal.

The passenger, seated in the back, was of such exceeding thinness that Denny would have looked like a wrestler by comparison. Wrapped in robes of dull grey from head to foot, it could have been either male or female. Only the barest hint of sharp pointed features were visible.

Without warning, the back seat passenger let out a sharp giggle, and the driver winced and cowered. He put his foot down and the elderly vehicle protested. It did not help; the passenger, displaying an agility that was clearly not human, leapt abruptly out of its seat and clambered out through the sunroof, flinging the robes away as it did so, revealing a long white sleeveless shift. Now it looked possibly female due to the long white blond hair that streamed behind the figure now swaying on the roof of the car with incredible balance. The driver sighed – *any minute now*.

A face, a beautiful yet androgynous face, appeared upside down in the windscreen; the driver reached for his sunglasses and put them on. A futile gesture. A skinny hand reached through the glass as if it were no more than mist and began clawing at the driver's face. The hand plucked the glasses away and scratched at the driver's eyes. It managed to extract an eye and the driver slammed the brakes on throwing the offending passenger several feet into a ditch.

'AA'll paay foor thaat laaterr,' he sighed, getting out of the car and sauntering with strange loping gait toward the prostrate figure.

He retrieved his eye from the side of the road and watched as his master picked himself up apparently unhurt and grinning. The figure definitely looked male now.

'Maake yoour miind uup' muttered the driver under his breath. But he bowed obsequiously as the figure approached.

'Fun eh?' said the person. 'Oh I *like* it in this place! Everything's so … so … *fun.*'

'Yaass,' agreed the driver, in tones that suggested that he thought it anything but.

'Seems almost a pity really,' said the other looking around, then added crisply, 'Come on Fulk, we have work to do.' He looked at his driver sternly. 'And if you ever do that again during a test I will personally rip out your entrails and use them for a hat, all right?'

Fulk bowed his head. 'Yaass maaster,' he said. He believed him. He still remembered what he had done to the unfortunate customs official when they had arrived off the boat in this benighted country.

'Good,' he said softly and then the face became feminine again. She smiled archly. 'Come on big boy,' she added roguishly. 'If you're good I'll let you have some fun later.'

Fulk grinned wolfishly. 'Yaass Missteress,' he said.

'Good boy.'

* * *

Tamar woke up in a darkened room. She was on the floor; there was no furniture, and there were blacked out glass windows all around her, she panicked and tried to teleport, but it did not work. Now she was really panicking; she began thumping on the glass.

A door opened, and a smooth looking man in a dark suit appeared and bowed courteously. 'I am sorry about the glass,' he said. 'We didn't think. I'm afraid the unnerving effects of being surrounded by glass on a former Djinn did not occur to my underlings.' He smiled at her face as he said these words.

'Oh yes,' he affirmed. 'We know who you are Miss – Black?' He looked mockingly at her.

Tamar raised a hand threateningly but the ball of lighting that she had expected to throw at this horrible smarmy man (who calls their employees *underlings*?) failed to materialise. She looked at her hand in confusion.

The man laughed. 'I'm afraid there's no magic here,' he said.

And Tamar realised that she must be in a pocket universe like Hank's forest or the Faerie realm. *Damn! These people, whoever they were, obviously knew their stuff.* But it did not explain how she had got here in the first place. The last thing she remembered was … was weird now she came to think of it. She refocussed on the immediate problem.

'I could still rip your arms off and stuff them down your neck,' she observed calmly.

'Yes,' he agreed. 'You could, but you won't.' he laughed a surprisingly high pitched, tinkly laugh that scraped across Tamar's nerves like a file.

They had been so afraid that something like this would happen again if they decided to get married. And now it had.

'What do you want with me anyway?' she asked suddenly. *Please not another "collector"*

The man seemed pleased. 'Ah, straight to the point,' he said rubbing his hands together.

'You might try the same,' said Tamar sourly.

'Well,' he said. 'You might say we need your expertise. We did try to recruit you, but now – you might say you've been drafted.'

'You make it sound like there's a war on.'

'Quite, quite,' said the man looking happier by the minute. 'That's exactly …'

'Quinlins!' A sharp voice came from the air. 'That will be enough, send her to me.'

'The Director wants to see you,' said the improbably named Quinlins seemingly unperturbed.

'I heard,' said Tamar. 'I'm not sure I want to see *him,* though.'

Two smartly dressed soldiers appeared in the doorway and saluted her respectfully. 'This way ma'am,' said one of them gesturing to the open doorway.

Tamar sighed. 'Why not,' she said. She turned back as she left the room with the soldiers and fixed Quinlins with an unfriendly eye. 'If I see *you* again,' she said. 'I'll snap your neck.' then she swept away haughtily.

'I'm not sure what you were trying to prove with that piece of bluster,' said The Director from behind his desk. 'Do sit down,' he added gesturing to the folding chair facing him.

'Not that I haven't felt the same way occasionally about Quinlins, a nasty little bureaucrat, but useful. Please *sit.*'

He said this last with such quiet force that it took all of Tamar's considerable willpower to prevent her legs from folding automatically under her. She remained standing her arms folded defiantly.

'God, if I were a younger man ...' said the Director appraising her approvingly. 'You're impressive. Quite magnificent really.'

She remembered coming across the two agents who had visited the house, the younger one (what was his name, Dobbins? Dawson?) had not seemed to recognize her. No, that wasn't it. They had been following her again, just as if they had never... and then ...

'We need your help,' said The Director cutting across her thoughts.

'You could have just *asked,*'

'We *did* ask. You refused.'

'Then I probably had a good reason, don't you think? What makes you think I'll ...?'

'One word,' snapped The Director. 'Curiosity.' He passed a hand over his face and smiled. 'What am I saying?' he said. 'I meant to say "blackmail".' He swung the board behind his desk revealing the list of names that had puzzled him for so long. The information on it was a lot more comprehensive now.

Tamar paled and sat down suddenly. 'How did you find out all that?'

'I know a lot more,' said The Director. 'But I do not intend to use it. Not unless I have to.' he leaned forward over the desk. 'We are not the bad guys Miss Black.'

Tamar was staring at the first entry.

Denis Sanger (Denny) … *Denny, Denny, Denny. Oh god, not Denny.*

'Denny will find me,' she asserted.

'He won't even *look* for you,' said the Director. 'Do you think we are such amateurs that we haven't thought of that. We have – *dealt* with him.'

'What have you done to him?' Tamar gasped gripped suddenly in a horrible nameless terror. After all these people had managed to kidnap *her*, they might be capable of anything.

'He's fine,' The Director assured her, 'but indifferent. He believes you have left him, that's all. I believe you have been having problems lately. Arguments and so forth?'

Tamar denied it instantly and vehemently. 'Where do you get your information?' she sneered with convincing scorn even though her heart had sunk. *They* had *been fighting – terribly, what if Denny... but he would never believe it; he would know she wouldn't just leave – wouldn't he? What if he didn't? What if he – horrible thought – was glad, or at least relieved, that she had gone?*

'I assure you,' The Director was saying, 'we are confident in the information our agents have supplied us with.

Those agents! Now she remembered. Dawber and Rook. She had been walking in the fields behind the house, just thinking, when she had spotted them again trying to keep out of sight, following her, and she had turned to confront them and ...

'Perhaps you would like a tour of our facility now Miss Black,' said The Director suddenly. 'I think if you knew what we do here, what we *really* do, you might be persuaded to join us without the need for all this distasteful cloak and dagger stuff.'

'X files,' said Tamar vaguely, her mind was elsewhere.

'Ha!' said The Director. 'If you like. The main difference being, we *know* what's going on out there. The truth, Miss Black, is not "out there", it's in here.' He tapped his head. 'And I'm pretty worried about it to tell you the truth.'

Tamar snapped back to attention. She was interested now, despite herself. 'Okay,' she said. 'Let's hear it then.'

'It would be easier to show you,' said The Director. 'If you would please come with me.'

Tamar rose to follow him, her curiosity rising.

* * *

'I'm not sure what to do,' Denny said, after the note had been read by Stiles and Cindy.

'*Do*?' erupted Stiles aghast. '*Do*?' he repeated. 'You go after her and bring her back that's what you *do* – for God's sake!' he passed a hand wearily over his forehead as if it hurt.

'She'll never forgive you if you don't,' put in Cindy sagely. 'I wouldn't.'

'So, it's a kind of test?' said Denny.

'Of course it is you maniac,' snapped Stiles. 'Haven't you learned *anything*?'

'But she doesn't say where she's gone,' said Denny.

'She doesn't have to,' said Stiles impatiently. 'As she pointed out herself in the note, you can find her anyway.'

'This could be a good sign actually,' said Cindy. 'Women don't pull this kind of thing unless they want some action. I mean she's testing you, to see if you still want to sort things out.'

'But she *knows* I do,' said Denny now hopelessly out of his depth.

'Women are not obliged to be logical,' said Stiles, earning himself a dirty look from Cindy.

'But Tamar always is,' pointed out Denny.

'Not about you,' said Cindy. 'You must have noticed.'

Denny shrugged. He ran a hand through his hair wearily and said. 'So you think I should go after her then?'

'*Yes*!' they both shouted at the same time.

'Even though she says not to?'

'*Yes*!'

Denny still looked unsure. He knew Tamar better than anyone else did and she was not given to playing games of this nature. She always said exactly what she meant and did exactly what she wanted to regardless of the consequences. On the other hand, there *was* something funny about the note, it just did not sound like her. If he tried to imagine her *saying* those things he just could not. He decided on a compromise. He would find her but not necessarily confront her yet. He made this decision in the full awareness that if she really did not want to be found, she would not be.

He concentrated, reaching out with his mind to her. After a few minutes, he relaxed and let out a sigh. Now he knew.

* * *

There had been something very strange about Agent Dawber's reaction when she had confronted him. Almost as if he had no memory of ever having been in her company. Agent Rook had looked uneasy and had tried steer his companion away.

'Stop following me, I already said no,' she had yelled, and the younger Agent had appeared confused. In exasperation, she had teleported away and then ...

'We have a number of elite teams in the field,' The Director was saying, 'we want you to lead our primary team.'

'I already have a team,' Tamar pointed out.

'And we want them also,' said The Director placatingly. 'But first, we decided, we would have to persuade *you* to join us. We had hoped that if you came on board they would follow you.'

Tamar was unsure of this; all her instincts told her not to believe too much that this man told her. 'You *had* hoped?' she said demonstrating her unerring knack of pouncing on the one thing in a statement that you hoped she would not notice.

However, The Director answered smoothly. 'Your boyfriend's attitude, so I am told, when approached was less than receptive. We have decided that he, at least, is independent of your influence, wouldn't you agree?'

Tamar reluctantly had to admit that this was true. She nodded shortly.

'A pity,' The Director continued. 'I had hoped he might also lead a team. He has qualities of his own; second only to your own.'

'Sexiest man in the world,' murmured Tamar.

'I was not referring to his attractions,' replied The Director, apparently hearing this. 'Nor yours for that matter,' he added as an afterthought. 'Ah, here we are.'

He showed her into a large room equipped like a cross between a laboratory and NASA mission control. Tamar's internal radar went on the alert at once. The room was dim, lighted only by banks of small computer monitors on benches, which blinked and hummed constantly, from a very large LCD screen across the back wall, and from small lights fixed above the laboratory equipment, which was set up on a long bench running along the adjacent wall. To Tamar it was a weird, alien world.

There were seven people in the room, four men and three women. Two of the men were working at computer consoles, as was one woman. Standard geeks, thought Tamar, who ought to have known better than to make snap judgements like that. Another man, extremely good looking with white blond hair and an air of extreme arrogance, was leaning back casually with his feet on a desk, one hand running through his hair the other hand contained a phone, into which he was talking animatedly. He looked like a stockbroker, but Tamar's sixth sense said "con man". She disliked him immediately. Two others, one man and one woman appeared to be soldiers, standing to attention at the opposite door. The last woman was more interesting. She was unquestionably a witch, but not like any witch Tamar had met personally. She was wearing a lab coat for one thing and wore her hair in a tight bun. Her face and hair looked faded like an old photograph from which the original colour had drained. She might have been a redhead once, and her eyes may have been blue, now the hair was sandy and the eyes grey. To the untrained eye she looked a lot like a high school science teacher. She was using the lab equipment to mix a potion or something like it. She looked up and smiled, the only one who did, Tamar smiled back, but she had reservations. These people did not look to her like a field unit. She wondered how any of them would handle an encounter with a werewolf, for example, or a vampire. She was willing to bet that not one of them had ever faced such an encounter. And there were worse things out there. She would rather have Denny at her back in that kind of a situation than any of these people. Especially that blond man, who looked as if he might crease up in a shower of rain; and all of them looked like they would faint at the sight of blood. Even Cindy would have been an improvement.

She gave no sign of what was going through her mind, however.

But The Director seemed to read her thoughts. 'I can see you're impressed,' he said dryly. 'But I wonder if you have considered that your own erstwhile little band of soldiers do not exactly look like a formidable front line in the fight against evil and yet … they have proved to be just that – with you to lead them.'

Tamar did not answer. '*Erstwhile?*' she thought. 'He's taking a lot for granted isn't he?'

'Perhaps I should introduce you,' he added.

But Tamar had already moved away from him. She stood silently behind the blond man on the phone for a few minutes listening to his subtle blandishments to a girl named Tiffany before suddenly darting forward and cutting the connection.

'Does anyone ever actually fall for that?' she asked him.

He grinned up at her. 'A surprising amount of people,' he told her. 'People are gullible, 'specially when you tell them what they want to hear. My name's Tony Rackham, and you must be Tamar.' he held out a hand.

'Tony,' acknowledged Tamar coldly ignoring the proffered hand. 'If that's your *real* name.' And, just for a second, Tamar saw his poise slip and a worried look creep into his eyes. However, he masked it quickly with a glib compliment and Tamar allowed herself to smile.

'Pretty slick aren't you?' she said.

The girl in the lab coat hurried forward and held out a hand. 'Hi, I'm Melissa Cuthbert, my *real* name,' she grinned nervously. 'It's a great pleasure to meet you.'

A people pleaser, thought Tamar, shaking hands absently.

'I was just running some tests on ...' Melissa stopped and glanced at The Director uncertainly as he coughed abruptly. 'Oh,' she faltered. 'But I thought ...'

'Miss Black has not yet agreed to join us,' said The Director firmly. The girl's face reddened and she blinked rapidly. 'Oh, but you *will*, won't you?' she asked earnestly. Tamar gave her a noncommittal smile.

'This is Ray Evans,' Melissa said, showing Tamar a scruffy looking man in his thirties with long reddish hair and an emaciated appearance, as if he were a zoo exhibit. 'He's a genius with computers.'

Ray, Tamar noticed immediately blanked the screen on his computer as she approached. He turned faded blue eyes on her for a split second and gave a disinterested shrug before turning away again. Tamar was fascinated by his skin, which looked parched and yellow, the colour of old newspaper.

'And this is David Collins,' continued Melissa. 'He's computers too,' she added but did not explain further.

Exhibit B was younger and tidier, thought Tamar, than Exhibit A. And at least he smiled when he was introduced. But it was an empty smile, and there was no warmth in the dark brown, almost black eyes looking out warily from under a thick shock of dark brown hair that fell almost to his nose in an elaborately dishevelled style.

Tamar disliked him immediately too. 'I'm doing well,' she thought ironically.

'And this is Valerie Byrnehil,' finished Melissa. Introducing a stark, severe looking woman, with smooth pale skin and light blonde hair, and who would have been quite pretty had her face had more life in it. She turned sea coloured eyes on Tamar and gazed serenely at her as if she wanted to penetrate her soul. 'Good luck with that,' thought Tamar who was not at all sure that she even had one.

'Valerie coordinates the team when we're in the field,' explained Melissa.

'Ah,' thought Tamar. 'The Boss. No wonder she doesn't look happy to see *me*.'

At that moment, they were interrupted by a loud droning sound followed by a lot of cursing. Tamar turned to see what appeared to be a bumblebee the size of her fist making a noise like a road drill, followed by a man chasing it with a net. 'Damn the bloody thing, how the hell they keep getting out I'll never know,' he said apologetically.

'They're Fons,' said Tamar. 'You'll never contain them,'

The man looked interested. 'They're what?' he said.

'Fons,' said Tamar. 'And it isn't an insect whatever it may look like.'

'We thought it was some sort of genetically engineered ...'

'No, no,' Tamar laughed. 'Fons are mystical creatures, perfectly harmless and not at all interesting. Sometimes the babies are mistaken for queen bees, but they don't sting and aren't at all interested in flowers. I'd let them go if I were you. The rest of the tribe will be coming for them, and you don't want that believe me.'

'We believe we *have* the whole – er tribe, did you say?'

'I doubt it,' said Tamar. 'How many have you got?'

'About a hundred and fifty.'

'You're about a million short of a whole tribe then,' Tamar told him. 'When they turn up they'll cause chaos.'

'I thought you said they were harmless,' said The Director.

'Oh they are,' said Tamar, 'just not very bright. Can you imagine a million of these things buzzing around the place like so many giant bees? Chaos!'

The Director turned to the man with the net. 'Let them go,' he said decisively. 'Now!' Tamar nodded.

When the man had hurried off Tamar turned on The Director. 'What else have you got caged up here?' she asked severely.

'Why don't I show you?' he said imperturbably. 'Maybe you can help us with some more identification.'

'So, what exactly is this place?' asked Tamar as The Director led her along more corridors. 'What's it all about? Is it government?'

'No.' The Director was firm. 'We work for no governments. They work for us. The Agency – we have no other name – is like a "Men in Black" organisation for the supernatural. We assess threats and eliminate them. In absolute secrecy. No one knows we exist.' He gave Tamar a sideways glance. 'And yet,' he continued, 'despite considerable funding, top flight experts and state of the art equipment we do not possess the impressive track record of a small rag tag group of mavericks, who work apparently off the cuff, when it comes to saving the world from supernatural threats.' He sighed. 'We need your help. That's the top and bottom of it.

'Of course we had no more idea of your existence than you did of ours until recently. People who do what we do have to work in secret out of necessity, and you kept your secret effectively for some years until this recent Faerie debacle. Something slipped I should say.' He looked sideways at Tamar who nodded.

'Something,' she said quietly.

'Of course we were aware of something else working away there in the background. Threats we had anticipated suddenly and inexplicably vanishing. And when you were exposed, we knew we had found you. All we had to do was backtrack events, and we found out a lot more than we ever imagined. So many threats averted that we had known nothing about, things that had never happened because of your interference, things that *did* happen and then, mysteriously, did not.

'But the most amazing thing was you,' he added. 'I still can't get used to the idea that you are five thousand years old. It's incredible. And I've seen a few things I can tell you.'

Tamar smiled.

'What it comes down to is this,' he resumed. 'You are now compromised, reporters on the doorstep and so on. We can help. With us, your anonymity will be restored. You will effectively disappear. You can continue to do what you do best which is what we all want.' he smiled. 'We might have left you to it had you not been exposed, but under the circumstances ...' he shrugged.

'If we hadn't been exposed, you'd never have found out about us,' Tamar pointed out. 'It's not a question of leaving us alone. You'd have had no choice.'

'A good point,' The Director agreed. 'But we *did* find out, because you *were* exposed. *C'est la vie.*'

'We, on the other hand, have *not* been exposed. We are in a position to help each other now, do you see?'

Tamar did see. She hated all the publicity that had descended on her lately. The chance to retreat back into obscurity was extraordinarily tempting. *And* to be able to continue to fight. It all seemed too good to be true. She remembered what Denny was wont to say about that. "If something seems too good to be true – remember the Djinn code. There's always a catch." No one knew better than Tamar, that this was true.

'Denny'll never go for it.' She voiced the thought without meaning to.

'Perhaps he might be persuaded,' said The Director, 'when he considers the alternative. Spending the rest of his life in the spotlight – never getting anything useful done. However, you wanted to see our holding pens, here they are.'

The Agents had been waiting in their car when she had returned to the house. Tamar had been furious and had gone and released the dragon from the garage. To her immense satisfaction, it had landed heavily on the car. The Agents had seemed to panic, they scrambled out of the car, and Tamar had decided that they had learned their lesson. She called the dragon off and sent him to the back garden. But Agent Dawber had been ...? It was as if he hadn't known. *Hadn't known about her,* or *her powers. The look of shock on his face... But he had been in her house! He had* seen! And *earlier that very day, he must have seen her teleport. Then Agent Rook had dragged him back to the car and taken off, but she could not remember what had happened next.*

However, she now had a shrewd idea.

~ Chapter Four ~

IN A HORRIBLE little motorway café, two strange people sat uncomfortably in the plastic moulded seats and looked at their plates with a mixture of intrigue and horror. This is perhaps not unnatural, and it certainly caused little comment from the other patrons, many of whom were engaged in the same activity.

'What do you suppose it is Fulk?' said his mistress poking her plate suspiciously.

'Err, the menuu, saays it's caalled aa fuull Englishh breakfaast,' said Fulk.'

'Yes, but what *is* it? What's *this*?' She pointed at the plate.

Fulk leaned forward. 'Shoe leather?' he suggested.

'I'm not hungry,' she said decisively pushing the plate away.

Fulk hesitated, and then reached forward and scraped the plate onto his own and devoured the lot in one mouthful.

'I do wish you wouldn't do that,' she snapped. 'It's so uncouth. People will stare.' She took a tentative sip of her coffee and a look an agonized indecision came over her face; aware that people *were*, in fact, staring. The eternal conundrum faced her – to spit or swallow?

She swallowed, to the great disappointment of one youngster at the next table who had taken a bet with himself that she would spray the foul liquid all over her companion's face and had been looking forward to seeing it.

'Now, how long have we got Fulk?' she said, ignoring her empty stomach.

'AAbout a weeek,' mumbled Fulk through a mouthful of food.

'Ah, good. And how long will it take us to be ready?'

Fulk swallowed hastily. 'AAbout a month Missteress,' he rapped out and ducked behind a menu.

'Hmm,' she said calmly. 'That should about do it. All right Fulk, let's get out of here.' She rose and walked out without a second thought for the bill. The manager went after her angrily but something in her face when he confronted her must have made him change his mind , and he decided instead to go home and have a lie down.

* * *

Denny sank down on his bed – his own bed, no point in sleeping in the spare room now – so, now he knew. Tamar did *not* want to be found. At least *he* had not been able to find her, which could only mean that she was hiding from him.

Why? He wondered. Why would she just leave like that? Surely, things had not been *that* bad. He remembered the lightning slinging. Okay, so pretty bad then, but still … he had a nagging feeling that he was missing something, something important. Maybe, if he relaxed and stopped worrying at it, it would come to him. He lay back and closed his eyes waiting for inspiration to hit him.

* * *

Tamar had been hanging around aimlessly for the last few days. She had been given new quarters and treated with deference. But still, she sensed that if push came to shove, she was a prisoner here. Of course, she would not have been Tamar if she had not already found a way out, but she was hanging fire on that for now.

'Why?' she wondered. Was it to find out what was really going on here, or was it that she was not ready to leave this place yet? The truth, she decided, was that she was seriously considering The Director's offer. But she had not made her mind up yet. The Director, perhaps sensing this, had left her alone since that first day and she had been given free access to the whole complex – more or less. She knew that she would not be given total access or any more information until she said definitively that she would join them and she did not resent this attitude. In fact, she was led to believe that it was as much for her sake as for theirs. That if she knew too much, she would *never* be allowed to leave. They were not to know that she would find a way out anyway.

She had spent most of her time hanging around with the so-called Alpha team that she was expected to lead (*if* she decided to stay that was) pumping them for information, about themselves (which they were happy to give) and about The Agency (which they were not). Still she had managed to find out more than they realised, particularly from Tony the con man.

'*Takes one to know one,*' she thought ironically, and she was better at it than he was. She refused to call him Tony, being certain that it was an alias and, as she had said, 'if I don't know your real name what shall I call you?'

He demurred, finally admitting that his name was embarrassing, which was tantamount to an admission, so she compromised and referred to him constantly as "Slick"

Slick was easy to pump for information being a talker by trade and, on top of this, almost insupportably arrogant. None the less, despite this, or perhaps because of this, she was beginning to rather like him. He did have a charm of his own, which he used shamelessly, rather like herself.

Melissa was another talker; she chattered on inconsequentially all the time, which Tamar recognized as a defence against actually *telling* her anything. However, she was a talented witch, Tamar surmised, and only needed experience to be as good as Cindy, maybe even better.

Ray turned out to be an amiable slacker (which was what he looked like) a computer geek and severely allergic to soap. There was not much below the surface there, Tamar decided. He spent his time following supernatural trends on the Aethernet, occasionally taking a break to play computer games of unparalleled viciousness and difficulty, and became pro-Tamar very quickly after she repeatedly beat him at "Demon Slayer II" having never played before – and with no intention of ever playing again. She forbore to point out that the demons were very unrealistic, inasmuch as they looked nothing like any of the demons she had previously met.

David was a different story though. Tamar decided he was sly. Outwardly friendly, she sensed that he did not like her at all, or, in fact, anyone at all. David was no hacker; he was a programmer and weapons designer. It took Tamar two days of subtle espionage to discover what she suspected that the rest of the team did not even know; that weapons and computer programs were not all that he designed. She kept her knowledge to herself but resolved to keep an eye on him. She suspected that he was working independently of the team, directly for The Director and that he had been placed on the team to hide his true activities which, when viewed in the abstract, were horrifying.

Valerie was rarely there; she stopped in occasionally to show her face and cadge a coffee, but was not a part of the team's activities. She monitored the teams when they were out in the field and had direct control (under The Director) of the base including the field agents like Rook and Dawber, handing out assignments etc. but otherwise had little to do with any of them.

Tamar thought she was disposed to resent her own presence but could not find any solid reason for thinking so. On the few occasions that they met, Valerie greeted her with a neutral remark and a bland smile, which was how she treated everyone – except Slick, who often got the favour of a wider smile and a light touch on the shoulder.

The team were definitely getting more relaxed around her now; it seemed that the longer she stayed the more they accepted that she was likely to stay for good.

'Six more of these today,' said Ray suddenly. 'A definite trend I should say.'

Tamar was alert at once although she gave no sign of this, but rather continued to stare aimlessly out of the window.

'Six more of what?' asked Slick impatiently. And Tamar blessed him silently.

'These spontaneous combustion cases,' said Ray patiently. 'You know? That's sixteen altogether – that we know of anyway.'

Melissa coughed meaningfully, and an awkward silenced fell in which every head turned to Tamar who, feeling eyes on her, turned around slowly and stared blandly back in Denny's best "who me?" manner.

After a few moments, Ray cleared his throat and said, as if nothing had happened. 'So, any more ideas about what's behind it?'

'It could be firestarters?' said Melissa.

'Dragons?' supplied Slick.

'Some sick bastard with a flamethrower,' said David.

'Dark matter,' added Ray.

'How's that?' said Slick

'Dark matter,' repeated Ray.

'And how would that manage to incinerate someone?' asked David disdainfully.

'It wouldn't,' said Tamar taking a hand. 'But nice thinking anyway, I can see where you're going with it. It makes more sense than an external source of flame like a dragon or a firestarter or – what was it, "some sick bastard with a flame thrower"?' She threw David a contemptuous glance.

'Spontaneous combustion occurs from the *inside* out. That's why it's regarded as spontaneous.' she added.

'What do *you* think it is?' said Ray. They all looked hopefully at her.

She shrugged. 'What am I, an oracle? I don't research things. I point and shoot at them.' She sighed. 'Okay, I'll need more information,' she said. 'What can you tell me? Are the cases connected? Did the people know each other? Where did they happen? When?

'Well,' said Ray, 'there's no connection as such, but there *is* a pattern emerging. The cases are moving south.'

Tamar's eyebrows shot up. 'Let me see that data,' she barked.

Ray hesitated.

'If you want my help,' snapped Tamar, 'then, let me see it. Let me see it *now*!'

She had them all thoroughly nervous, she thought as she slipped gracefully into the seat that Ray had been previously occupying. She looked at the data; it made no sense to her whatsoever. However, it did not need to; she already knew what they were dealing with. Crettins.

If they were nervous, she thought, it was no more than they should be. With Crettins on the loose, they had a big problem.

* * *

Agent Dawber was considering leaving the Agency. He had been having a bad day. He had run into the new woman on team Alpha. Literally run right into her, and the way she had looked at him … That stare was terrifying. But that was not the real problem. The feelings that he was forgetting something had greatly intensified after this had happened. Perhaps it was the way she had looked at him. As if she recognized him, which was clearly … Well he had never met her, he was sure of that. But she had gazed searchingly at him as if she expected something. It was a relatively minor incident, so why was it preying on his mind so much?

Of course, Dawber was used to being stared at by women, he barely noticed these days, being completely obsessed with his work. Mind you, this was a woman that any man would notice and, besides, it had not been that kind of stare.

Then there was the strange note he had found in his inside pocket. It had to have been her, but how the hell had she done it? And why, what did it mean?

He had noticed it after he had gone to check his badge (the FBI one) they were required to hand these in periodically to have them changed and today had been his day, a small, crumpled piece of paper that he was certain had not been there before. As soon as he had officially become "Agent Lowry", he had escaped to the men's washroom to see what it was.

Now, in the relative privacy of a cubicle, he looked at it again to see if it made any more sense than it had the first time. Amazingly it did.

Agent Dawber,

Go to the house on the hill "Vir Domas" currently in Staffordshire; you will know it when you see it. Ask for Denny, he will help you. I think you know you are not safe here. You will be safe with him. Show him this letter, the words on the back are for him. Go as soon as you can.

Tamar Black

Dawber pondered on this note for a long time trying to make it out. Who was Tamar Black? How did she know that he didn't feel safe? Who was Denny? And what did she mean "*currently* in Staffordshire"?

"Vir Domus" that was Latin wasn't it? 'Home of Heroes' – modest! Still, parts of it made sense, in that she was right, he didn't feel safe here. But you did not just leave the Agency. *No one* left The Agency – not alive anyway. But somehow, her promise that he would be safe reassured him. There was something he had felt from her, brief though their contact had been, that engendered trust. She was not what she seemed. Then again, he had felt for a long time that no one here was.

He read the note again and then curiously turned it over. There were no words on the back only a few scratch marks in pen, like something that had been written by a chicken in a tremendous hurry. Some sort of shorthand perhaps, but not one that Dawber recognised. "They are for Denny," he thought.

His instinct was to burn the note, as he had been taught, but he could not; she had trusted him with it. All the more reason, he argued. If this note fell into The Director's hands, she would be in trouble. She had, rather foolishly, in his opinion, signed it openly. But there was no reason for it to fall into The Director's hands. Not unless he meekly handed it over and he would *not*. His expression grew grim. He would *not* betray her who was trying to help him. Somehow, it never occurred to him to doubt her. He made his mind up. He *would* go. He would find the house and this Denny character and see what happened.

Now he just had to find a way to escape Rook and get away unnoticed.

* * *

'Crettins' Tamar tried to explain, 'are remnants of a far older world. I suppose you would call them fire spirits, but that isn't the half of it. They were born in the beginning, long before there was life on this planet when it was still clicking hot and covered in molten lava.' She became aware that they were hanging on her every word in a most gratifying fashion. Her own little gang never looked at her like that. 'They live now in the earth's core but sometimes they accidentally find their way to the surface, and when they do they become disorientated and afraid. It's far too cold for them up here.'

'Is that why they are heading south,' asked Slick, 'because it's warmer?'

'No, all temperatures on the surface are the same to them,' said Tamar. 'Freezing. 'It's like the difference to us between one part of the arctic and another. It all feels the same. Only it's worse for them.' She thought for a moment. 'It's not the direction *per se* that's important; it's the fact that they go in *one* direction whatever it is. Crettins always move in more or less straight lines following the invisible lava currents beneath the earth's surface.'

'You seem to know a lot about them,' said Ray.

'I've seen this before,' said Tamar vaguely. 'It happens every so often. You always know when Crettins are around because of the spontaneous combustion, usually of animals but sometimes people. You see, they are attracted by the warmth. They enter a body and begin to use the heat within to warm themselves, they get hotter and hotter until ...' she gestured with her hands KABOOM! 'They don't mean any harm. They're just trying to survive. The sad thing is, it doesn't really heat them up enough. The body disintegrates long before the Crettin within feels any benefit at all. But they keep trying it.'

'So what do we do about it?' said Melissa practically.

Tamar hesitated. 'I can handle this on my own,' she said. 'They can't hurt me, but you would be in a lot of danger.'

This remark received blank stares all round. Even from Slick, who she had been certain would grab at the straw of relative safety.

'So what else is new,' said Ray eventually.

'I'm not afraid,' said Melissa. And looked as if she meant it.

'We *want* to go,' said Slick. 'It's what we do.'

'Hmm,' Tamar appraised them uncertainly. 'Are you sure you ...'

'We know what you think of us,' said Melissa suddenly. 'You haven't exactly tried to hide it. But we *can* handle ourselves, and we're wasting time here. Tell us what you need us to do.'

'All right,' said Tamar. 'Ray, where was the last incident recorded?'

'Venezuela,'

'Okay, when was that?'

'Yesterday at around two ...'

'Right, Crettins move fast. They'll be at least two hundred miles away by now. Does that fit in with your data?'

Ray looked surprised. 'Yes,' he said, 'exactly.'

'Good, so we all know where we're going. How does One get out of here?'

Tamar did not need all this really; she could have sensed the Crettins easily once she was out of the complex. But she felt that these people were uneasy without a plan they could follow and data they could rely on. Not like Denny, Stiles, and the others, who acted on instinct and improvised most of the time. Tamar preferred acting on instinct. Nine times out of ten it worked for her. There were some things you could not plan for and she dealt with most of them on a regular basis.

It was no wonder, she thought, that her batting average against supernatural forces was better than theirs. They thought about things too much. Try to out-think a werewolf for example and see where it got you. Dead is where it got you. Because, while you were trying to decide what it might do next, the werewolf, acting on instinct, had already torn your throat out.

She was thinking a lot about wolves recently, she realised. She docketed the thought and decided to come back to it later. Her instincts told her there was probably a reason for this and she never ignored her instincts for long.

She surveyed the team before her, eager to be off. Right now, her instincts were telling her that at least one of them was going to die.

* * *

'She sent you to *me*?' Denny was bewildered. He read the note again. No doubt about it, it was her writing and the shorthand on the back was pretty conclusive. Only Tamar could have written it.

'You'd better come in then,' said Denny shortly. 'And we'll see if we can't sort this out. You have no idea who I am, do you?' he added astutely.

'No,' said Dawber baffled. 'We've never met.'

'We have you know,' said Denny. 'Cindy!' he bawled.

Cindy appeared suddenly behind him causing Dawber to step backwards suddenly in shock.

'What?' she snapped. Then she saw Dawber. Her eyes narrowed sharply. 'What's *he* doing here?'

'Tamar sent him,' said Denny. He handed her the note.

'He doesn't remember us,' he added when she had read it and handed it back to him with a mystified look. She drew her eyebrows together in an effort to understand. 'What?' she said eventually.

'Tamar says that his memory has been tampered with,' explained Denny. 'Probably magically. Can you help him?'

'He's lost his memory?' said Cindy.

'More like, had it taken from him,' said Denny.

'And Tamar sent him *here*? Why didn't she just fix him herself?'

'I think she's in trouble,' said Denny. 'We'll know more when – *if* we can get Agent Dum Dum here to remember.'

Cindy just stared at him blankly.

'Cindy!' snapped Denny. 'This is no time for the dumb blonde routine, can you help him or not?'

Cindy shook herself. 'Okay, okay,' she said testily. 'There's no need to get all bent out of shape, I was just thinking … It depends on how it was done but probably he hasn't actually *lost* his memories, just had them blocked off.'

'Which means?'

'Which means I probably *can* get them back for him, but it won't be pleasant for him.' she looked at Dawber. 'Give me your hands,' she ordered.

In a daze, Dawber did so.

'Thanks Cindy,' said Denny quietly.

She inclined her head coldly. After a few minutes intense concentration she released his hands and announced. 'There's at least three months worth in total of missing memory, although it's not consecutive. It's from all over the place, a bit here, a bit there. It adds up.'

'Three *months*!' exclaimed Denny. 'How long have they been doing this to him?'

'Several years I would say,' said Cindy sombrely. 'Pretty bad.' she looked at Denny. 'And Tamar's with these people?'

'I bloody hope not,' said Denny.

'She is,' volunteered Dawber.

'Shut up "Memento",' snapped Denny. 'What do you know about anything? You probably don't even remember your name.'

'It's Dawber,' said Dawber mildly.

'Are you sure about that?'

'It probably is,' said Cindy. 'I mean, he's had his name his whole life hasn't he? They've only been messing with him for the last few years or so.'

'So, who are *they*?'

'That's what I'm hoping he can tell us, when I've finished with him.' said Cindy. 'They wouldn't have bothered to do this if he hadn't found out what they didn't want him to know.

'I wouldn't worry about Tamar,' she added gently. 'If anyone can take care of herself ...'

'I'd just feel better if I was there,' muttered Denny.

Cindy turned to Dawber. 'I can restore your memory,' she said. 'But three months of disjointed memories returning all at once will be an overwhelming experience. You won't like it I'm warning you.'

'Three months doesn't sound like all that much,' said Dawber uncertainly.

'You'll see,' said Cindy. 'It's more than you think. Ready?'

'No,' said Dawber nervously.

'Too bad,' said Denny. 'Cindy, get on with it.'

Cindy ignored the peremptory tone. The truth was that she tended to go gooey inside when Denny bossed her around. But she would be damned if she was going to let him see it.

She moved gently toward Dawber. 'Don't be afraid,' she whispered softly, caressingly almost seductively. Dawber was hypnotised, and Denny could quite see why. Cindy certainly had a way with her when she wanted to.

She took his face in her hands and closed her eyes. '*Dea Hecaté audite meus placitum, permoveo obex solvo is mens.*' she muttered in a voice not her own. '*Teneo obex quod distraho is in nusquam, restituo mens, refero monumentum.*'

Her eyes snapped open and were blank without irises. Denny had seen this before, but it was still disconcerting.

'*Dea Hecaté audite meus placitum, permoveo obex solvo is mens.*' she repeated in commanding tones. '*Teneo obex quod distraho is in nusquam, restituo mens, refero monumentum.*'

Denny had to admit it; Cindy was impressive when she did this.

'*Solvo mens, solvo. Redigo is ita.*' at these last words, the meaning of which Denny could only guess at, a strange light descended on Cindy and enveloped her. Dawber screamed.

'I told him, he wouldn't like it,' said Cindy, whose voice and eyes had now returned to normal.

Denny stared in shock at the prostrate figure of Dawber lying whimpering on the floor. 'Will he be all right?'

'Give him a kick,' said Cindy heartlessly. 'He's over-egging it a bit if you ask me, it can't be *that* bad.'

'Depends on what it is he's remembering,' said Denny grimly.

They stared at each other for a second or two, contemplating this and imagining all sorts of horrors that might have been suddenly revealed to the mind of the poor man now twitching feebly on the floor.

Denny recovered first. 'That was some pretty impressive gobbledygook.' he said hastily, changing the subject. 'I sometimes forget what a first-class witch you really are.' He unthinkingly laid a hand on her shoulder as he spoke.

She shook it off irritably. '*Don't*,' she said, with what Denny thought was disproportionate vehemence

'Don't what?' said Denny taken aback.

'I can't have *you*, but I don't need your pity!' she yelled, her eyes blazing suddenly, and then she ran away.

Dawber, who had recovered enough to be watching this scene with curiosity from his prone position on the floor, temporarily forgot his own problems and asked in some surprise. 'What was all that about?'

Denny turned to Dawber with a carefully neutral expression. 'I have no idea,' he lied.

* * *

Tamar surveyed her troops with a critical eye. 'The neoprene catsuits and the radio mike headsets?' she asked. 'Are they absolutely necessary?'

'We always wear them,' said Melissa.

'Even if we do look like complete dicks,' muttered Ray under his breath.

'And small children don't follow you to find out where the circus is going to be?' asked Tamar.

'Sometimes,' again this was Ray speaking *sotto voce* so that only Tamar's sensitive ears caught the words. She smiled.

I thought the idea was to be *covert*?' she pointed out. 'You lot might as well be wearing signs around your necks saying "secret government special ops team".

'You look like the X men,' she added cruelly, 'only dorkier.'

Ray stifled a laugh. 'That's what *I've* been saying,' he said. 'Well. Actually I said we look like the Fantastic Four.'

Tamar tried to imagine Jack Stiles wearing a neoprene catsuit and suddenly burst out laughing.

'The outfits go,' she said firmly and snapped her fingers and putting them back into their normal clothes. 'I mean, look at this,' she snapped them again, and she was wearing the catsuit. 'What does this look like, really?'

They stared at her as one man. The catsuit fitted her like a second skin.

'Wow!' said Slick.

'It looks … pretty amazing really,' said Ray. 'On you, anyway.'

Tamar frowned. 'Do I look inconspicuous though?'

'No,' said Slick trying unsuccessfully to drag his eyes away from her legs. 'But, then again, you never do.'

'Okay,' snapped Tamar dryly. She was annoyed that her point had not been made. 'Put your eyes back in Casanova.' She dressed herself in her regular combats and T-shirt. 'Let's go.'

'Er, what about the headsets?' said Melissa. 'How will we keep in contact?'

'We won't need to,' said Tamar wearily. 'We'll all be together.'

'No, she's got a point,' said Ray. 'What if we get separated?'

'*I'll* find anyone who's daft enough to get lost,' said Tamar. 'And maybe make them wish I hadn't too. Are we going or what?'

She looked them over. They were nervous, edgy. This was no good. If they got this nervous about a few Crettins, how would they react when the universe pulled out the big guns?

'Neoprene catsuits!' she muttered. 'What we really need are thermal regulators,' But she knew that she would just have to do the best she could to protect them by elevating her own body temperature enough to attract any Crettins in the vicinity to herself. She did not bother to mention this though. They were anxious enough, and she was afraid that if she brought this up there would be questions, and she would be compelled to admit that it might not work.

~ Chapter Five ~

ONCE THEY WERE out of the complex, Tamar knew that she was now free to teleport anywhere in the world in the blink of an eye. She also knew that she had been tagged, and they *would* find her again, should she try to escape. Of course, she had a way round this; but for now, it would not do to let them know this. Perhaps they already knew, perhaps The Director was banking on her curiosity or his threat of blackmail to keep her in line and the tagging was just a way of keeping score.

She knew now, that this was how she had been brought to the complex. The Agents who had visited her house had done it. They had tagged her with a mystical isotope – she had never even known about it – and when the time was right, they had brought her in telekinetically. She now remembered the room. They called it the teleportation room (Ray called it the departure lounge) although Tamar knew that this was not strictly accurate. Teleportation was not used, only something (and she was not sure what, but it felt familiar) that looked and acted like it. They had used this room again today to transport the team outside; it was the only way in or out of the complex.

They had then selectively wiped her memory in the same way that they had done to Agent Dawber and left her in the glass plated room to observe her reactions.

As angry as this had made her at the time, she now knew several things:

1. That the memory device had not had a permanent effect on her. Her mind was not the same as a human mind. It had taken time, but eventually all the memories they had blocked had found a way back into her consciousness.

2. That the Director and his cronies were not aware that this was the case (and she had no intention of letting them know it either)

3. That if her own memory could be re-routed by magic back into her conscious mind, then Agent Dawber's could be also. Only in his case, an outside source of magic would have to be employed. Tamar had no doubt that Denny would have Cindy do it.

4. That there was no possible chance of escaping directly from the complex. Once inside, her magic was useless. It was a bit like being back in the bottle. Only when she was released, could she access her powers.

5. That the isotope, like chemical isotopes, dispersed after 26 hours and had to be reapplied. Now that she was outside of the complex, all she would have to do would be to keep them off her trail for that length of time, after that, they would no longer be able to get a fix on her. She knew that she was more than capable of doing this, and suspected that they knew it too. She could only conclude, therefore, that since she had been allowed out of the complex, they were unaware that she knew about the isotope.

Strangely, she did not resent the actions they had taken. In their place, she would have done the same. And they had not hurt her.

She wondered if the lack of resentment was because she felt that, in a way, they had done her a favour.

It *was* interesting here. She could see the possibilities. She had wondered how to escape the notoriety that had descended on her and continue to work in secret, and they had shown her a way. She did not ignore the fact that this advantage had been shoved down her throat as a strong piece of propaganda and that there might well be more to it. But she could give this place a chance and see what developed. After all, she had a way out if she ever needed it.

So why didn't she take it and go home?

She faced the truth; she was not ready to go home. Being brought here, although she had not planned it, had given her a chance to stand back and think about things. She would never have taken such a course of action on her own, preferring to stay and face things head on, but now that she *was* here, there was no point in not taking advantage of the situation. She *liked* it here. It was peaceful and, unlike the current situation at home, there were no problems here that she was not more than equal to solving.

Like the Crettins.

Back to business. She closed her eyes and concentrated. She had to admit, having a definite area to focus on did make it easier; in any case, it took her about three seconds to isolate the Crettins' location.

She held out a hand to Melissa. 'Ever tried *real* teleporting?' she said. 'All grab hands and *hang on*!'

They had been transported from the teleportation room to a hangar full of interestingly high tech aircraft that made Tamar feel even more like she was participating in a comic book adventure.

'Sod that,' she had decided. She gave the gang no opportunity to argue. Her way was better. And after all, she was supposed to be team leader. This was why they had wanted her, because what she did *worked*.

The reactions of the group varied from Slick – 'Cool! Can we do that again?' to Melissa 'I think I'm going to throw up.' Ray admitted that it was more efficient than flying, but could he have some warning next time? David maintained a taciturn silence. He had said almost nothing from the beginning, in fact. Tamar had the impression he was keeping mental notes on her.

'Sod him,' she decided. 'We have work to do.'

They were on a dusty road, apparently deserted apart from a stalled bus full of both people and livestock. A buffet for the Crettins; all it would take to stall the bus was one Crettin in the gas tank burning off the fuel.

A man staggered from the bus looking oddly shiny. His eyes were glazed he was clutching desperately at his stomach.

'Any minute now,' murmured Tamar.

'Is that …?' said Melissa looking slightly sick.

'He's had it,' Tamar confirmed. 'It's too late for him. I wouldn't look if I were you.' She did not, however, avert her own eyes. She wanted to see the moment when the Crettin emerged.

'Ray, Slick,' get on that bus and get everyone off,' she ordered. 'And be careful. Anyone who looks like *him* is to be avoided.

The man who had staggered from the bus exploded. And Tamar saw it; a shape against the air, almost invisible, shimmering like the air around a heat mirage, moved fast and with deadly accuracy toward Ray. No time to think, Tamar moved, lightning fast, into the Crettin's path and swayed backwards as it entered her.

'*Tamar*!' Melissa had seen it too.

'I can handle it,' said Tamar between gritted teeth. 'Get on that bus like I told you.'

No one moved.

The heat was building up inside her; it felt like she had a volcano in her gut. And this was only the beginning. She was vaguely aware of the faces staring at her in horror.

'Well,' she thought, 'I daresay I wouldn't win any beauty contests at the moment.' But that was no reason to… they were just going to have to get used to this sort of thing. The heat was unbearable even to her. Had she been human, she would have been ashes by now. She felt her skin split under the intense heat; her eyeballs felt like they were boiling, flames flickered under her fingertips. No more choices, she could not hold it back any more. She burst into flame, knowing, as she did so, what would happen next.

The Crettins swarmed, attracted by the intense heat she was creating. She was punted backwards violently as three more entered her, within seconds, she was a mere pillar of fire. Melissa was screaming.

For a minute there, Tamar had panicked, but she had it under control now. The pillar of fire stabilised and began to burn steadily. She was in more pain than she had ever believed possible.

'Set the bus on fire,' shouted Slick.

'*No,*' thought Tamar but no words came out. It would not matter anyway. The heat radiating from Tamar was hotter than any fire they could hope to create. The only thing hotter than Tamar right now was the Earth's core itself or possibly the sun. *The sun, now there was an idea.*

The very air around her seemed to be on fire, and the ground for several yards in every direction was scorched. Trees caught fire and people from the bus began running and screaming, no need to set the bus on fire, it caught by itself. The team backed away helplessly keeping their eyes on the now complete wall of fire that had been Tamar. Time to end this, thought Tamar, she was sure she now had them all.

From the point of view of the team, the flames suddenly vanished, and Tamar, black as a sweep, came screaming through the air from high above like a comet, hitting the ground hard enough to dig a deep trench along her path.

She sat up grinning, and allowed Ray and Slick to haul her out. 'Not exactly what I had in mind,' she told them dusting herself off. 'But it pays to be flexible, I always find.' she smiled at their stunned faces. She would never tell them, she decided, that she had not been at all certain that she would survive. It would completely spoil what had been, by anyone's standards an impressive début.

* * *

What had possessed her to say such a stupid thing? Cindy castigated herself. How was she ever to face him again after *that*? It had been bad enough before, when he had only had a vague suspicion, now it would be impossible. She must have lost her mind.

'Cindy?' she jerked her head up in shock. It was Denny. Denny who always avoided her like the plague for at least a week after she so much as hinted at her feelings for him, who never wanted to know about it so that he could pretend it was not real, who skirted round the subject if it ever came close to coming up, to make sure it was never said. It was not possible that he had actually sought her out after such a huge blunder as she had just made. Was it?

'Cindy, are you in there?' It *was* him.

'Er, come in.' she said uncertainly, all embarrassment forgotten in surprise and curiosity.

He shuffled in awkwardly, and sat down gingerly on a pink satin chair and gazed past her ear out of the window.

'Not handsome at all,' thought Cindy. 'He dresses like a scarecrow, he never shaves, and just look at him sitting on that chair for all the world as if he thought it was going to break. There's no way he could ever fit into my life.'

He ran long, thin fingers through his hair nervously and let out a sigh.

'It's nice,' he said gesturing around the room.

'He thinks it looks like a tart's boudoir,' thought Cindy. 'And normally he would say so, what's up with him?'

'How's our guest?' she said.

Denny looked relieved. 'Better, I think, it's all been a bit of a shock for him. But he'll be okay.'

'Give him a day,' said Cindy. 'He should have sorted things out by then.'

Denny nodded. 'I wanted …' he began. 'I mean, I never said thanks for y'know, sorting him out.' he stopped and looked almost plaintively at her. *Please,* his expression seemed to say, *can't we just pretend it never happened, let's just go back to how it was before, when I could pretend I didn't know.*

Now she understood; she had gone too far this time. He had come to try to erase what she had said. He shifted awkwardly on the fancy chair and gestured unconsciously to his clothes, his hair, his three-day growth of stubble.

Look at me, he seemed to be saying, *why would you want me anyway? I don't fit in here.* It was what she had been thinking a moment ago. But it was no good. She still wanted him.

She took pity on him; didn't he have enough on his mind at the moment?

'Could you stand up a minute,' she said grabbing a towel and placing it on the chair as he rose. 'Sorry,' she said. 'It's silk.' Denny grinned in relief; this was the Cindy he knew.

'Where's Jack?' he asked conversationally. 'I haven't seen him.'

'Oh, didn't he tell you? He has a new case on hand. He and Hecaté are looking into it. Some spontaneous human combustion cases I think he said.'

'Oh, it's probably Crettins,' said Denny.

'That's what I thought,' agreed Cindy.

There was an awkward silence.

'Well, I'd better go and see what Agent Whatisname is doing,' said Denny eventually.

'I wonder why Tamar sent him here,' mused Cindy.

'I think it was a message,' said Denny his voice vibrating with hope. 'Of course she may just have wanted us to help him,' he conceded. 'Hard to imagine her needing rescuing really.

I know what you mean,' said Cindy.

'She … I mean why wouldn't she come home, if she could? Mind you, we *were* arguing a lot,' he answered his own question. 'All that "being normal" crap,' he continued, 'Facials and shopping and stuff like that … not that I blame you of course.'

There was a frosty silence.

'What's *that* supposed to mean?' said Cindy.

'Well, nothing, I just …' Denny backtracked desperately.

'You think this is *my* fault?' Cindy was outraged. 'After all the stuff *you* did. Acting like a chauvinistic prat, telling her what to do all the time, lightning bolts in the kitchen.'

Denny was furious. He leaped angrily to his feet. '*You* were the one who got her into all that stuff in the first place. *And* you encouraged her, even though you must have known that it was driving me mad. I wouldn't be surprised if you hadn't done it on purpose, just to drive a wedge between us, you're quite smart enough for *that*!' he went on relentlessly. 'That dumb blonde routine of yours might fool the others, but I know better.'

'Why would I do that?' snapped Cindy. 'God knows she's welcome to you,' she continued hurriedly before he could answer. 'I saw the way you treated her before she left. She was in tears some nights after you had been having a go at her. *You* drove her away. It had nothing to do with me. And I don't blame her for walking out. I wouldn't have put up with it either.' She stopped. Denny's face was white. He knuckled his eyes to stem the sudden tears that had sprung up.

Cindy was horrified. *What had she said?*

'Was I really that bad?' he stuttered.

'No-no, I didn't mean it, I was angry. I'm sorry. Don't …'

'I *was*,' said Denny. 'Jack warned me I was behaving badly too, only he put it a bit more tactfully than you did.' he slumped back into the chair and covered his face with his hands.

Cindy put a tentative arm around him. 'I'm sorry,' she repeated. 'I miss her too.' There did not seem to be anything else to say.

'I just want her to come back,' said Denny.

'She *will*,' said Cindy vehemently. It was terrible seeing this side of the normally laid back Denny.

Denny looked up at her face. 'I'm sorry I tried to blame you. I didn't mean it. I guess I've treated you pretty badly too. I just didn't want to face the truth – that it was me. *I* drove her away.'

'I'm not at all sure that you did,' said Cindy thoughtfully. 'I mean it's not like her to just leave like that. You can forget all that stuff I said before. I was just being emotional. I guess we'll know more after that Agent tells you what he remembers.'

'You don't have to be nice to me,' said Denny. 'I don't deserve it. I'm a shit.'

'You *are* a shit,' said Cindy but without accusation in her voice, 'lately anyway. But you didn't use to be. And I don't think you've changed that much, not deep down.' she took his face in her hands and turned it gently towards her as if he was a small boy. 'What's wrong with you Denny? What's happened to you?'

'I don't know. It's like it's not really me saying those things. Only I know it is.'

'All *I* know,' said Cindy. 'Is that you have always been one of the sweetest, gentlest, kindest men I ever met. And Tamar knows it too. *I* wouldn't have left you over a few silly arguments ...'

'Cindy ...'

'... and I don't think *she* would either.' finished Cindy. 'She's too wise for that. If *I* can see that you haven't been acting like yourself lately, if *I* can see that something is wrong, that this isn't the real you then *she* certainly can.'

'I don't think she did see,' said Denny miserably.

'Tamar knows the real you,' said Cindy firmly. 'She'll be back.'

Denny risked a smile. 'You don't think you're biased?' he asked wickedly.

Cindy stiffened imperceptibly.

'I mean because you want her to come back too,' he added.

Cindy relaxed. 'I *know* she'll come back,' she said. 'She can't do better than you.' she touched his face lightly. 'If there's a better man than you out there, *I* haven't met him.'

This was dangerous ground. 'Maybe *she* has,' he said glumly.

'If she hadn't in five thousand years,' said Cindy. 'What are the chances of it happening now?'

* * *

Tamar was sat in the commissary nursing a coffee of unparalleled toxicity, when a hand touched her lightly on the shoulder and a familiar voice said. 'Hello gorgeous.'

'Hello Slick,' she turned with a mocking smile. 'What can I do for you?'

'Dinner,' he said promptly.

Tamar laughed. 'When you tell me your real name I'll consider it,' she told him. She was beginning to enjoy his company. She liked his refreshingly direct admiration. He found her beautiful and did not see any reason to pretend otherwise. It was nice to be appreciated. He would look at her at odd moments with undisguised and fervent desire. Denny had looked at her that way once. Of course, he was no Denny, but he was handsome and charming and he exerted that charm in her direction at every possible opportunity. Sometimes she would screw her eyes up to distort his image. With the floppy blonde hair and long lean physique, he looked a little like Denny, and he had the same hands, the same long sensitive fingers, artistic hands. Tamar had always appreciated Denny's hands.

She wondered idly what it would be like to let herself be tempted by this man. And would she be pretending all the time that he was Denny? The way Denny used to be …

'Sorry,' he was saying. 'That's the one thing I can't do, even for you. It's a secret.' He put his fingers to his lips.

'It can't be *that* bad. I knew a guy called Eugene once, but I never thought less of him for that.'

'It's worse than that,'

'Not Cyril?'

'No, and I'm not telling you.'

'So it *could* be Cyril.'

'It could be, but it isn't.'

'Cecil? Torquil? Tarquin? Denzil? You know, I once knew a guy called Florid Underdrawers. Whatever it is, it couldn't be worse than *that*!'

'You made that up.'

'I swear, although to be fair, he was a dwarf.'

'Okay, it's not worse than that, but I'm still not telling you.'

'Okay, suit yourself,' she turned back to the heinous coffee. 'It's your loss anyway,' she added.

'Believe me, I know,' he said.

They were interrupted by a wailing siren accompanied by a screeching voice announcing to the complex "INTRUDER ALERT, INTRUDER ALERT... TEAM ALPHA TO THE HOLDING ROOM."

'Intruder alert?' said Tamar, getting off her seat. 'How can there be an intruder alert? A mouse couldn't break into this place.'

'If we're being called to the holding room, then it means they've caught someone,' said Slick, 'probably sneaking around outside. Usually they aren't trying to get in at all. Why would they be? It's not as if anyone knows this place is here.'

Tamar found her heart sinking; although she had not even realised, until it did, that it had soared for a moment when the alert came through. She realised that she had irrationally hoped for one split second that the intruder might be Denny. Now, she realised, that it probably was not. Even if it was then, according to Slick, he had been captured, and that would not be a good thing.

She knew where the holding room was and she was not looking forward to seeing it again under any circumstances.

The rest of the team, along with The Director and a gaggle of scientists were crowded outside the holding room talking excitedly.

'Oh, Tamar, there you are,' said Melissa, her eyes shining. 'It's so exciting. We've caught a demon.'

'*Probable* demon,' corrected The Director.

'A demon?' said Tamar, her eyes narrowed. She thought it extremely unlikely that they had caught a demon. Many of the people here had bite and scratch marks on them, but, interestingly enough, there were no scorch or burn marks on anyone. Demon indeed?

'What kind of demon?' she asked.

'We don't know,' said The Director. 'We were hoping you might identify it.'

'There are fourteen million demons in hell,' said Tamar. 'I've been there, but I didn't meet them all personally. There wasn't time.'

This remark drew surprised gasps from the onlookers crowded around the door to the holding room.

'I meant, identify the species,' said The Director calmly. 'Shall we go in?'

Tamar shrugged. All this excitement over a demon, what was the big deal?'

As she entered the room, she almost laughed out loud. Of course, she could see where they might have been confused. The horns, the cloven feet, the tail. However, she suppressed her amusement. To laugh now would be to escalate what was already shaping up to be a diplomatic incident. She just hoped she could sort this out.

She bowed low before the figure on the chair. 'Your Highness.' she said to astonished gasps from behind her. She ignored these.

'It's your Majesty now,' said the figure on the chair in a high squeaky voice. 'The old one passed away in the fight against the Sidhe. Is that Tamar Black?'

'It is your Majesty,' said Tamar keeping her voice carefully respectful. 'Please allow me to apologise for this terrible misunderstanding ...'

'They called me a *demon*,' said the figure indignantly.'

Tamar whirled. 'You *called* him a demon?' she asked in horrified tones. 'To his *face*? This, as any person might know, is Slev, Prince ...'

'King!'

'*King* of the Satyrs.' she turned to King Slev. 'Please forgive the ignorati over there,' she said. 'They didn't know any better.

Slev twisted his face into what might have been a smile. *Ignorati*! That was typical Tamar.

Tamar turned round to the Director. 'I suggest you let him go immediately, unless you want a diplomatic incident that I doubt very much you are equipped to handle.' she leaned in a whispered. 'Let me talk to him alone, they're very touchy, and calling him a demon was the worst thing you could have done. But I think I can handle it.'

The Director nodded in a bemused fashion. 'Whatever you think,' he said. Clearly, this had got beyond him. He signalled a guard to release the Satyr King and said loudly. 'Everybody out,'

'What are you doing here, Tamar Black?' said Slev when they were alone.

'Long story,' said Tamar. 'And I might ask you the same thing.'

'I was captured,' said Slev.

'There's a lot of it about,' said Tamar vaguely.

'Not you too?' Slev was astonished.

'*Were* you hanging around outside the complex?' said Tamar, who did not believe it for a second.

'I don't think so. I was in my forest when suddenly …
'D'you know, I'm not sure …'

'Hmm,' was Tamar's only response.

'Is that how they got you too?' asked Slev shrewdly. 'Are they going to let me go?' he asked when she did not answer this.

'Yes,' said Tamar.

'I think you should get out of here too,' he said. 'This is not a good place Tamar Black. And that Director man, I know a wolf in an alpaca wool suit when I see one, or rather smell one.'

'Wolf?' snapped Tamar. 'As in …?'

'As in a *wolf*, Tamar Black. As I think you know.'

'Oh shit,' said Tamar. 'You don't mean a werewolf do you?'

'No I do not. I mean a wolf disguised as a human, a very dangerous creature.'

'Yes I thought that's what you meant. Oh shit,' she repeated.

She did not ask him if he was certain. Satyrs do not make mistakes about things like that. It explained her current obsession with wolves too. She must have sensed it on some level.

'Thanks for the heads up Slev,' she said. 'Now, let's get you out of here.'

'You aren't leaving too?'

'Not yet,' said Tamar. 'I have some things to do here, before I go.'

'Be careful Tamar Black. Wolves are dangerous creatures when backed into a corner, but they are also seductive. And this place too is seductive. Make certain you understand your own motives in deciding to stay.'

* * *

After Denny had finished grilling the Agency man, and was certain that he had got as much out of him as possible, he let him go and get some food and sat alone in the vast, empty study pondering on what he had heard.

There was a lot to assimilate, but first up and most bewildering was the fact that Tamar had apparently chosen to stay and work for the Agency. He had cross-examined poor Dawber on this point extensively but had been reluctantly forced to accept that, unless there were things about the situation that Dawber had never known, she had indeed made that choice. It was almost funny.

'I *knew* that the next thing would be her getting herself a job,' he thought. Well, he could not stop her; apparently, it was just something that she had to get out of her system. 'She could have *told* me at least,' he thought resentfully. But then again, given his recent attitude to her quest for all things ordinary, he could hardly blame her for not doing so. And after all, she *had* sent Dawber to him; that was a *kind* of message.

He forced himself to put this issue to one side for now and thought about some of the other things that Dawber had told him.

One thing he decided almost immediately was that he had to take a trip to Hank's mythological forest and find out just how many creatures were missing and what, if anything, Hank was doing about it.

He would take Agent Dawber with him – just let him try to argue about it.

* * *

Before he could go, Stiles appeared with the news that he had seen Tamar in Venezuela sorting out the Crettin problem. She seemed fine if a bit hot and bothered, Stiles reported.

Denny told him about Tamar's message through Agent Dawber. Stiles was sceptical as he always was, but had to admit that, for the moment, there did not seem to be a lot he could do about it.

'And the wedding's booked for two weeks on Saturday,' said Denny mournfully.

'Don't cancel it,' Stiles advised. 'I reckon she'll turn up if she can.'

Denny's face lit up for a moment. 'D'you reckon?' he said hopefully. 'Do you really think so?'

'Absolutely,' said Stiles, with far more conviction than he actually felt.

But Denny felt better immediately. If Jack thought so, then it was probably right. Stiles had an almost uncanny prescience when it came to people's reactions and motives. That was why, deep down, he had serious misgivings about Dawber's story.

He offered to come to the forest with Denny and Denny accepted his offer with alacrity, he did not like Hank very much, and Dawber was a bit of an unknown quantity as yet. It would be good to have a friendly face along. This may have been Stiles's motive for making the offer since, on a practical level, there was no reason to suppose he would be needed.

* * *

Dawber, already considerably unnerved by the teleporting and the strange method of entering the forest – which looked pretty intimidating to him in itself, was then made irremediably nervous by the appearance of Hank who greeted them heartily.

'DERRY!' he boomed cheerfully and gave him a slap on the back that would at one time have knocked Denny flat on his face.

Denny raised an eyebrow but made no attempt to correct him, as Tamar would have done. He knew perfectly well that Hank knew his name and that this was a low attempt to hide his extreme jealousy over Tamar by pretending that Denny was of no account to him at all.

'And who are these chaps?' Hank asked. 'Wait, I know this one,' he indicated Stiles. 'We've met before I'm sure, I never forget a face. Jake isn't it?'

'Jack,' said Stiles.

'Jack! Of course,' he pumped his hand vigorously. 'Nice to have you back, I take it all went well with the Hart's Blood?' Hank's heartiness was threatening to go into overdrive, but both Stiles and Denny sensed a strain in his voice.

'Fine,' said Stiles laconically.

'Good, good. And who is this fine fellow?' He smiled widely at the cowering Dawber.

'Missing any animals Hank?' said Denny abruptly cutting off this line of dissembling.

'How did you know?' said Hank, too surprised to try a denial. His *façade* of heartiness crumbling like the walls of Jericho.

'Because I know, or rather this man here knows where they are' said Denny.

'Does he, by god?' said Hank peering closely at Dawber who shrank back. 'What's been going on then? I didn't think too much about it at first. There are always a few who leave in the summer you know. They normally come back eventually, but there's been an awful lot gone lately, more than usual. What's been going on then?' he reiterated. 'You seem to know all about it.'

'They've been taken,' said Denny. 'More than that, I can't tell you. Tamar could probably tell you more.'

'Where is the lovely one anyway?' asked Hank.

'Unavailable,' said Denny shortly.

'Trouble in paradise?' asked Hank, looking absurdly pleased about it.

'She's with them,' volunteered Dawber unexpectedly.

Denny gave him a black look.

'Ah, undercover,' said Hank, looking slightly disappointed.

'Well, if she's on the case, what do you want from me?' he spread his hands.'

'Well, actually,' Denny admitted reluctantly. 'We aren't at all certain that she *is* on it.'

Hank frowned. 'Then what is she doing with the swine who are taking my creatures?'

'She might not know ... Look *we* are looking into this. What can you tell us?'

'How many are missing?' put in Stiles interrogatively. 'When do they go, is it at night or what? Have you seen anything? Anyone?'

'All right, all right,' said Hank. 'Give a chap a chance to think.'

'They just seem to vanish,' he said eventually. 'Not at night especially I don't think, I've never seen it happen. And I've never seen anyone here who doesn't belong here, except you of course. There are about sixty missing creatures of all different species. That's all I can tell you. Can you find them?' he added anxiously.

'We'll damn well try,' said Denny grimly looking at Dawber. 'Can you get us inside?'

'I-I suppose,' said Dawber. 'But it's risky. They won't just let me in now.'

They turned to go when a thought struck Stiles; he turned back. 'I don't suppose any of them have ever come back have they?' he asked.

Hank looked surprised at the question. 'No, not as far as I know,' he said. 'I mean, some of the Fons that went off returned recently, but they're always disappearing and coming back again, you'd think this place had a revolving door on it the way they carry on. Anyway, no one'd be interested in Fons.'

'*They* would,' said Dawber darkly. 'They're interested in *everything*.'

'You can't question Fons, though,' said Denny. 'Too stupid.'

'That's true,' said Hank. 'And they can't talk anyway.'

'It was a good idea, though,' said Denny. 'We'll keep in touch Hank and let us know if any of them do come back, we might learn something.'

Right ho,' said Hank.

* * *

That night Denny dreamed about wolves. Snapping, snarling, growling wolves with foam flecked muzzles and mad fiery eyes. He woke up in a cold sweat. Denny was used to this sort of thing and usually dismissed it summarily. It was either a normal dream evoked by his unconscious mind or, if it wasn't, then it had been planted there deliberately by someone who wanted to mislead him in some way. This time it felt different. Although Denny did not believe in precognisance of any sort, he felt as if he had just been given a glimpse of something like it. Someone, he thought, was trying to tell him something.

He got up and went to the kitchen to get a drink and found Cindy there reading the paper.

She looked up at him and grinned. 'Is Denny Sanger the sexiest man in the world?' she read out in a singsong voice.

'Don't' he groaned putting his head in his hands. 'I thought I got rid of that.'

'It's not a very good picture,' said Cindy. 'In fact, I wouldn't swear to it being you at all.'

'That's what I said,' Denny agreed. 'Now can we talk about something else – *anything* else?'

Cindy flipped the paper into the bin. 'Such as?' she queried.

Denny shrugged.

'What you are doing up in the middle of the night, for example.' she said.

'Couldn't sleep,' he said.

'I know,' she told him. 'You woke the whole house shouting and going on in your sleep. That's why I'm up.'

'Oh, sorry.'

'That's all right.'

'Are the kiddies asleep now?' he asked. 'Did I wake them?'

'They're fine,' Cindy waved a dismissive hand. 'Kids can sleep through anything and Fin just turned back over and started snoring which pretty effectively "murdered sleep" for me, so I got up. And fascinating though all this must be, I want to know what's bothering *you*.'

'Nightmare, nothing serious.'

'Balls,' said Cindy. '*You* don't get up and come downstairs over a nightmare.'

'Don't push it Cind,' said Denny. 'I really don't want to talk about it right now.'

'Suit yourself,' said Cindy a little snippily. 'I think I'll go and make up the sofa, there's no point in me going back to bed now, with him snoring away like a road drill.'

'*You've* had premonitions haven't you?' said Denny suddenly.

Cindy started. The last premonition she had had, had involved Denny in a rather personal way but he didn't know about that surely? He *couldn't*.

Then she realised what he was getting at. 'Is that what you think it was?' she asked, 'your dream?'

'I don't know,' he said. 'How – how accurate are they?'

'Depends,' she said. 'Mostly they're allegorical or, at best, pretty vague. I shouldn't worry about it, if I were you.'

'But they *are* accurate sometimes?' he persisted.

'Almost never,' she assured him. 'The last one I had didn't exactly come true,' she blushed as she said this but Denny did not notice.

'I thought it *did*,' he said. 'Wasn't it about Finvarra and how he wasn't dead like we all thought?'

'That was *part* of it,' she said. 'The rest was ...'

'Pretty vague?' finished Denny.

'Absolute bollocks,' said Cindy firmly.

'What was it?' asked Denny curiously.

'I died,' said Cindy tersely, which was partly true, but not the whole truth but certainly enough to explain why she did not want to go into details and hopefully dissuade Denny from asking any more questions.

'Oh, I'm sorry,' said Denny and clammed up.

'Sometimes it's the past you're seeing and not the future,' she said. 'It can be hard to tell the difference.'

'That doesn't really make me feel any better,' said Denny. 'It might have even been the present by that standard.'

Cindy shifted uncomfortably; she wanted this conversation to end. It was making her feel oddly exposed, and being alone with Denny was becoming a trying experience at the best of times. Without Tamar around as a buffer, Cindy was constantly fighting the irrational urge to spill her heart out to him. If she did, she knew it would be a catastrophe. There were some things he just did not want to hear.

After a few moments of silence, she got up to leave.

'Don't go,' he said surprisingly. She turned; Denny was looking steadily at her with such an expression as she had long wished to see on his face.

She hesitated. Then she went to him, and he put his arms around her in silence. And then ... Oh God it was bliss, just as she had known it would be.

'I'm lonely,' he muttered into her hair.

'Me too,' she told him. His hands were sliding up her back and into her hair. She hovered for a moment, poised between uncertainty and desire, and then she pulled away.

'This is a mistake,' she said, hardly believing her own ears.

He looked questioningly at her.

'This can only end in disaster,' she said. 'I'll end up devastated, and you'll feel guilty. It's not *me* you want. I wish it *was*. Maybe you can live with that,' she continued. 'But I *can't*. And I find it pretty hard to believe that you could either. This isn't *like* you. Even under the Faerie spell, you wouldn't have done this. You *didn't* do this.'

Denny looked at her like a man coming out of a trance. 'What's the matter with me?' he asked despairingly. 'I'm *so* sorry Cind, I never meant to …'

'There's something going on,' said Cindy briskly. 'Something magical. And it started a while ago too. First, you acting like such a prat with Tamar – No, *First* was her wanting to be ordinary and *then* you acting up about it. Then Tamar leaving, and not coming back either, and now … Well anyway, neither of you have been acting like yourselves for a while now, don't you think?'

'When you put it like that,' said Denny. 'I think you're right.'

But did he really? He wondered. Or did he just *want* to think so? It was far less painful to believe that it was some magical conspiracy that had made his life fall apart rather than his own foolishness – and worse than foolishness. He was ashamed of his behaviour to Cindy. It had been selfish and ultimately cruel, but was it *him*? Had he, *would* he – under no influence but his own – have done such a thing? Cindy clearly did not think so, but he had never been in this position before. Tamar was gone, and Cindy was almost as beautiful, almost as strong … A pale shadow of what he had lost.

And if he could have done *that*, wasn't he capable of just about anything, even driving Tamar away in the first place?

Cindy was watching him shrewdly. She guessed some of what was passing in his mind – she had entertained the same doubts at first, and had even told Stiles categorically that it was not magic at work. But now she thought differently. Denny's recent behaviour had decided her. He would *never*, under any circumstances, have tried to seduce her. She knew it.

'It *is* magic,' she told him firmly cutting across his welter of self-recrimination. 'And I can prove it.'

~ Chapter Seven ~

THEY WERE ALL sitting in the Team Alpha control room, where Tamar had first been introduced to them, watching a series of still photographs flit across the large screen while Valerie briefed them about the man in the photographs and what they had to do about him. Tamar could not have told you so much as his name. She had other things on her mind and, as far as she was concerned, all this was unnecessary. Valerie, she was vaguely aware, was ranting about atrocities and burbling about the creature's background and other irrelevant details. Tamar had picked up at the beginning of the briefing, while she was still listening, that they were talking about a minor sorcerer who had recently gone into terrorism. Tamar could deal with such creatures without breaking a sweat; therefore, she had immediately switched off and begun staring out of the window. The blinds were down, but that did not stop her.

She had not forgotten Slev's warning about The Director. In fact, it was this – among other things – that was preying on her mind. Who, or what, was capable of bringing about such a transformation? Denny would know, she thought with a pang, or, at least, he would be able to find out. She was almost certain that The Director himself had no idea of his lupine origins. Although, if pushed, she could not have said what had given her this impression, but it was a very strong feeling. He certainly did not *act* like a wolf. And, despite what Slev had said, she did not think he was particularly dangerous.

The other question, of course, was *why* someone would do such a thing? No matter how many ways she canvassed this question, she simply could not come up with a satisfactory explanation; it just did not make sense.

So why was she still here? Common sense dictated that she use her escape plan and go home to Denny who would almost certainly be able to help her to find out the answers to these questions. But her *un*common senses told her ... What? That if she left now, she might never get back in. *So what?*

That there was much more to find out about this place – like how she was being held inside. And what was that familiar feeling she had experienced when she had exited from the so-called "Teleportation Room" that was anything but? She had a feeling that these two questions were related. And that if she could only use the room a few more times it would come back to her.

She had not forgotten Slev's other warning either, but Tamar was not given to introspection at any time and particularly at the moment, when she knew in her heart that any deeper examination of her motives would probably reveal things that she did not want to know.

The briefing was winding down, and Tamar had made a decision. She would deal summarily with the sorcerer,* he *was* a bad guy after all. And then ... there was one other person who might be able to help her to answer some questions ... and fortunately, she knew exactly where she could lay her hands on him.

*[It would never have occurred to Tamar that she could fail to do this. Even Cindy could deal with a small time sorcerer.]

* * *

'The only kind of magic that we know of that can do this, is the Faeries' magic,' said Denny sceptically. 'And even then, it wasn't this strong. I managed to fight it the last time. I don't think it's magic.'

'Trust me,' said Cindy. 'It is. And I can prove it.'

'Prove it how?'

'I'll have to show you. Come on.' she began to lead him through the house.

A thought struck Denny. 'We *do* have, not one, but *two* Faeries living right here in this house,' he said, following her. 'Although I can't imagine *Finvarra* wanting to make me ... us ... I mean ...what we ...'

'He didn't.' Cindy said firmly. 'It wasn't him. It's not Faeries.'

'And yet,' Denny mused. 'If anyone could ... I mean he has access, we trust him, trust him enough to let him live here anyway and if our guard was down ... he could, theoretically, have a far stronger influence than the Faerie Queen did. I mean we were wary of her.'

'Have you finished?' said Cindy somewhat astringently.

'I'm being ridiculous aren't I?' said Denny, looking slightly ashamed.

'It isn't your fault,' said Cindy briskly. 'I'm just going to assume, for the time being, that you don't really mean *anything* you say.'

'Really?' said Denny. Then added mischievously, 'I like your hair, have you had it done?'

'Very funny,'

'No really. Oh, all right then, I'll say I'm sorry if you like. But how will you know if I mean it?'

Cindy laughed. 'Do you ever?'

'Hey?' Denny was indignant until he realised that he had asked for this.

'So, what do you mean, it's *not* Faeries?' he asked still trotting along behind her obediently.

'I mean it's something else,' she said. 'And I have an idea what, and so would you, if your brain was functioning on all cylinders, like it should be.'

'Something that uses mind control magic like the Faeries, but clearly far more powerful,' pondered Denny.

Cindy grinned. 'Think about it,' she said just a little smugly.

'Oh, you're loving this, aren't you?' said Denny.'

They had arrived at the room that Tamar had recently converted into a nursery. This was where Finvarra was usually to be found during the day, which was why Cindy had come. He was sat on the floor with the boys; they were playing with some plastic dinosaurs.

Denny had never been in here before, and as he walked in, he let out an involuntary. 'My God!' which he tried, unsuccessfully, to cover with a cough.

Cindy gave him a dirty look, which he protested against. 'We're ignoring everything I say, remember?' he tried.

'No, no,' said Finvarra rising gracefully to his feet. ''Tis a bit … ahem. Well it's not a man's style let us just say.' He looked quizzically at them both.

'What state of mind do you think Tamar must have been in to design such a room?' Cindy asked Finvarra abruptly and as far as he was concerned, irrelevantly. Even used, as he was, to Cindy's sharp non-sequiters, Finvarra looked nonplussed at this one.

'Well, she did it for the kiddies, didn't she?' he asked. 'I mean … Well, all right, I see what you mean.' he conceded. 'If I didn't know better, I'd say she was a little bit … perhaps not quite herself maybe. Never really had her down as the decorating type at all really,' he admitted.

'How is this helping?' interrupted Denny impatiently. 'We *know* she hasn't been herself – assuming you're right,'

'What could do that to someone as powerful as her, do you think?' said Cindy ignoring this.

Finvarra looked perplexedly from one to the other trying earnestly to understand what they were getting at. 'Well, I don't know,' he said eventually, hoping this was right.

Cindy lost her temper. 'Oh, for God's sake Fin,' she snapped. 'They're still here, aren't they?'

'Who?'

'The Tuatha de Danann,' she said quietly, as if they might be able to hear her. 'Leir's race.'

Light finally dawned on Denny. 'My God,' he said softly.

Finvarra froze. 'Don't talk about them,' he said.

'We *have* to,' said Cindy firmly. 'Tell us what you know.' She took Finvarra's hands gently. 'It's important darling,' she said. 'We need your help.'

Finvarra looked nervously behind him at the two little boys who were watching this scene avidly. 'Not here,' he said, indicating pointedly at the children.

'Let's go downstairs then,' said Denny.

* * *

'They fled into the hills,' said Finvarra, 'The Tuatha, many centuries ago. Long before the Sidhe were banished by men. Their power had dwindled, so it was said, and now they are supposed to be nothing more than spirits that haunt the hills and forests.'

'But they never actually left?' asked Denny. 'I thought they had left, or died or something.'

'Where would they go?' asked Finvarra, not unreasonably. 'And gods do not die. Rather do they diminish as the world moves on without the need of them.'

'So, they *are* still here, then?'

'There's one way to find out for certain,' said Cindy. 'Where's Jack?'

* * *

Having dealt summarily, as predicted, with the sorcerer, Tamar had suddenly vanished from sight. The Director, when the bewildered Team Alpha had reported this to him, had taken it very well. 'Don't bother looking for her,' he said. 'She wouldn't have done this if she hadn't worked out how to beat the isotope tracking. But she'll come back,' he added confidently. 'This was just something she had to get out of her system. No, I don't blame any of you. This was foreseen, but not how or when it would happen. You can go now.' he dismissed them. It is doubtful, that had he known where Tamar had gone and for what purpose, he would have been quite so blasé about it. However, he did not.

* * *

In a scene never witnessed before in any male prison in the whole of history, an attractive woman traversed the entire cellblock, passing cell after cell of humanity's worst and wickedest to the accompaniment of not a single catcall, whistle or jeer.

At cell 420, she stopped and passed, apparently unimpeded, through the bars without the need of a key. 'Matthias Greyholme,' she said to the cell's present incumbent, who was reading a book about crochet. 'You haven't changed a bit.'

'Tamar the Black?' he said apparently undisturbed by this sudden and unorthodox intrusion. 'Neither have you.'

He looked up at her. 'But I am wrong,' he said. 'I see that you are no longer a Djinn.'

'Well,' Tamar laughed. 'There's not much gets past you anyway.'

'But it is very obvious,' said Matthias.

'To you maybe,' she said shortly. 'Look Matthias I need … why are you reading a book about crochet?'

'Ah, when one is given a sentence of three hundred and forty years, it is not expected by anyone that one will have to serve every last day of that sentence. In such a case, one passes the time any way one can.' Which was not really an explanation, but it did raise another question.

'So why do you stay here? You don't have to.'

'I like the peace. Besides, how to explain?'

'Explain what? That you are not an ordinary prisoner but a 500 year old necromancer?'

'That too.' he said.

'But you wouldn't *have* to explain,' pointed out Tamar. 'You'd be gone. How are you going to explain being here so long anyway? They'll be expecting you to die eventually. What did they get you on anyway?'

'I think I'll be asking the personal questions actually,' said Matthias suddenly. 'After all, I don't suppose you came here for a social visit. You want my help with something I take it? Well it's going to cost you.'

'Cost me what?' sighed Tamar in a resigned tone.'

'Tell me how you became human. I'm just bursting with curiosity on that one I have to admit.'

'And that's it?'

'Yes.'

'Oh, Okay, well I got a new master about six years ago and he freed me.'

'How?'

'We found Askphrit together and tricked him back into the bottle. It was all Denny's idea actually.'

'Denny?'

'He was my master. That was … that's his name.'

'And, I'm sorry, I must have missed a bit. Who is Askphrit?'

'Of course,' Tamar thought. 'Until Denny, I never told anyone about Askphrit – well no one ever asked.'

*

She had met Matthias four hundred years earlier when he had been the court magician to a horrible Emperor in one of those savage rural fiefdoms that were pretty much everywhere in those days. She had been the Emperor's Djinn, and they had struck up something that approximated a friendship. "The enemy of my enemy is my friend" as Matthias said.

Of course, the Emperor had not really been an Emperor; he had given himself the title and had Tamar enforce it. When Tamar had become free upon the Emperors untimely death, Matthias had also mysteriously disappeared.

Tamar suspected that he was now in prison for grave robbing – he was a necromancer after all.

She had kept in touch with him in a desultory way over the years, often not seeing him for years at a time but still, until Denny, he had been the closest thing she had had to a friend in five thousand years. She had found out that he was in prison from himself; he had contacted her in the usual way – that is to say, along the mystical grapevine. She had actually had the news from a passing gnome, who could not remember where he had heard it. That had been twenty-seven years ago, and she felt suddenly ashamed that she had not visited him before. This guilt, she recognized as Denny's influence. However, Matthias seemed neither surprised nor injured that she had not come before.

*

For the next twenty minutes or so, under Matthias's patient questioning, Tamar found herself explaining the whole story of how she had become a Djinn and how she had met Denny and how he had saved her.

'And you are still with him?' asked Matthias at the end of the tale.

'Y-yes.'

'And I bet he is neither handsome nor rich, is he?' asked Matthias ignoring her hesitation. 'Or powerful, eh?'

'Well, he is powerful – now,' said Tamar, thinking of the Athame. 'But he wasn't then. He was just ordinary when I met him.'

'Ordinary?' said Matthias. 'Oh I don't think he was ordinary. Do you?' he asked with a twinkle in his eye.

'No,' said Tamar thoughtfully. 'He's anything but ordinary.'

There was a silence. 'So, what can I do for *you*, then?' said Matthias after a long few minutes of this.

'Hmm, what? Oh yes, I was miles away there, sorry.' she turned to face him and said abruptly. 'What can turn a wolf into man?

'I take it you don't mean a mere glamour,' said Matthias.

'No, I don't. I mean the full transmogrification – brainwaves and everything. I mean who or what has that kind of power?'

'Hmm,' Matthias looked thoughtful. 'That's some powerful magic. Odin used to be fond of that sort of thing of course. Very into the genetic engineering thing, as they call it now in quantum circles.'

'Odin?' but he couldn't do *that*. He was just a god … wasn't he?'

'Ah, but if he was only a god, then why didn't he go the way of the rest of them?' Matthias said.

'What do you mean by *that*?' asked Tamar, in sudden alarm.

'Oh, old Odin's still around.'

'He *is*?'

'Oh yes, most certainly.'

So, *not* just a god then?'

'I have no idea my dear. No idea, not my area. I *do* know he still has many worshippers, which might account for it if he were.'

'That wouldn't explain the, what did you call it, genetic engineering?'

'I don't know about that,' said Matthias. 'Anyway, I didn't say for certain that he was your man ...'

'God.'

'... God. Just that he *might* be.'

'So, what else is likely responsible?'

'Could be a Djinn of course,' said Matthias. 'But I doubt it.'

'So do I,' said Tamar emphatically. She had already discarded this idea at the beginning as unlikely, being as the Djinn could only access their power by means of a direct wish from a human, and what human would make such a wish? Humans were crazy, but not, in her experience, as crazy as *that*.

'A bio engineer looking for a Nobel Prize,' said Matthias as if reading her thoughts.

'Bollocks,' scoffed Tamar.

'I suppose, so,' said Matthias mildly.

'I should be going,' said Tamar. 'Thanks for your insights anyway. I'll have a think about it. And Matthias?'

'Yes?'

'What's with the shaggy beard? You look like an old hermit'

'Well, it's a look, isn't it?' he said in a hurt voice. 'I thought it made me look venerable.'

'Just scruffy really,' she said scathingly and vanished.

'She hasn't changed at all.' said Matthias to the space that she had just vacated.

* * *

Jack Stiles gingerly slipped his hand into the gauntlet and waited. It only took seconds before the filigree tendrils began extending through the skin and into the nerves in his arm. Although they had seen it before, (except Finvarra) they all watched fascinated as the tendrils writhed under the surface of his skin extending up his arm and into his central nervous system.

When it stopped, Stiles looked up sharply and opened his eyes – they glowed briefly and then faded to normal.

'Are we *certain* this is absolutely necessary?' he asked, somewhat belatedly.

The problem here was that once the gauntlet was attached, there was no way to remove the damn thing. It just came off when it wanted to – or at least so it seemed. The last time he had worn it, it had removed itself after its purpose had been served. Created by the Tuatha god Leir as a means of preserving and passing on his power, the wearer became the Avatar of Leir possessing his knowledge and power as a means to continue the fight against the Sidhe. As far as anyone knew, no previous owner of the gauntlet had ever been able to shed it until their death. But then, none of them had ever fulfilled its purpose and defeated the Sidhe. Stiles had.

Now he was putting it on for a second time, and who knew whether it would ever come off again. He had not even been certain that it would attach, and a part of him had fervently hoped that it would not. It was not pleasant having another's thoughts and memories roaming around in one's head.

'Well?' said Denny.

'Give me a minute,' said Stiles impatiently. He closed his eyes.

'The brethren of Leir fled into the hills and mounds,' he said somewhat pompously. He always talked like this when he was channelling Leir; it was very different to the way he normally talked which made it easy for the others to tell which one of them was speaking.

'Some diminished, but a great many more did not. A way was found to survive. They became wraiths, spirits. Ascension was achieved. They left their physical bodies. They are now the spirits of wood and water, of lakes, rivers, forests and hills. To answer your question, yes, they are here still, in a manner of speaking. But there is fear. A great enemy of old seeks them now. I feel its presence also. A terrible war approaches. The Tuatha will rise again, take new physical form, and fight the enemy, though they have little hope of victory, and this world and all its people will be swept away in the ensuing battle for dominion.'

This extraordinary statement was met with shocked silence. They had asked the question and been told much more and far worse than they had expected.

'It *is* the Tuatha who have been influencing your minds,' said Stiles in his ordinary voice. 'All that stuff about taking a new physical body – they've been doing that for a long time. All it means it they can inhabit a human body if they want to. They can take over completely and run the body or they can just live there and make suggestions – you'd never know they were there.'

'You mean I'm *possessed*?' screeched Denny in absolute horror. (This was getting worse and worse.) 'Tamar too?'

'They were not intentionally influencing your behaviour,' said Stiles as if he was reading from some invisible script inside his head and incidentally answering Denny's question. 'It was a side effect of the inhabitation. They chose the strongest – you, Tamar, and others like you, in order to be ready for the enemy that is coming.'

'And when this enemy arrives they were just going to take over our minds completely and have us fight this enemy for them? I don't *think* so,' said Denny. 'How do I get it out of me?'

'The spirit has already gone,' said Stiles. 'Once you knew it was there, you were no longer a viable host. You would have fought for control and probably won. Taking control of the body relies on the host's obliviousness to the spirit's presence.'

'The element of surprise,' said Denny with grim humour. 'I see.'

'But Tamar is still …' began Cindy.

'It's strange,' said Stiles shaking his head. 'But the one inhabiting Tamar was cast out shortly after she left here.'

'How do you know *that*?' snapped Denny.

'Leir is telling me, we can hear their thoughts.'

'"*We*" *again,*' thought Denny. Stiles had talked like this the last time. It had been unnerving then too.

'Cast out how?' he asked.

'I do not know, it was not her. She had no idea of its presence.'

'So, she didn't come home because …?'

'We don't know *what* her reasons might have been,' said Cindy. 'Don't jump to conclusions.'

Denny looked mutinous but kept silent.

'How many others have been affected?' Cindy asked, and Denny realised that he should have asked this himself.

'Many,' said Stiles enigmatically. 'Sorcerers, Witches, Necromancers. All humans with extraordinary powers. There are more than you think.'

'Me?' asked Cindy nervously wondering if she wanted the answer to be yes or no.

'Indeed,' said Stiles.

'I'd have preferred no,' thought Cindy.

'But no longer,' he added, to her relief.

'So, let me get this straight,' said Denny. 'We have all been acting out of character because we have been possessed by the spirits of the Tuatha de Danann. Who wanted to use our bodies in some great battle that's coming up, is that about right?'

'You have not been *possessed*,' corrected Stiles. 'You have been *inhabited*. The spirits are not *making* you do anything – as yet. But you may have been prey to subtle influences that have exacerbated your behaviour. Perhaps you were even aware of them on a subconscious level, and it made you behave in certain uncharacteristic ways. I cannot say.'

Denny looked at Cindy. 'Oh, I think we've been acting in *very* uncharacteristic ways at times,' he said

'Of course, an inhabitation can adversely affect your moral centre,' said Stiles. 'The Tuatha have a different set of moral values to humans, perhaps equally valid perhaps not. But their influence would probably be felt. You might follow an impulse toward behaviour that you would normally restrain in yourself out of a sense of morality or shame. The Tuatha do not understand shame. Perhaps that is what you mean?'

Denny nodded. 'I think that *is* what I mean,' he said.

Cindy looked at her shoes; she was scarlet with embarrassment.

'But the original impulse toward that behaviour would have been your own,' added Stiles.

'All right, all right,' said Denny testily. 'There's no need to hammer it home. We get the picture.'

'Well, said Finvarra suddenly, 'now that we have got all that out of the way. What about this wretched war that's coming? I mean I thought all you hero types would have been all over that one.'

'That's right,' said Denny with no apparent sense of irony. 'What's the deal with that, anyway? You said the world would be swept away. By whom? Who *is* this enemy that they're all so afraid of anyway?'

But at that moment, the damn gauntlet fell off. Stiles gave Denny a blank look. 'What are you talking about mate?' he said.

Denny groaned. 'Oh hell!'

~ Chapter Eight ~

'IT'S ARMAGEDDON,' said Denny flatly to the others now assembled in the study. Cindy and Finvarra, of course, already knew. Dawber, Stiles and Hecaté, by reason of their being absent, (either in body or at least in Stiles's case, in mind) when the revelations of Leir had been made, did not.

'What – *again*?' said Stiles and Hecaté in unison.

'Hey, what do they mean, *again*?' asked Dawber nervously.

'Don't worry about it,' advised Cindy. 'It's par for the course around here, it'll all be sorted out in the end, you'll see.'

'We need Tamar,' said Denny. 'You,' he pointed to Dawber, 'can you get me into this agency or not?'

'I-I can try.' stammered Dawber.

'When?'

'Er … now?' asked Dawber uncertainly.

'We'll leave in an hour,' confirmed Denny.

'That'll give you time to make your peace with God before you go. I would.' said Stiles wickedly.

'*Jack*!' said Hecaté in a shocked voice. 'That was *not* kind.'

'We'll try to find out about these animal abductions while we're at it,' said Denny apparently not hearing this exchange. 'But our first priority is to find and retrieve Tamar, okay?'

'Okay, sir,' said Dawber reflexively and without apparent sarcasm.'

Denny raised an eyebrow. 'There's no need for that,' he said.

'Now, how can we find out who else has been "inhabited" by the Tuatha? Any ideas?'

'I'm not putting that sodding gauntlet back on,' said Stiles.

'No one's asking you to,' said Denny shortly. 'I doubt it would help anyway. Leir clearly didn't want to tell us any more than he did.'

'But without his help, how can we hope to track down the others?' said Cindy.

'There is more than one god in this room,' said Hecaté unexpectedly. 'I shall try to sense their location.'

'Good,' said Denny. But I need a backup plan. Anyone?'

'We'll come back to that,' he said, when no ideas were forthcoming. 'The other thing we need to do is find out who the enemy of the Tuatha is and how much of a danger he – or she poses. Also, when they are expected.'

'That sort of research is usually *your* thing,' pointed out Cindy.

'I'm going to be busy.' said Denny. 'Give it a try, it's not hard.'

'I'm no hacker,' said Cindy, 'but I suppose I'll do my best.'

'I'll get you started,' offered Denny.

'Investigation is really more *my* area,' said Stiles. Clearly wondering why this detail had been palmed off on Cindy. 'Oh, *I* get it, you don't know if you can trust me.'

Denny looked awkward. 'You and Cind work together,' he said coming to a decision.

'And what shall I do?' asked Finvarra expectantly.

'Oh, er,' Denny floundered. 'Well ...'

'He is the distant kin of the Tuatha,' said Hecaté. 'He shall also see if he cannot locate their whereabouts. I shall show him the technique. It may well be that he shall have more success that I. he is closer in nature to them than I am.'

'Okay, good,' said Denny recovering his poise. 'That's a good idea. He gave Hecaté a warm smile.

'We also have a wedding to arrange,' she said suddenly. 'Armageddon or not, some things are important. Too often do we put our lives on hold for these things and what is the result? Unhappiness, disruption, dislocation. Do not argue with me Denny.'

'I wasn't going to.' he said. 'I think you're right, but everything's already arranged – except the bride.' he added *sotto voce*.

'*You* are taking care of that.' said Hecaté crisply.

'Wedding?' said Dawber. 'Oh my god, *yes*. I remember. All those dress fittings.' He looked at Denny compassionately. 'For what it's worth, I reckon she'd turn up anyway. No one would go to all that trouble over an outfit, if she didn't intend to wear it.'

'That's the spirit,' said Stiles slapping Dawber heartily on the back and Denny remembered Stiles himself saying much the same thing recently.

They all looked at Denny. 'So, why hasn't she come back yet?' he challenged.

Everyone looked at the floor.

'Right,' said Denny. 'Let's get on with it.'

* * *

They had come by car, there being no way to teleport to an unknown location, and Dawber had lost his way several times to Denny's ill concealed chagrin. However, they were now standing in a large aircraft hangar, which Dawber insisted was the right place. Denny was sceptical.

'Okay, how do we get in?' he said.

'I swiped this from Agent Rook,' said Dawber, holding up what looked like a security card. 'They'll read it and bring us in. I just hope Agent Rook is out at the moment, otherwise … ah, here we go.' A bright red light beam shone out, and Dawber immediately waved the card in front of it. There was a loud beep. 'Confirmed,' said Dawber. 'Be ready to fight in case there's anyone in the control room,' he said.

'I'm ready,' said Denny grimly. And then they were brought inside.

It was the most horrible sensation Denny had ever experienced – since the last time he had experienced it anyway, which had been quite recently.

'Who the hell *are* these people anyway,' he said when they arrived in the control room which was, fortunately, empty. He sounded frightened. He was. He had a feeling of being trapped that was so strong he was close to panic.

He looked around the room, frantically seeking a way out, while Dawber watched him curiously.

'The way out is there,' he said pointing to a door.

'No,' gasped Denny, 'that's just a way further in. This whole place is one big trap,' he said. 'Can't you feel it?'

Dawber shrugged. 'We should go, before they find us in here,' he said.

Denny pulled himself together. 'Right,' he said. But he could hardly believe that Tamar, of all people, would have chosen to stay here. Not her, not *here*. Of course, it had been specially designed to prevent escape. He was not even sure that he himself would ever get out. Perhaps Dawber had been wrong; perhaps she *was* trapped here, just as he feared *he* was. He felt his throat tighten. 'Don't panic,' he admonished himself. 'You've got out of worse situations.'

But the truth was he had not. No one *ever* had – not without outside help. That was kind of the point of a Djinn's bottle.

It was massive inside, much larger than Tamar's bottle had been, but he knew that theoretically her bottle *could* have been this large inside if she had wanted it to be. A horrible thought struck him; this could not *be* her bottle, could it? No, that had been destroyed. What did it matter *who's* bottle it had been. The result was the same; no one got out from the inside. Someone outside had to be pulling the strings on this operation. He was going to find out who it was and shove the bottle down his throat. The thought made him feel a little better.

'Where's Tamar?' he said to Dawber.

'Team Alpha control room, probably,' answered Dawber. 'This way.'

Denny followed him cautiously down an endless corridor. They passed several people, none of whom took the slightest notice of them. This was not too surprising. Evidently, there were hundreds of people here, and no one could be expected to know them all. Unfamiliar faces were probably not unusual, and the chances were that there had never before been a security breach here.

The Team Alpha control room was deserted, and Dawber shrugged helplessly. 'There's always the cafeteria,' he said. 'Or we could wait here. They're bound to come back eventually.'

'Here's better,' said Denny. 'Less people, but … let's have a look at the canteen then. We can just see if she's there and then maybe wait for her outside.'

It was not much of a plan, as Denny was painfully aware, but there was nothing better, and it was probably pointless anyway. There was no way out of here even if he did find her. He realised that he just wanted to *find* her, no matter what happened next. He just wanted to *see* her, *needed* to see her, to tell her he was sorry.'

His thoughts skidded round in the midst of his despair. 'Wait a minute,' he said. 'How did you escape from this place, anyway?'

'I just gave Rook the slip when we were on surveillance,' said Dawber. 'I thought I told you.'

'Yeah, that's right, you did,' said Denny suddenly subdued. 'So, why did you take Rook's card, then? Surely you didn't think, back then, that you'd be coming back?'

'Oh, no, I didn't. The truth is I never expected to get away from Rook. If he hadn't gone for a leak, I'd never have gotten away. I took the card to escape from *here*. I don't have one. Only senior Agents have them.'

'So, we *can* get out of here?' said Denny.

'Of course we can. You don't think I'd've come back if I couldn't get out?' He shuddered.

'Thank Odin,' said Denny; apparently never noticing what a strange thing this was to say.

'What's that room?' he said as his attention was drawn irresistibly to a large plain oak door.

'It says on it,' said Dawber. 'That's The Director's office. *Don't* go in … ah shit!'

Denny had not, in fact, just blithely walked into The Director's office. He had merely pushed the door slightly ajar and was listening to hear if anyone was in there. Someone was. Denny could hear voices.

'Don't bother looking for her,' said a deep voice. 'She wouldn't have done this if she hadn't worked out how to beat the isotope tracking. But she'll come back. This was just something she had to get out of her system.'

'We're terribly sorry Director,' said a female voice. 'She just disappeared. I never saw such a thing before.'

'Well, she was a Djinn,' said another voice, this time male. 'We should have been prepared for this.'

'No, I don't blame any of you. This was foreseen, but not how, or when it would happen,' said The Deep voice again. 'You can go now.'

Denny dodged back as the four people filed out of the room. Dawber was hiding in a handy alcove.

Denny dragged him out. 'We're leaving,' he said tersely. 'She isn't here,' he added before Dawber could ask any questions.

* * *

Tamar woke in the glass room. Her eyeballs hurt. 'Oh no, not again,' she thought.

But it was not the same this time. For one thing, this time she remembered how she had got here. She had made her own way back – she was certain of this. She had teleported back to the aircraft hangar and waited for them to bring her in, and that was all she remembered. So why …? She struggled up onto her elbows and looked around the familiar room dispiritedly.

Was she being punished? That would make some sense, she supposed. But it seemed unlikely. They *needed* her; they had made that pretty clear. Or was that a lie? Suddenly she felt weary. 'Why does this sort of thing keep happening to me?'

'Ah, you're awake,' it was The Director. 'We were getting concerned.'

'You were?' Tamar was nonplussed.

'I am sorry that we put you in the containment room again,' he said smoothly. 'I know you don't like it in here. But your behaviour was, quite frankly, rather alarming.'

'It was?' *he's lying*, she thought.

'Oh, yes,' said The Director smoothly. Tamar was beginning to loathe that unruffled, smooth demeanour of his. She knew also that he had her at a disadvantage here. She was feeling uneasy in this room, like a trapped animal. That, she thought, was probably the idea.

'Don't you remember anything?' The Director asked.

'Yes,' she thought. 'I remember getting the hell out of here. I should never have come back.' But she did not remember anything after she had returned to the hangar. What had they done to her?

'No,' she said. 'I can't remember.' for a split second, no more, an expression of satisfaction flitted over The Director's face. Then he looked sombre. 'Well, he said. When you and the Alpha Team returned from your mission, you began exhibiting erratic behaviour. We have tried to account for it. The mission itself, you remember that?'

Tamar weighed it up and decided. 'No,' she said.

The Director nodded sagely. 'It was a success anyway,' he said, 'as far as we could tell anyway. Target neutralised – by you, I might add, and most efficiently. However, your behaviour after your return … It is possible that the target was warned in advance and may have activated some sort of magical booby trap in the event of his own demise.'

'Warned by whom?' said Tamar, obediently following the script. She wanted to see just how far he was going to push this ludicrous rigmarole of lies.

'We are investigating the possibility of a leak within the agency,' he said. 'I can't tell you any more about that at the moment. What I *can* tell you is that you were rambling incoherently about going home, just as if *this* wasn't your home. And wolves and – oh, all sorts of nonsense, then you became violent and we had to sedate you.'

'He doesn't know,' she thought.

The Director was clearly hypothesising on her motives for her sudden departure, and he was counting on the fact that they had been fooling around in her memory again, in order to plant doubt in her mind by making up this ridiculous story.

'He doesn't know where I went. They didn't have me followed. And he knows that I know he's a wolf. He must have been listening when Slev warned me, so he's trying to make me believe it was all a fantasy, in case I remember. Imagine trying to convince me that this place is my *home*.'

'Just how much of my memory did they try to remove?' she wondered. Was she have supposed to have totally forgotten her former life? Surely not. No, they had tried to remove just enough to cause her to doubt the memories she had. To wonder if she *had* been attacked by some "booby trap" that had affected her mind.

It was damned clever, she realised. In the face of such doubt most people would agree to just about anything they were told in order to allay suspicions that they were unreliable – or worse, crazy. It was a way of chastening her, making her behave herself in future, to make her want to behave as expected and not argue, and probably, in time, to come to accept whatever they told her as the truth. But their memory modifications had not worked this time. And because they had not, she would never know just how much they expected her to have forgotten. She would just have to guess. Then she realised that it did not matter in any case, whatever she *did* remember they would not expect her to admit to anyway. She would not want anyone to think she was crazy now, would she?

'Wolves?' she said now. 'That's weird,' she added and treated him to her most innocent stare.

He appeared to swallow it because he smiled. 'Why don't we get out of this unpleasant room?' he suggested.

She wondered idly why the process had not worked on her memory this time.

With a sudden guilty feeling Tamar realised that, while she had been wondering how much of her memory they had tried to access, she had thought of her life with Denny and her friends as a *former* life.

'What if they *had* been successful?' she wondered. What if she had truly been made to forget everything up to this point? Her life, her friends and oh God – *Denny*!'

Suddenly, watching the broad back of The Director as he walked calmly ahead of her, she became choked with hatred.

*

Things, on the surface anyway, had returned to normal. Tamar was back on the team as if nothing had happened. She suspected that Team Alpha had no idea what had happened to her. They had probably all had their own memories altered at times. Certainly, there was no restraint between them and no one asked her where she had been. She wondered how long she had been missing. Probably not more than a day. But she would never know for sure.

But it was not the team's behaviour that was puzzling Tamar, it was her own. Now, more than ever, surely, she should be trying to get herself *out* of here. It was not as if it would be difficult. She had allayed The Director's suspicions, she was sure. They would not be expecting an escape attempt again so soon. So, again she wondered. 'Why am I still here?'

The same mixed motives as before applied of course. She was still here, because she was not ready to leave.

She became aware that Slick was saying something to her. Instead of focusing on him properly, she squinted up her eyes and sighed heavily.

'You're imagining I'm someone else when you do that, aren't you?' asked Slick with frightening perspicacity.

Tamar was too astounded to deny it. 'How the hell did you know that?' she sputtered in a shocked voice.

Slick seemed unperturbed. 'It happens to me all the time,' he said. 'I have a kind of generic face. A bit of "soft focus" and I can be anyone you want. Hey whatever works for you babe, I'll take it.'

'You wouldn't mind that?' Tamar thought of herself as broad minded, but this seemed outrageous.

'I told you, it happens all the time. I'm used to it.'

'Well, I'll leave it if you don't mind,' she said stiffly.

'Who is he?' asked Slick curiously. But Tamar pretended she had not heard and moved off with her nose in the air and her head in turmoil.

'That chick is off the map,' said Slick to Ray who happened to be sat close by and had heard everything.

Ray grunted noncommittally and then said. 'You're just pissed off because she said no again. If anyone's gotta problem round here, it's you. Why don't you try keeping it in your pants for a change? Give us all a break.'

'What's *your* problem?' muttered Slick and slouched off to put the TV on.

* * *

Tamar was out on surveillance. She found this ironic, considering that she had recently been the object of this activity. Activity was the wrong word for it. It was hours and hours and hours of dull watching and waiting.

However, the good news was that her act had clearly been completely swallowed; otherwise, they would never have let her do this. Not that she was alone, of course. But Ray, who was partnering her, would have had no chance of stopping her had she decided to take off again.

As yet, despite three days of acute boredom, she had shown no sign of wishing to take off.

They were, not that it matters, watching a house that was suspected of being a Troglodyte stronghold. There had so far been no evidence of it. Trogs were hard to miss, being reptilian in appearance and between five and seven feet tall. From being a feudal society of warring clans, they had developed into a strong part of the mystical underworld. The magic community's answer to the Mafia, dealing in drug peddling, murder for hire, kidnappings all the usual crimes. The scum of the otherworld. The warring clans still existed, only now they were more like factions, but the wars went on.

Still, if they *were* in there, they weren't coming out – even at night.

Ray yawned widely. 'Mind if I put the radio on?' he asked. 'It'll help me keep awake.'

'Sleep if you like,' said Tamar. 'I don't need to. I'll wake you if anything happens.'

'Naw, I'm not tired, just bored.' He flipped the radio on.

The song playing reminded Tamar poignantly of Denny. He had sung it to her once, but it could, she had felt at the time, quite reasonably, in fact, more appropriately, be sung by her, to him.

'Cause I wanted to fly. So you gave me your wings
And time held its breath. So I could see ... you set me free.
You're in my heart
The only light that shines there in the dark
When I was alone, you came around,
When I was down
You pulled me through,
And there's nothing that I wouldn't do for you

'*You set me free*,' she murmured under her breath. She was not listening she realised, to the radio. The words running through her head were not in tune with the radio. She was remembering ...

More than three hundred miles away, as Denny swung the car round bends, slamming the accelerator viciously and furiously, he unexpectedly started to sing.

When I was alone, you came around,

When I was down
You pulled me through,
And there's nothing that I wouldn't do for you
Cause I wanted to fly. So you gave me your wings
And time held its breath. So I could see... you set me free.

Dawber looked curiously at him. 'That's nice,' he said. 'What brought that on?'

'I don't ... I'm not sure.'

'Well, at least you've calmed down,' said Dawber in undisguised relief. 'I thought you were going to get us killed, the way you were driving.'

Denny smiled quietly. 'Yeah,' he said, 'I feel better. It's going to be all right.'

'Dawber looked somewhat askance at this remark, remembering all the stuff he had heard quite recently from this guy. Most memorably a lot of stuff about, oh what was it? Oh yes, *Armageddon*!

'The hell you say?' he remarked sceptically.

* * *

'We're on the move,' said Ray snapping off the radio. 'There they go.'

Tamar snapped her focus back to the matter at hand. The three figures emerging stealthily into the dark streets were indeed Troglodytes. Tamar recognised the reptilian skin and the ungainly build. These were unbalanced – their walking strangely lopsided. Tamar realised suddenly and with some amusement the reason for their strange gait. They had had their tails docked.

'Cascar clan,' she said.

'How the hell do you know that?' asked Ray, impressed.

'The tattoos,' she said.

Ray peered into the shadows. All he could see were silhouetted shapes with the occasional blur of scaly skin highlighted by the ambient light from the night's half moon. 'What tattoos?'

'Clan tattoos, on the forehead. They are a bit hard to see in this light. I suppose you have to know what you're looking for.'

'Okay, you're the boss,' said Ray. 'What do we do now?'

'Follow them,' said Tamar unhesitatingly. 'I want to know where they're going.

'We won't need the car,' she added. 'Troglodytes don't move fast, and they can't drive.'

Ray looked unhappy about this, apart from anything else (like having to run away if they were spotted) it was starting to rain.

*

It was uncanny, Ray thought. He was soaked through, he squelched unhappily as he walked, but Tamar looked barely damp. How did she *do* that? His admiration for Tamar knew no bounds and he was unhappy in the extreme about her apparent bond with Slick, who he felt was an immoral womaniser; but he was rarely forthcoming about anything much and she certainly had no idea of the respect he had for her. If anything, because of his dour attitude and limited communication, she had the idea that he really did not like her much.

However, she did take pity on him when she glanced over at his miserable face with the rain running down it. 'Here,' she beckoned him. She waved a hand, and he felt a warm glow run through him which more or less dried him off from the inside out.

'Thanks,' he said in surprise.

Tamar grinned in the darkness. 'Well, you looked like a drowned rat,' she said. 'Look sharp,' she added abruptly. 'Looks like journey's end.'

It was a large abandoned storage facility. The Troglodytes showed their tattoos and were waved inside.

'Call it in,' hissed Tamar. 'Looks like a meeting. Could be a lot of them in there.'

'What are you going to do?' asked Ray fumbling for his radio.

'I'm going inside,' she said.

'Could be dangerous,' said Ray mildly.

Tamar smiled wickedly. 'That's their problem,' she said.

* * *

Tamar had her feet up on The Director's desk. She was, perhaps unconsciously, copying a demeanour of Denny's that she herself often found irritating. So she knew she was annoying him.

The raid on the Troglodytes had been another unqualified success. Tamar had not actually been carried along the corridors in triumph on the shoulders of Team Alpha, but the sense of victory when she returned had been palpable.

The Director considered looking pointedly at Tamar's feet but decided against it. He knew that a crisis was coming. Now, if ever, was the time to placate her and bind her more closely to the operation. She had been chastened, now she must be given her freedom to choose. After this victory, he was certain that she would now decide for herself that her place was here. And when he was sure of her, it would be time to show her the real reason she had been brought here.

Unbeknownst to The Director, Tamar was fully aware of the impending crisis that was on his mind. She had been pushing it to the back of her mind almost since she arrived here, but now it was nearly upon her. What she did not know for sure, was whether The Director knew. Not that it mattered; nothing he did would change her plans.

The Director considered giving her a hint of the tremendous task the agency had ahead of it. The reason they so desperately needed her help. He decided against it for the time being. It was to be a decision he would regret.

Had he told her now, or had he simply told her from the beginning, she would very probably have decided, of her own free will, to help.

His own instincts from the start had been to be open with her and hope that she *would* help. But the one from whom he took all his orders, understood only manipulation and control, and was in any case, too proud, too arrogant to beg for help.

His motives may have been good. They *were* good, but his methods sometimes seemed … Well, it had to be faced, they were deceitful, devious and overbearing. Under the circumstances, the fact that he meant well, could well be disregarded if she ever found out how she had been used. She had a strong streak of independent pride of her own. But surely, if she knew the stakes …?

Tamar waited for him to speak. He seemed, for the first time since she had met him, uncertain of what to say. Well, she was not going to help him out. She stared insolently at him.

'Well done,' he said eventually, after pretending to read the report on the Troglodyte capture (he *had* to be pretending. It had been written by Ray whose handwriting Tamar knew to be as indecipherable as his computer codes). 'I see that because you insisted on following the suspects from their hideout, you managed to track down many of the clan leaders and their most trusted henchmen.' He did not say that this was all small potatoes compared to what was coming. But Tamar knew it was. Not that she knew what was coming, but she herself would never be terribly impressed by the mere capture of a few measly Troglodytes. Then she remembered Denny. 'Everything we do matters to someone,' he had once said. 'Sometimes, you just have to save the world one person at a time.'

'Add your light to the sum of light,' she murmured to herself.

'Beg pardon?' said The Director nonplussed.

Before she could stop herself, she said. 'I was just thinking about all the people who might have been, but won't be hurt by the Trogs now.'

'Quite,' agreed The Director. 'A nasty bunch, very dangerous. You did a good thing.' He smiled.

And Tamar remembered a flaming sword and the words "Protector of The People". 'I didn't do it for praise,' she said shortly. 'Once you start down that path, everything goes wrong.

'If that's all sir …?' she half rose in the seat – her mind elsewhere.

The Director nodded amiably, but he was vaguely perturbed by her sudden divergences and her apparent distance.

'Well,' he said to himself after she had drifted from the room. 'That could have gone better.'

* * *

'So, what has everybody found out?' asked Denny.

'That's easy to answer,' said Stiles sardonically. 'Bugger all – in a nutshell.'

'Nothing?' nothing at all?' Denny sighed.

'Sorry,' piped up Cindy. She brightened up slightly. 'But maybe now you're back, you might have more luck. I mean the computer hacking is more your thing really.'

They had been told about the washout at the Agency headquarters, but Denny seemed quite cheerful about it really, so no one liked to push it, or point out that actually, in a material sense, nothing much had changed.

But now his mood was changing again. 'So, we still have no idea what's coming to get the Tuatha?' he said. 'And if it wasn't going to cause a bloody disaster for the rest of the world. I'd say we just let them get on with it,' he added viciously.

'I'd agree,' said Stiles. 'But for the fact, that we're *already* involved. Those *spirits,* or whatever they are, have been inhabiting *people. Our* people. And we still have no idea who else.'

Denny rubbed his head wearily. 'I know, I know. Keep on it. I'll give the Aethernet a try again'

'Oh, no you do not,' said Hecaté firmly. 'You are exhausted. First you need to rest.'

'But we don't know what kind of time frame we're working in,' objected Denny. 'Whatever it is could be on its way right now.'

* * *

Two mud coloured figures writhed in the dirt, like creatures climbing out of the primeval ooze.

'Really Fulk,' said the smaller figure, 'why don't you look where you're going?'

'Biit diifficuult wiith juust the one eye,' muttered Fulk peevishly.

'*What* was that?'

'Nuuuthing,'

The car was ruined. Fulk had driven it headlong into a ditch, upon which it had toppled over impressively and bounced away sideways ending up in heap on the other side of the road. Fulk and his master (who had been on top of the car anyway) had been thrown clear and landed in a muddy puddle at the bottom of the ditch. His mistress was not in a good mood.

'I'll be glad when this is over,' she said. (She was currently a female).

They heaved themselves to the side of the ditch and sat almost companiably in silence, collecting their various thoughts.

'How much further Fulk,' she said suddenly revealing her train of thought.

'Twao aand a haalf morre daays shoulld doo iit,' he said.

'Hmm, without transport?'

'Steaal caar,' suggested Fulk.

She grinned widely cracking the dried mud on her face. 'I *like* your thinking,' she beamed. 'Let's do it!'

~ Chapter Nine ~

COUNTING DOWN to wedding hour… two hours and counting. Denny was nervously getting into his morning suit – nervous, not because he thought she would not show up – but just nervous in the way bridegrooms are always nervous.

Stiles, on the other hand, was terrified. If she *didn't* show up then Denny would be devastated, probably permanently. And it would be mostly his fault. Carrying on with the wedding had been his idea in the first place.

Cindy was applying her makeup for the fourth time. She kept crying and ruining it.

'Weddings make me emotional,' she explained to Finvarra (dressed to the nines in a beautiful and flamboyant velvet suit, in an elegant dove grey. He looked like a visiting prince) who seemed to accept this explanation without query.

Hecaté, already resplendent in clinging purple silk and a large floppy hat, was adding the finishing touches to the cake

Dawber had been invited at the last minute as a guest (the only one really) and was hanging around the house like a spare part. He only had one suit – the one he had arrived in. But since it was impeccable, no one had thought of offering him another.

'Everyone looks so pretty,' observed young Jacky One. Cindy's son and her stepson, for reasons not worth going into at this point, were both called Jacky. Jacky One and Jacky Two looked cute in miniature morning suits that they had uniformly protested against wearing until Cindy said that if they did not, they would not be allowed to come.

'Doesn't Mummy look beautiful?' confided Jacky two to Stiles, as she finally floated down the stairs in pink chiffon and a bright smile, and was quite surprised to find he agreed.

The small anonymous chapel that they had agreed on was in a beautiful and obscure part of Italy. They had decided to take their honeymoon there afterwards, but now it seemed that even if Tamar turned up, that part would have to be cancelled.

It would take them about five minutes to get there, they estimated. Less, if they had not been forced to teleport to an unobservable location first and walk the remainder of the way.

They arrived ten minutes before the ceremony was due to begin. Even in the cool shade behind the thick stone walls, Denny began to sweat.

* * *

There was no way in hell that they were going to let her out of here today, Tamar knew. Even though all the calendars in this place told her it was August 5th, she knew it was not, she knew exactly what day it was. And the fact that they were trying to fool her that it was not, meant that today of all days, they would be taking no chances.

She had a backup plan for this eventuality of course, but it was a long shot – a very long shot. She just hoped that she had not mistaken her man.

'Slick,' she said softly tapping him on the shoulder from behind. 'I need your help.'

'Sure,' he said amiably. 'What's up?'

She took a deep breath and crossed her fingers. 'I need you to get me out of here,' she said. 'Right now.'

* * *

She was now ten minutes late for the ceremony. Stiles, waiting at the door, to give her away (he also had best man duties, which I'm sure is not proper) was fingering his collar nervously.

Denny was in worse shape, but Dawber leaned forward encouragingly from his seat and whispered. 'Brides are always a bit late, it adds to the drama.'

Denny gave him a weak smile. 'She *does* like a bit of drama,' he acknowledged.

'There you are then,' said Dawber. 'Give it a bit long…' He was cut off abruptly by the sudden swelling of music filling the tiny church. The unmistakable strains of "Here Comes The Bride".

Stiles, walking beside an extremely pale and agitated Tamar, was grinning rather foolishly. Denny nearly fainted with relief.

She stopped at the altar and looked questioningly at Denny who swept her suddenly into a crushing embrace and held her as a drowning man might cling to a life preserver.

Only Cindy, turning away to dab her eyes, noticed, at the back of the church, leaning casually against the door frame with his arms folded, a very good-looking man with white blond hair, taking in the scene with a mocking gaze and a strange look of resignation on his face. She wondered who he was. He caught her eye and winked.

'What a fool,' he thought. He had known there was someone. There was *always* someone. And that someone was never him.

He had known, the minute that she had asked him to help her, that he might regret it. He had also known that he would. And no questions asked.

One day, he thought, he might learn, but he doubted it. He had always been a soft touch where women were concerned. It was this (perfectly genuine) softness and inability to hurt a woman or turn down even the slightest request that had made him such a success with women, of course. But you had to expect to get burned sometimes. He had been burned this time all right. She had read him perfectly. He did not regret it though. One look at her radiant face and how could he? 'I'm too soft, that's my trouble,' he thought.

The blonde looked interesting though. He wondered vaguely if she was attached. Probably to that stick in the poofy suit sat next to her.

Then there was the other dark haired woman, a real beauty that one, but she had "married" written all over her. He almost laughed aloud at himself. 'At least you don't have a broken heart, he told himself.'

*

'Man and Wife.' intoned the padre in heavily accented English. It was done, finally. They were married at last.

'You may kiss the bride,' the padre informed Denny, who was way ahead of him.

End of Part One

Part Two

HUNTING FOR LOKI

~ Chapter Ten ~

MANY PEOPLE HAVE their wedding night ruined in a variety of interesting and upsetting ways. From an ex lover – or even spouse turning up and laying claim to one half of the happy couple right down to the hotel catching fire, being flooded or taken over by terrorists. Sometimes it is because the hotel has not actually been built yet (but there are worse things than camping out on the beach with someone you love). However, it could only happen to Tamar and Denny that they had *their* wedding night ruined by the inopportune arrival of a large wolf in an Armani suit.

Denny took it calmly, as was his wont. Nothing, but *nothing*, was about to disturb his happiness at the moment. But Tamar – as was *her* wont – was ready to take his head off.

Even The Director seemed to have realised that his timing could have been better. He shifted awkwardly and backed away as Tamar, wrapped in a hastily grabbed sheet, advanced on him with such a look of ferocity on her face as would have intimidated the gods.*

*[She practiced this look regularly – shattering quite a few mirrors and leaving a trail of transmogrified household object in her wake]

Denny lay back on the bed with a look of amused chagrin on his face. 'I wouldn't want to be that guy for any money,' he thought.

Of course, he did not know who the man was. He and Tamar had already agreed to save all explanations until the next day – there were other things they wanted to do tonight. But his senses told him that:

a) Here was trouble (so what else was new?) And …

b) What was standing awkwardly in the small honeymoon suite backing away from his enraged wife (*wife?*) was not, strictly speaking, a man.

Tamar was swearing fluently in Greek and Arabic and backing The Director into a corner, while he was holding his hands up defensively and trying desperately to placate her. He looked terrified. Denny was trying hard not to laugh. It was pretty obvious to him that Tamar was not actually going to hurt the intruder, whom she clearly recognised – she would have done it by now if she were going to. Denny decided it was time to take a hand. He rose lazily from the bed and casually interposed himself between Tamar and the interloper (phenomenal cosmic powers will make a person feel at ease in almost any situation).

He grabbed Tamar by the arms (no one else would have dared, but Denny had never been afraid of Tamar even before he had his own powers)

'Who is he?' he asked quite naturally.

Tamar spat furiously. 'νόθος,' she said.

Denny knew what she had said (she had used this word to describe Askphrit all the time) but this remark, being no more than an insult was not sufficiently illuminating. He tried again. 'But who *is* he? Or rather, *what* is he?'

'Λύκος,' said Tamar, who seemed unable to revert to English. Denny did not know this word. It sounded like it might be another insult, but he was not sure.

'What was that?' he said calmly.

Tamar took a deep breath; Denny's calm was translating itself to her. She looked steadily at him and said clearly. 'I said, he's a wolf,'

Denny's face cleared. 'I *thought* he wasn't human,' he said. 'What does he want?'

'Ask *him*,' Tamar said stroppily.

'I'm asking *you*?'

'I don't know.'

'Help,' interposed The Director. 'I need your help,'

'You've got a nerve,' snarled Tamar, turning on him again.

The Director responded quite mildly. He seemed to have recovered his equilibrium quite rapidly since Denny's intervention. 'I suppose you could say that,' he agreed. 'But I was only following orders.'

'Whose orders?' asked Denny, before Tamar could take off at him again.

'Why should we believe anything you say,' she snapped at him before he could answer. 'You're a *wolf*.'

'Tamar,' said Denny warningly.

She turned on him. 'No, she yelled. 'You don't know – what he did, what's he's done.'

'I think I have a pretty shrewd idea,' said Denny. 'Kidnapping, memory modifications, imprisoning a load of people in a disused Djinn bottle.'

Tamar's eyes widened. 'You've been there?' she asked aghast. There was no other way he could possibly have known.

'Looking for you,' he affirmed.

Tamar melted at once. 'You did?' I didn't know.'

'No, you weren't there,' he said.

The Director interrupted again at this point. '*You* were in my facility?' he asked in surprise. 'How on Earth …?'

'Shut up,' snapped Tamar and Denny together.

'It took me *ages* to work it out,' said Tamar. 'But you must have figured it out right away. You'd have thought that I, of all people …'

'Perhaps you felt sort of at home there, sort of familiar you know, but hard to pinpoint.' said Denny. 'Whereas I … I just recognised it as a horrible place that I had been in once before. I knew it as soon as I was taken inside.' He shuddered feelingly. 'That horrible feeling when you get sucked in – urgh.'

'Okay, why don't you tell us what's going on,' said Denny turning to The Director.

'Oh *Denny*,' wailed Tamar. 'Can't we just get rid of him? Surely this can wait until tomorrow?'

'There is no time to waste,' said The Director. 'My new orders are to tell you everything. A terrible war is coming ...'

At this Denny looked up alertly.'

'If we don't stop it ...' he shrugged helplessly as if words failed him.

'Terrible devastation?' said Denny. 'The world will be swept away in the battle for dominion,' He was quoting Leir directly.

'Ah, nuts!' said Tamar in comic resignation.

'What do *you* know about it?' asked The Director in surprise.

But Tamar had long since ceased to be surprised by anything Denny did or said. It seemed perfectly natural to her that he knew all about it.

'Clearly not as much as *you* do,' Denny told him. 'I know the Tuatha are preparing for a war. Who is their enemy?'

'I should start at the beginning,' said The Director. 'You don't know a good restaurant in these parts, do you? I'm starving.'

*

'My master is Odin. You have met, I think,' said The Director wiping barbeque sauce of his chin. He had just eaten, to Tamar's disgust, five large plates of special ribs.

'Then you are Fenrir,' she said in surprise. 'Why didn't you just *say* so?' A thought struck her. 'Hey, you're even older than *I* am. Why were you acting so surprised at my age? '

'I didn't remember,' he explained. 'You have experienced the memory modulator. Odin used it on me also. I did not know who I really was for many years, very many years actually.

Odin sent me to Earth over a millennium ago, in the form of a man. And I formed the agency in a crude shape even then, to fight the evil underbelly of the magical world in Odin's name, but he always kept me in the dark.

'But now, finally Odin has revealed his plans to me and returned my memories. For, you see, now the final challenge is at hand, the day that Odin has foreseen. Loki has escaped from Valhalla.'

'*Loki*?' oh no, that's bad.' Tamar was horrified.

'It's worse than you know. You have heard of the Tuatha?'

'I should say so,' said Denny ironically.

'Of course, of course, you said,' said Fenrir. 'Well, Loki is the enemy of the Tuatha.

'That story goes back a very long time.' he continued. 'Needless to say, it was Loki's fault in the first place.'

'No kidding,' interjected Tamar sourly.

'Wasn't Loki stripped of his power by Odin?' asked Denny.

'Not stripped,' said Fenrir, 'it was more that he had it hidden from him, and … Well, he's looking for it, here on Earth. When he finds it, he will go into battle with the Tuatha and, as you said, this world, and its people will suffer the consequences of a battle that has nothing to do with them. My master aims to stop that from happening.'

'How exactly?' asked Tamar, getting interested despite herself.

'With your help,'

'And this is where we came in,' said Denny leaning back in his chair.

'Why should we?' said Tamar. 'After all you've done?'

'Oh, come on Tam,' said Denny chidingly. 'Terrible devastation, innocent people caught in the crossfire, Armageddon. You know we *have* to.'

Tamar rolled her eyes.

'I realise my master has gone about this all the wrong way,' said Fenrir, glancing apprehensively at the ceiling as if expecting a vengeful thunderbolt from above. 'But he doesn't understand humans too well you see? He understands using his power to achieve what he wants. He does not *ask* for help, he gives orders, he manipulates. But he means well.'

'You mean he's proud and arrogant and ... All right, all right.' Tamar held up her hands in disgust. 'I suppose he *does* mean well.'

'Would we be any better than he is, if we refused to help just because he hurt our pride?' asked Denny softly. 'You're better than that Tamar.'

'No, *you're* better than that,' she said. 'I just know that you're usually right about these things. Okay then, what do we have to do?'

'Stop Loki from finding his power.'

'Sounds easy.'

'It will not be. If it were easy, we wouldn't need *you*.'

This was gratifying to hear, although Tamar would never admit it.

'Well,' said Denny. 'We need some more facts. Like what is Loki's power? Where is he likely to be looking for it? We know the Tuatha are inhabiting powerful agents of magic – do you know who they are? How did Loki escape from Valhalla in the first place? – Although I don't suppose that really matters now.'

'I think that might have been *my* fault,' said Tamar hesitantly.

'You are correct,' said Fenrir. 'It was you who opened Valhalla and allowed Loki to escape. However, *fault* is too strong a word. This was foreseen from the beginning. You were merely the instrument of fate so to speak.'

'There you are,' said Denny showing no surprise at this revelation (it was all too familiar). 'No one's blaming you.'

'I'm always doing things like that though,' said Tamar. 'You'd think I'd learn.'

'You couldn't have known,' said Denny. 'And it's not important now anyway. What's important is fixing it. So ...?' he looked at Fenrir.

'Loki's power resides in a pool in a hidden place. Loki lost his powers in the water when Odin and Thor caught him hiding there, disguised as a fish, after he killed Balder. They used his own fishing net to catch him – there's irony for you.' He snorted with laughter.

'Like the Holy Grail, if Loki drinks from the water with the cup of Odin (which Loki has stolen) then his power will return (unfortunately) tenfold.'

'*Tenfold*?' Tamar snapped. 'Whose bright idea was that?'

Fenrir shrugged. 'You can't argue with mythology,' he said. '*You* should know *that*.'

Tamar shrugged. 'In my experience, you can argue with just about anything,' she said.

'But Loki *doesn't* have any power at the moment?' asked Denny.

'Shape shifting,' said Fenrir. 'That's all.'

'Shape shifting?'

'Loki can be either a man or a woman,' explained Tamar. 'But he – or she, I suppose – always looks pretty much the same. *I'll* recognise him all right.'

'This is wild,' said Denny. 'Anything else?'

'We believe he has Fulk with him,' said Fenrir. 'But he's my problem.'

'Fulk?'

'Loki's wolf.' said Tamar. 'Oh, this just keeps getting better and better.'

'*I* will deal with Fulk.' said Fenrir. 'Wolf to wolf.'

And before Denny's vision there rose the image of two snarling wolves fighting to the death.

'So where is this hidden pool?' asked Denny. 'Surely all we have to do is get there first and grab Loki before he uses Odin's cup.'

Fenrir shook his head. 'There's the rub, unfortunately,' he said. 'It isn't in a *place* as such. Only Loki himself can find it – because it's his power and he will be drawn to it. As for us ...'

'We need to find Loki,' supplied Tamar. 'Loki will lead us to the pool.'

'What do you mean, it isn't in a *place*?' asked Denny the literal.

'He means it's like Hank's forest or something. Not in the world, but still accessible from the world. They'll be an entrance somewhere, but we'll never find it.'

'Doesn't Odin know where the entrance is?'

'Why should he?' asked Fenrir. 'They aren't *his* powers.'

'But Loki knows where he's going presumably.' said Tamar.

'Yes, but he'll have to travel the mortal way, and therein lies our only hope.'

'I still don't get it,' said Denny. 'How can Odin not know where he put Loki's powers?'

'It's *mythic*,' said Tamar. 'It doesn't have to make sense. Besides, I might ask you how come you never know where you left your keys.'

Denny frowned. 'It's hardly the same,' he said.

'It's exactly the same, actually,' said Fenrir.

'Odin can't *remember*?' said Denny appalled.

'It *has* been three thousand years,' said Fenrir defensively.

Denny could have sworn he drew his lips back slightly into a snarl, and his hackles definitely rose a little.

'Wait until you've been hanging around a few more thousand years,' said Tamar. 'See how your memory stands up. I know mine's terrible.'

Denny did not believe this, but he knew a losing argument when he saw one, so he held his peace. 'The point is,' he resumed. 'We don't know where Loki is, and we don't know where he's going. That about sum things up?'

'We need Jack,' said Tamar.

Denny agreed, but he also thought – and said. 'We're going to need a lot more than just Jack on this one.'

* * *

The honeymoon was effectively over. Neither Tamar nor Denny were particularly surprised about this.

As Tamar said philosophically, 'It's always going to be something.'

No one was terribly surprised to see Tamar and Denny back in the middle of their wedding night. Hecaté made some half-hearted disapproving clucking noises, but even she accepted it, in the end, as more or less unavoidable.

On the other hand, it was good to have Tamar back where she belonged. Tamar herself had been uncharacteristically nervous about coming home. Before the others were told about Fenrir's revelations, she decided, she would have to do some explaining of her own.

As it turned out, it was not as bad as she had feared. Much of what had happened was already known, mainly from Dawber. And her friends had some surprising revelations of their own. It was Cindy, in the end, and in her own inimitable way, who put into words what they all wanted to make clear.

'Oh, God,' she said dismissively. 'If we all fell out every time one of us did something stupid because of a maniac taking over our brains, we'd never speak to each other again. Forgive and forget. That's what I say.'

Tamar had already been apprised of the Tuatha situation and the probability of her own judgement having been compromised in this way, so this statement was not as unintelligible as it might otherwise have been. But she wondered at the comment coming from Cindy. She also did not miss the glance that passed between Denny and Cindy as she made this remark, but she decided, just this once, that she would never ask.

'I'm not sure the Tuatha count as maniacs,' she said. 'But I see what you mean.'

Tamar, having gathered everyone together (including Dawber and Slick, who had not wanted to return to the Agency after what he had done in helping Tamar and had begged for asylum) now went over the salient points of the situation as told to them by Fenrir.

'We have two main problems,' she summarised. 'We need to find Loki, and we need to find the Tuatha and, if necessary, bang all their heads together.'

'We've already *tried* to find the Tuatha,' said Cindy.

'So, we keep trying,' said Tamar. 'In any case, it's far more important at the moment, to find Loki.'

'And how are we supposed to do that?' asked Cindy. 'You said yourself, we have nowhere to start.'

'I think I might have an idea about that,' said Stiles.

Tamar smiled. 'Yes,' she said. 'We were hoping you would say that.'

Stiles's idea, like so many good ideas, was simple in its inception, but would be complicated to put into practice. They would simply need more bodies. Fortunately, that would not be a problem.

What he proposed, put simply, was a manhunt.

'You said that he's headed straight for the source of his powers,' Stiles said, 'which reside in a pool, right? Now a pool could also be a well or even a lake but definitely a body of water. And you can bet your life it won't be an ordinary body of water. Now, no matter what the true facts may be, the fact is that legends build up around such places. We've seen it before. It's like the magic leaks out into people's consciousness. There are probably a lot of places which fit the bill. I can think of one or two right off. "The Fountain of Youth legend for example, which fits our criteria perfectly, in that it's a known legend with a supposed location, but which no one has actually ever found. That's what we need to look for. Personally, I think the fountain of youth is a bit too obvious, but that's the sort of thing we're after.'

'Now, the *most* obvious place to start would be the river Rhine, supposed home of the Rhine Maidens and the Rheingold – which has never actually been found, by humans I mean – has it?' He stopped to look questioningly at Tamar.

She shook her head. 'It hasn't.'

'The river Rhine is on maps,' Denny pointed out. ' and people take crusies on it … But – that's not what you mean is it?' he added.

'No,' agreed Tamar, 'he means the Rheingold and the maidens and all that guff.'

'It's in the right area, more or less.' Stiles resumed. 'And it might be that that makes it a bit *too* obvious. But we can't afford to eliminate it until we've tried it. However, there will be others. Not as famous or as identifiable with the Norse Legends but we should try them all. What do you think?'

'Only women should go to the Rhine Maidens,' said Tamar. 'I know – I've met them. No man is safe. Cindy and I will go.' This was as good as an endorsement, and the plan was accepted.

'I'll get researching other possible sites,' said Denny. 'I'll also have another go at looking for the Tuatha.'

'We need to advertise,' said Stiles. 'A manhunt depends on luck; mostly on the chance that someone has seen who you're looking for and lets you know. "Have you seen this man?" sort of thing. 'I know it goes against the grain, but we may not have much time here. And we needn't say who he actually is.'

'I can put the word out to the magical community,' said Tamar doubtfully.

'Do it,' said Stiles. 'But it won't be enough. You can bet your life that he'll be avoiding that ilk as much as possible.'

'It's a good idea,' said Denny. 'He'll never expect it, that's for certain.'

'We could do with more people,' said Stiles, 'as many bodies out looking as possible really. I have a feeling that Denny's research is going to turn up a lot of possible sites to investigate.'

'The other thing we need is some information on what exactly Loki's powers are,' Stiles continued. 'It might help us narrow down where we need to look. Some possible sites can be eliminated on the basis that they don't fit with Loki's known powers.'

'He's a shape shifter,' said Tamar. 'He uses magic spells like a wizard – there's a fountain of eternal youth in Brittany near Merlin's Tomb at Broscelainde.'

'Get that down,' said Stiles to no one in particular. 'That sounds like a good possibility.'

'He isn't a god,' said Tamar. 'He's part giant and part ... oh something else, I can't remember Odin adopted him as a foster brother and ... anyway, technically, he's not an immortal.' Stiles was scribbling furiously, there being no volunteers to do this for him, despite his peremptory order. Sometimes he missed being the boss.

'He was an inventor,' Tamar said. 'He designed weapons for the gods and other useful things (Thor's hammer was one of his and the flying ships) not just for the gods though. He gave his inventions to humanity too. Which the gods did not like, but he basically told them to stuff it.'

'He doesn't sound all that bad,' said Denny.

'He wasn't really, he was just shifty, mischievous, you know. They called him the trickster. Until he killed Balder. He crossed a line there and, well ... I don't know what else I can tell you.'

'Any idea what his beef is with the Tuatha?' asked Stiles. 'Motive is key in this sort of investigation.'

Tamar shook her head. 'No idea at all. It makes no sense to me that they would even know each other. The Tuatha are Celtic gods.'

'That's not necessarily a problem,' said Denny. 'The Vikings conquered the Celts after all and besides, mythologies are always getting mixed up with each other. Look at the Romans and the Greeks, and even the Egyptians got in on the same act. Many of their gods are the same as the Greek gods only with different names. And Hercules was supposed to have visited Asgard one time. It happens all the time. Mythology is mythology, once you accept that it's real, then it's all the same thing.'

'So, the fact that the Tuatha apparently pissed Loki off is not so surprising after all?' said Stiles.'

'I never heard about it though,' said Tamar. 'And I still think it's weird,' she added stubbornly.

'Maybe the Tuatha weren't *just* Celtic gods,' said Cindy. 'Maybe they were also, like um, in the Norse legends somewhere, but like Denny said, with a different name.' She shrugged; everyone seemed to be staring at her. 'That's stupid isn't it?' she said, feeling uncomfortable and wishing she had said nothing.

'That's *brilliant*,' said Denny. 'Abso-fucking-lutely brilliant. Why didn't *I* think of that?'

'You can't think of everything,' said Tamar with a grin, 'It *is* a good idea though. It makes sense, except I can't think of anyone in the Norse legends, either, who Loki had a grudge like that with. Well, except the Norse gods of course, and they're all accounted for.'

'You moved around a lot back then,' said Denny. 'You once told me there was a lot you missed in history. It probably happened after you moved on.'

'That's true,' Tamar admitted.

'Well, anyway, I'll do some research on it. A grudge big enough to cause Armageddon must have left a trail *somewhere*. I'll find it.'

'I *know* you will,' said Stiles.

'We could really do with someone else who's good with computers,' said Cindy. 'There's so much research to do.'

Er, hello,' said a hesitant voice from the door. Everyone turned. Fenrir had returned with the rest of Team Alpha (whom only Tamar recognized – although it was perfectly obvious to everyone else who they were) in tow. It was Ray who had spoken. 'I'm pretty good with computers,' he said diffidently.

'Ever surfed the Aethernet?' asked Denny challengingly without waiting for introductions.

'Oh, yes, frequently.'

'Ever hacked the mainframe?'

'Occasionally,'

'Right, you can start on the possibles for Loki's power source. Jack will fill you in. I'm Denny by the way. You've probably heard nothing about me. I don't care who *you* are. That's Jack over there, don't let his jolly demeanor fool you into believing that anything he tells you is not an order.'

Stiles's face was a grim as human face could possibly be, without being the face of a corpse. Ray gave him a nervous smile.

'Hi Ray,' said Tamar.

'I'm pretty good at computers too,' said David coming forward with a sly, cocky look on his face.

Denny raised an eyebrow. '*Pretty* good?' he said sceptically. His eyes bored into David's interrogatively. David stared back defiantly for as long as he could then dropped his eyes.

Tamar snapped her fingers suddenly. 'That's enough,' she said. 'Get him out of here. I'm not having that scum in my house.'

Fenrir did a very passable imitation of an extremely startled man.

'What?' he began, 'why …?'

'And I want him voided,' said Tamar. There was a gasp from the room. To be voided (put into the void) was a fate worse than death, as everyone in the room knew very well. Denny grabbed David by the arms as he tried to run. He was stronger than he looked, but Denny managed to hold him, with some difficulty, as he struggled violently to get free.

'On what charge?' asked Fenrir in an outraged tone.

'He's been genetically manipulating free magical creatures. I saw the data. And I'm pretty sure he's a spy too, although I don't know for whom.'

'Hank's forest?' said Denny tightening his grip, his face white with fury.

'What?' said Tamar, surprised in her turn.

Fenrir appeared to come to a decision. 'Void him,' he said, as David let out a howl of protest. 'We can question him later, if we have time.'

Tamar instantly made up her mind that he would be questioned as soon as possible – by her.

There was a long awkward silence after David had been dragged away by Fenrir and Denny. A high, thin scream had been heard which cut off abruptly, then silence.

It was Fenrir who broke the silence; coming back into the room, preceded by a grim faced Denny, he said heartily. 'There's always one bad apple in every barrel eh?'

No one replied. There really did not seem to be anything to say.

Suddenly, with great relief, Ray noticed Slick and hailed him in surprise. 'Hey Tony, what are you doing here?' he looked questioningly at Tamar.

'Yes, I got her out,' said Slick sighing heavily. He indicated Denny. 'I think you've met Tamar's husband.'

'Husband?' He turned to Tamar, who was trying to suppress her laughter. 'You never said you were married.'

'I wasn't,' she said. 'The wedding was yesterday, that's why I asked Slick to get me out.'

'And he *agreed*?'

Slick glowered and looked as if he might be about to say something cutting.

'I'm Melissa.' The owner of that name hurried forward to pour oil on potentially troubled waters. 'Anything I can do to help, you know.' She was looking at Denny, whom she had, quite naturally, assumed to be in charge.

He gave her a weak smile. 'What are you good at?' he asked.

'Potions mainly,' she said perkily, 'some incantations.'

'Don't believe a word of it,' said Tamar. 'She's good.'

'How are you at toiling through the jungle?' asked Stiles suddenly.

'Er ... what?'

'First potential hit, he said, waving a newspaper advertisement. 'Say's here there's a supposed "Fountain of Youth" in Peru.'

~ Chapter Eleven ~

RHINE MAIDENS ARE, in modern parlance, "bimbos". Or at least, that is the myth. Tamar knew better. Rhine maidens are vain – no one could be more so; even Tamar could not match them. They expend a lot of energy on fun as opposed to work and they tend to chatter on inconsequentially in a manner that Tamar found maddening. But they are not stupid.

Rhine maidens will attempt to seduce anyone, male or female, they are not fussy. Admiration is what they want. But Tamar reasoned that she and Cindy would be safe from this kind of attack. Safer than any of the guys anyway. Still, she warned Cindy what to expect.

She was not really expecting to find Loki here, or anything much except irritation. There was something about the Rhine maidens that got under her skin. They were too much like mermaids and Tamar despised mermaids. However, Stiles was right. They could not afford to ignore any leads, even one as obvious as this. And Stiles was in charge of this investigation.

'Just keep them distracted,' Tamar told Cindy. 'Compliment them and let them chatter on. They'll try to seduce you. Let them think they can. Keep them out of my way, while I have a look around. Okay?'

Cindy nodded uncertainly.

'Don't worry,' said Tamar. 'They'll love you. It's the golden hair, just like theirs.'

'I never expected to wish I was a brunette,' said Cindy wryly.

Tamar laughed. 'Are you a witch or aren't you?' she said. 'What are you so afraid of?'

'It's just icky – that's all.'

Tamar pupped her lips dismissively. She clearly did not see what the problem was. 'They won't hurt you,' she said. 'Anyway, I won't be long.'

'Did you …?' Cindy asked curiously.

'Did I what?'

'Oh, never mind, I suppose not.'

'Not my style,' said Tamar.

Tamar had been right; the Rhine maidens greeted Cindy with enthusiasm. It was creepy the way they arched their backs and pouted their lips, the way Cindy herself sometimes unconsciously did around an attractive man. It was not working on her. However, she decided, she had a role to play, and if Cindy knew anything, she *knew* how to flirt.

After half an hour, Cindy knew more about the Rhine maidens than any sensible person wants to know. She was getting restless, and she sensed that the Rhine maidens were aware of it. *Where the hell was Tamar?*

There was tension in the air. She felt their bewilderment. She should have been totally enamoured by now, and she clearly was not and yet she had not left. It was incomprehensible.

The Rhine maidens were inclined to blame one another. The constant bickering that took place when no mortal was around was threatening to resurface. Flosshilde was already pouting.

Cindy decided, since there was still no sign of Tamar, to take a line that had been successful in the past, although how well it would work on *women* was uncertain, this being uncharted territory for Cindy.

She chose Woglinde, who she judged to be the most susceptible. If she had been a man, she would have been the one hanging around the bar nervously, getting progressively drunk and fully expecting to slope off home around midnight alone. In other words, Woglinde had a self esteem problem.

Slowly, Cindy reached out, shyly and yet as if she could not help herself, and she gently touched Woglinde's hair. Then she pulled back her hand as if she had been burned. The blush that spread over her face as she did this was genuine.

The effect was immediate and electrifying. Woglinde smiled at Cindy; a message passed between them. Cindy caught and held Woglinde's gaze and for a few moments they just stared, smiling at each other.

She switched her gaze, first to Flosshilde and then to Wellgunde, they smiled. And then, it was as if she was falling into deep water. This may have been because she was. But she was unafraid. As soon as she hit the water her head began to swim, as if she had been exposed to a powerful narcotic. This was the power of the Rhine. She was vaguely aware of the Rhine maidens swimming alongside her, laughing merrily, guiding her towards the darkness at the bottom of the river. Her last coherent thought was. '*This* wasn't part of the plan.'

She awoke in a lighted cave to find Woglinde stroking her hair gently and murmuring comforting words that she did not understand.

There was no water in the cave, apart from a pool, which glowed with a strange golden light. Cindy knew what it was; she had heard the stories. The Rheingold! She felt a sudden lust like a sharp salt taste in her mouth.

Woglinde's hands were wandering, and Cindy sat up abruptly and pushed her away.

'Where am I?' she asked harshly.

Woglinde cowered away looking hurt and confused. 'In my home,' she said. 'Isn't that what you wanted?'

'Where?' snapped Cindy.

'In the river of course – Darling …'

Cindy had known it. Now she could see – outside the cave was a wall of water held back by God knows what power. She was at the bottom of the river.

'Where are the others?'

'Oh, they aren't here, now,' said Woglinde giggling. 'It's just us.'

'Good!' said Cindy, and hit Woglinde over the head with a rock.

She judged that she if she had managed to swim down here, then she ought to be able to swim to the surface. On her way out of the cave, she grabbed the Rheingold from its pool. '*No*,' called Woglinde, whom Cindy had thought was unconscious, 'unless you have forsaken love, it will destroy you,'

Cindy turned and gave a bitter laugh. 'I *have* forsaken love,' she said. 'It has forsaken *me*, after all.'

'But *I* love you,' said Woglinde despairingly.'

'Tough break,' sneered Cindy heartlessly and was gone, leaving poor Woglinde in a distraught heap on the floor of the cave.

She found Tamar pacing up and down by the river bank looking cross and fed up.

'Nothing,' she snapped. 'I *knew* this was a waste of time. Where the hell have *you* been?'

'Distracting the Rhine maidens like you told me to. It isn't *my* fault that Loki isn't here either, so don't take it out on me.'

Tamar was immediately contrite. 'Sorry, she said. I guess I'm just pissed off about the whole thing really.'

'Want to go home and spend some time with your sweetie?' asked Cindy slyly.

'Well, *yes*, actually.' She sighed. 'Oh well, I suppose it can't be helped. Let's get out of here. At least we can cross this one off the list.'

Cindy nodded distractedly. Her hand clenched around the Rheingold hidden underneath her jacket. For a moment her face flushed and her eyes burned feverishly. But the face she turned towards Tamar was bland and innocuous.

'What a wash out!' said Tamar as they disappeared.

* * *

Stiles was holding what he called a "bull session" whereby everyone sat around throwing ideas, good, bad or indifferent and sometimes just ridiculous, into the hat for the consideration of the group. No one was allowed to pass judgement on these ideas, no matter how silly or irrelevant. That was the number one rule. And everyone had to contribute at least one suggestion.

The idea was to supplement Denny's research into possible sites of water with mystical or mythical properties. These had so far ranged from "Loch Ness" – Melissa, to "Lourdes" – Cindy.

Tamar stuck with Broscelainde in Brittany. But there were many other sites that mirrored this one all over Europe.

The Aethernet search had turned up a grand total of seventeen legendary bodies of water most of which had their origins far in the past. Shangri La in Tibet, (said to contain a fountain of youth) the secret kingdom of Borges, (the location of which is entirely unknown) where Borges supposedly met Homer and other ancient Greeks, who had been alive there for centuries. Dragphug Maratika in present day Nepal where Guru Rinpoche had supposedly gained immortality in Maratika after drinking the water, and many others spread all over the globe. It was a frightening conclusion given the time factor. Somehow, they had to narrow it down.

In the meantime, there was nothing else for it but to start visiting these locations, but there was a feeling of futility about the whole thing.

* * *

Melissa was discovering that trekking through the jungle was *not* her strong suit, as she had suspected. Stiles, however, who had elected to join her on this one, was taking to it like Indiana Jones. It was hard not to admire him really, she thought, slashing his way through the undergrowth thoughtfully and persistently pausing only occasionally to puff on an outsized cigar. Melissa, on the other hand, was hot, sweaty, dirty and out of breath. She hated it here. The whole place was *alive*. Every other minute she saw something that made her want to scream. Snakes, spiders, and huge, scary birds with beaks like razor blades. She hated it all.

The Peruvian fountain of youth turned out to be a series of pools, lakes and muddy puddles, none of which looked very mystical to Melissa, but she obediently took samples and tested them for genuine magical properties. There were none that she could detect.

Stiles was philosophical about it. 'You can't expect to hit the jackpot right away,' was all he said about it.

* * *

Cindy was in Lourdes; she had insisted on this and had taken no one with her, saying she would be better on her own. She checked the waters quickly, found nothing in them (which was what she had expected) and then took off to regions unknown for quite some time. At least, she was gone far longer than anyone had expected her to be. And when she returned, she would not say where she had been.

* * *

'Do you think Merlin's really in there? Denny was peering over a wall at what was purportedly the last resting place of the world's most famous wizard (not even saving the presence of Harry Potter).

'Well if he is, it's only his little finger,' said Tamar. 'That's all that'd be left if the poor man is in all the graves he's supposed to be in.'

'Oh,' said Denny feeling slightly disappointed.

I think … wasn't he supposed to have been frozen in some cave somewhere?' she added uncertainly. Denny was supposed to know this stuff.

But he just shrugged. 'Dunno,' he said. I always assumed it was just a story. Well, what about it, is there any real magic here or not?'

'Not.'

'So, not even his little finger then?'

Denny and Tamar were on a European tour starting with Brittany and then taking in Geneva, Russia, Glastonbury, supposed location of the mysterious lady of the lake – she was not in (something about this nagged at Tamar's brain) and Loch Ness, which was worth a try. Tamar gave the monster a scare, and they went home, empty handed and dispirited.

* * *

After several more abortive trips to Mongolia, Nepal, Pakistan and other places too numerous to mention, it was time to make a start on those places that were legendary in themselves – as opposed to being real places with legends woven around them.

The problem with these places was that they were legendary; no one knew where, if anywhere, they existed. However, the legends gave clues.

Shangri La was supposed to be in Tibet for example. This was a start.

Mulehet, where the old man of the mountains trained his assassins in a magical paradise was said to be within the Alborz mountains south of the Caspian Sea. It was not exactly a map reference. But it was better than nothing.

Bimini, the mythical land of the Fountain of youth that was the object of the explorer Ponce de Leon was reputed to be somewhere in the Bahamas.

` And so on.

* * *

'I don't understand why we're even *doing* this?' said Melissa to Ray. 'I mean, it's not that I mind helping, but we're wasting our time, aren't we?'

The two remaining members of Team Alpha (Slick did not count; he had left the agency officially when he took asylum with Tamar's gang) tended to stick together, keeping themselves apart from the rest of the household. There was plenty of room in the house for fifty people to be alone somewhere. Melissa and Ray were in the second conservatory.

An empty, forsaken part of the property, furnished only with cracked plant pots. Two of these, upturned, were being used by Melissa and Ray as seats.

'It may *seem* like a waste of time,' said Denny appearing like a pantomime demon in the doorway to the extreme surprise of them both. 'But we've learned the hard way, that you don't get results without putting in the work. You have to go through all the wrong answers before you get to the right one. Usually from the most unexpected place, where you weren't even looking for it in the first place. But there are no shortcuts.' He grinned wolfishly. 'We appreciate your help,' he said and then left as suddenly as he had arrived.

'Is it just me,' said Melissa, 'or is that guy scary?'

'Very intimidating,' agreed Ray cautiously looking around as if he expected Denny to suddenly pop up again. 'Funny really, I mean, he doesn't *look* like he should be scary, but he is.

'I kind of like him though,' he added.

'Yeah, me too,' said Melissa. 'Strange, isn't it?'

* * *

'Okay, you hang around looking like potential assassin material, and I'll stay out of sight.'

'How *exactly* am I supposed to look as if I'm potential assassin material?' asked Denny pettishly

'Just look like you always look,' said Tamar. 'Moody.'

'Yeah, like that,' she said, as Denny's face creased into a frown.

'Nice to see being married hasn't changed our relationship,' said Denny caustically.

'That's right,' said Tamar smiling cheerfully.

'They were dressed as hikers, this being the modern equivalent of "lost in the mountains" which was, according to the tales of Marco Polo, the condition of the young men normally associated with the legends of the old man of the mountains.

Tamar vanished from view, leaving Denny apparently alone and feeling horribly exposed. This was not the kind of honeymoon he had envisaged. It was, however, the kind of honeymoon he had *expected*. It was just the way their life always was.

The story went that these young men were lured to a hidden paradise and then, once they had become addicted to its pleasures, sent back into the world and told that they would only regain admittance by doing the old man's bidding. The assassination of various princes, kings, sultans, viziers etc. So desperate were these men to get back to their Earthly Nirvana, that they became the deadliest band of men in the world.

If the old man was still around (and there was good reason to suppose that he was) Denny was not looking forward to meeting him.

However, it had been decided that he was the best qualified of all the men in the group to face the test. Still, Tamar had insisted on going with him.

He sat on a handy rock looking despondent (or moody, as Tamar would have it) and waited.

It did not take long. From apparently out of nowhere there appeared an old man. Denny knew he was an old man from the bent back and the constant litany he was muttering along the lines of. 'Oh, dear, my poor old legs,' etc.

'It's him,' came a voice in his head, *Tamar*. He fought the urge to shush her and stood up slowly, his face a mask of concern as the old man approached. He was not at all convinced that it *was* him, yet who else …?

'Who do you think you're kidding?' said the old man unexpectedly. He looked Denny right in the eye and winked. 'You're no ordinary hiker. Do you think I'm daft?'

Denny sighed. Every *single* time, it happened. These encounters always turned out this way. You met a beautiful goddess, and she harangued you like a fishwife or a hideous spider demon who turned out to have an inferiority complex. If Denny had awakened the Sleeping Beauty, she would probably have said 'What time do you call this?' and gone back to sleep.

Any minute now, the old codger was going to start complaining about how it "wasn't like this in the old days" or something similar.

'What are you anyway?' said the old man surprisingly. 'You're not a demon, nor a wizard, *definitely* not an angel. What's your power?'

'I'll show you mine, if you show me yours,' said Denny, quick as a flash.

'Ha, so that's the game is it?' said the old man. 'You want to see my little paradise. Well, why should I?'

'Because if you don't,' said Denny, suddenly uncloaking the hidden menace that lurked behind his friendly smile. 'I *will* show you mine. Do you stay immortal if your head comes off?'

It was a long shot, but from the way the old man quailed, it hit its mark. 'No need for that,' he said with a slight quiver in his voice. 'I never said I wouldn't. Just wondering why you wanted to see it, that's all.'

Denny grinned nastily. 'Just curiosity,' he said. 'A professional interest you might call it.'

'You won't like it,' the old man warned him.

'I thought it was a paradise,' said Denny. 'Who doesn't like paradise?'

'It's not a paradise to the likes of us,' was the reply. 'Not for those with eyes to see the truth. It's hell on Earth.

'Dancing girls!' he added in a contemptuous tone. 'The youngest one must be three hundred years old. And she looks every day of it too – if you can see through the glamour. As for the rest of it … it's a bloody hell hole I tell you. Still, come on then.'

'Three hundred?' said Denny following him round a rock. 'So there *is* a fountain of eternal life.'

'Who said there wasn't?' said the old man obscurely. 'Be more to the point if it was a fountain of eternal *youth*. What's the point of immortality if you have to spend it looking like *this*?' And he pulled at his own wizened features.

'Ah,' thought Denny. 'I was wondering when we'd get on to the complaining.'

'I see what you mean,' he said gravely.

'Ah, you're young,' said the old man. 'You don't really understand ... Wow, what a woman!' He had spotted Tamar. 'Yours?' he asked dubiously looking from one to the other.

'My wife,' said Denny just narrowly escaping bursting with pride.

'Must have money,' muttered the old man. Denny heard this but did not take offence. He was used to this attitude. It *was* fortunate, though, that Tamar did not hear it.

'Right,' said the old man. 'Welcome to my paradise.' he walked easily through a sweeping wall of water that was gushing down over a cave mouth. Denny had not even noticed it.

The old man had not been kidding. Hell on Earth was too good a name for what turned out to be a dank cavern, dimly lighted with grubby looking candles, spread far and wide over a vast area. In the approximate centre of the cavern was a pool of clear spring water. Denny wandered towards it.

'Don't do it lad,' said the old man. 'Eternal life isn't all it's cracked up to be. Just look at me.'

To the old man's surprise, Denny did not drink any of the water. Most people just ignored him and drank anyway. People always thought they knew better. He just looked at it for a few minutes with a frown on his face, and then called Tamar over. Then *she* looked at it for a few minutes. Neither of them seemed remotely interested in drinking the water. The old man could not understand it.

'You see them?' said Tamar. 'In the water.'

'Yeah, what the hell are they?'

'See what?' said the old man, alarmed.

'Nanobes,' said Tamar. 'Very very tiny er ... things. That's what's prolonging your life, not the water.'

'Are they dangerous?' asked Denny.

'Let me put it this way,' she said drawing him aside and talking in a low voice so that the old man could not hear. 'That's not an old man, not any more. That's a swarm of nanobes. It just doesn't know it. It *thinks* it's an old man. It's like vampires. They take over the host body, but the old personality remains. It has the old man's memories and personality, but it isn't him.'

'A swarm?' asked Denny.

'Like cells in a body, all packed together. They can form any shape and follow any brain patterns. But they don't have a central intelligence of their own. Just like humans.'

'That's horrible.' said Denny shuddering. 'What do we do?'

'We can't do anything,' said Tamar. 'And it doesn't matter anyway, he can't leave. If he leaves here, he'll die for sure. He has to drink every day.'

'So he – *it* isn't going anywhere then?'

'No and neither are they,'

Denny spun round at these words to see three ... well to call them ancient, raddled hags was being charitable. They were walking corpses dressed in disturbingly girlish and revealing outfits. There was nothing about them that Denny wished to see revealed.

They homed in on him, lurching toward him like night of the living dead, and surrounded him cooing flirtatiously. Denny was reminded irresistibly of the Houris – this was worse though. He shrank away nervously.

'Forget it girls,' said the old man laughing until he coughed at Denny's horrified face. 'He can see you.'

The creatures stopped immediately and backed away looking embarrassed as if caught doing something wrong. Denny's feelings changed instantly from disgust to pity.

Tamar saw this and smiled. He *was* a good guy.

'Just doing their jobs,' said the old man. This is Hasti, Mahnoosh and Zohreh. I can never remember which is which. Okay girls you can go. No point in staying here, this one's not for turning.'

'*Stop*,' ordered Denny as they turned to leave. They turned and looked hopefully at him. One of them nudged her neighbour suggestively, and Tamar heard a *sotto voce* reference to '... handsome boy.'

Even Tamar did not think of Denny as handsome, not exactly. (While at the same time, being convinced that he was the most attractive man in the world and prepared to flatten anybody who said different.) But she supposed it depended on your point of view. Considering what they had had to look at for hundreds of years Denny probably *did* look pretty handsome – comparatively.

Denny caught some of what was going through Tamar's head, and he said absently 'comparatively?'

'Compared to *him,* you are.' said Tamar out loud.

'That's close enough ladies,' said Denny, noticing the surreptitious approach of the old man's harem. He held up his hands defensively, and they stopped confused.

'I want to ask you some questions,' said Denny, whereupon they all turned, as one, to look at the old man.

'Don't mind him,' said Denny. 'He can't hurt you, not as long as *I'm* here.'

There was a collective sigh. Tamar smothered a laugh. *What was it with Denny and older women?*

'But what about when you've gone?' asked one of them, pragmatically.

'You are …?' asked Denny.

'Mahnoosh,' she said.

'Pretty name,' said Denny.

And Tamar realised what it was. Just as Stiles had a knack for all boys together camaraderie, Denny was good at talking to women. Old women, young women, he treated them all the same, the same careless courtesy. He would never have dreamed of addressing a woman of any age, as "Madam". Older women did not *feel* older with Denny. It was a gift really.

'Thank you' said Mahnoosh.'

Denny leaned in conspiratorially. 'How long have you been stuck here with this old bastard Mahnoosh?' he asked.

'Long enough to wish I was dead,' said Mahnoosh.'

Denny raised an eyebrow. 'Really?' he said sceptically. 'And if you could leave?'

Mahnoosh shrugged. 'Where would I go, looking like this?'

Tamar was frowning. What was he up to?'

Denny turned and beckoned Tamar into a private corner. 'These nanobes?' he asked. 'Why don't they keep the hosts looking like they did when they were young?'

Tamar thought for a moment 'Because they follow the host's brain patterns. They don't *expect* to stay young, so they don't.'

'You're just guessing,' said Denny.

Tamar shrugged. 'Makes sense,' she said.

'Yes it does,' agreed Denny. 'I have an idea.'

Denny turned back to the huddled women. The old man was getting increasingly restless. But he was too afraid of Denny to interfere, so he stood to one side muttering mutinously.

'How would you feel about being young again?' asked Denny. 'Not just a glamour but real youth that you can take out into the world with you?'

'It's not possible.' said Mahnoosh.

'What if I said it was?'

Tamar nodded. She saw where this was going now. 'He can do it, you know,' she put in. He's a very powerful sorcerer.'

The women looked at Denny doubtfully. 'He *was* a handsome boy, but he did not look like a powerful sorcerer to them. Powerful sorcerers tended to be bearded, black browed and forbidding.

'I am actually five hundred and forty three years old,' Denny lied shamelessly.'

'Show them something,' said Tamar. 'Do some magic.'

Denny hesitated, the way people do when, having talked easily for their whole lives, they are suddenly asked to "say something".

Everyone waited.

Come on, Tamar's voice resounded in his head. *You have to prove it. If they don't believe it, it won't work. It's all in the mind.*

I know! Denny replied snappily. *I can't think of anything.*

Oh, hell, start chanting some mumbo jumbo, I'll *do it. This was your stupid idea in the first place.*

Denny started muttering in Latin as he had often seen Cindy do.

There was a loud flash and a bang, presumably from Tamar (who did not usually go in for showy side effects, but felt that the occasion demanded it this time) and the cavern vanished.

The women gasped and clung nervously to each other in the open air for the first time in no one knew how many centuries.

Denny clapped his hands, and the cavern rematerialised.

There was a flabbergasted silence.

'What about Alaodin?' asked Mahnoosh, meaning the old man.

'He stays here,' said Denny. 'I'm afraid he can't be trusted.

The women nodded uncertainly.

'You certainly don't owe him anything,' snapped Tamar. This was like Stockholm syndrome on a bad scale.

But Denny was not worried. When they regained their youthful looks, they would abandon him like old cheese. Which he reminded Denny of in a way – perhaps it was the smell.

Denny started the mumbo jumbo and Tamar provided the special effects but really, it was the nanobes that were doing the work. The women just had to believe. And having seen the cavern vanish before their very eyes, they really believed.

Nanobes work fast, and it was only a few minutes before the crones had transformed into three moderately attractive young women. Without the aid of the old man's glamour they were not the ravishing beauties that other men saw when they entered the cave, but they were a vast improvement on what Denny had seen.

After the excitement had passed (and it lasted some considerable time) the women began to eye Denny speculatively again.

'Sorry ladies,' he told them. 'I'm married.'

'You're a good guy,' said Tamar as they made their way down the mountain.

Denny inclined his head. 'And I'm glad to see that you have finally realised to the full that I am comparatively handsome,' he said.

'I love you,' she said simply.

'Mmm, me too,' he said. But clearly, his head was elsewhere.

'You did a good thing,' said Tamar.

'They won't last five minutes outside of that cave,' said Denny.

'Who knows' said Tamar. 'Perhaps nature will find a way. She often does. In any case, you did the right thing either way, now at least they're free.'

'And he isn't.' said Denny.

'Exactly,' said Tamar. 'Isn't that how it should be? And now we *really* have to get on, Loki won't have been stopping to do good deeds along the way, and we're running out of time.'

~ Chapter Twelve ~

'OH THIS YEAR we're off to Shangri La,' warbled Stiles tonelessly. 'Eh, *viva* er um …'

'Do stop it sweetheart,' said Hecaté mildly. She was used to this. Every time her husband went on a trip to an unknown and possibly dangerous location, he felt the need to sing cheerfully about it, always the most ludicrous songs too. At least, she thought, Tamar was not here, it really got on her nerves for some reason. Slick, Melissa and Ray, however, merely looked nonplussed.

Stiles was taking Melissa along again; he said she was quiet and efficient – which was another way of saying that she did as she was told.

'Eh *viva* Shangri La-a-a.' Stiles finished defiantly.

Ray was staying behind to continue the research that Denny had left him with on possible alternate identities of the Tuatha within the Norse legends. Slick had been appropriated by Hecaté who felt an inexplicable motherliness toward him, and they were going to the Borges valley. Cindy was nowhere to be found. This was accounted odd, but they did not have time to worry about it right now and Hecaté assumed that if it became necessary, she would be able to locate her as she could all witches.

No one mentioned that they had covered a lot of ground in the last two days (had it really only been two days? – it seemed far longer) and had so far turned up nothing. Denny's little homily to Melissa and Ray had permeated the whole group and seemed to have affected everyone's thinking. There was a solid determination, all the stronger for being unspoken, to push on until the answer was found or it was too late.

Even Finvarra (who was even more laid back than Denny) was, in his lazy way, making a contribution by searching for the hidden Tuatha.

* * *

In the beautiful and fertile Blue Moon valley between the softly outlined snow capped mountains lay the earthly paradise of Shangri La. Stiles felt no desire to sing stupid songs about this place now that he was here. Unlike the hidden land of Alaodin, this was a real paradise.

They had found it in a most unusual way, as suggested by Melissa when she had been presented with the problem of finding the valley of Borges, for which there was also no known location. Having been briefed on the various uses if mainframe and its access to different files in history and mythology etc. she asked, quite ingenuously, if there wasn't a file for the valley?

It was not quite that simple of course, (it never is) but it gave Ray an idea.

All the accumulated data on these various legends could be said to constitute a file in themselves. Particularly in the case of that data that was accessed on the Aethernet. Ray assembled the data into a file on the Aethernet and saved it to mainframe. This was the easy part, accessing mainframe was the hard part, or would have been if Tamar and Denny had not been in and out of mainframe so many times in recent years that they might as well have installed a revolving door.

Ray had been astounded and frankly envious when he had heard this. He bowed down to Denny as his master. To actually break into the mainframe was, for Ray, the summit of all hacking achievement. However, Denny and Tamar had already gone to the Alborz Mountains so Ray was on his own with this one. Luckily he had paid attention to his teacher, and he knew a bit about computers in his own right in any case. Besides, mainframe was always open on Denny's computer anyway.

It was, as he explained it, a bit like stepping into a storybook.

So, it was in this way that he sent Stiles, and Melissa to Shangri La and Hecaté and Slick (or Tony as he still thought of him, although nobody else did) to find the Borges valley. It was not until after they had gone that he realised what an idiot he was.

* * *

'Is it real?' asked Melissa in a hushed voice.

'Oh, I think so,' said Stiles in a voice that meant "definitely"

'It's wonderful.'

'Yes.' answered Stiles dully.

'What's wrong?' asked Melissa nervously. These people seemed to have an instinct for trouble that she had not been endowed with.

'Nothing,' said Stiles to her immense relief. 'But it's *real*, you see. Not magical – or is it?' He looked enquiringly at her.

'There's magic here,' she said. 'But of an Earthly kind if you see what I mean. It's deep, old magic from before the mainframe and all the gods and well, everything really.'

'I feel like an intruder,' said Stiles.

'Yes, no human being has ever set foot here before,' she said. 'But I don't feel like an intruder here. It feels like home in a funny sort of way. There's a welcome here, can't you feel it? This place is filled with love.'

'No,' said Stiles stolidly. 'I can't feel it. We don't belong here. And Loki definitely wasn't, isn't or never will be here.'

'No,' said Melissa in a distant voice.

Stiles looked sharply at her. She was like a woman on drugs, lost somewhere far away in her own head. Stiles knew an instant addiction when he saw it. He could feel the power of this place too, but it was beating uselessly on his consciousness from the outside as it were. As a former addict (of alcohol) and a man whose brain was on permanent suspicious alert his resistance was stronger than hers. She was so far under the influence of this place that she could not feel the influence any more. But he could. He was going to have trouble getting her out of here; he could see that. And worse, when she left, she would suffer a terrible withdrawal. He had seen it before.

Best to take her by surprise he decided. If he gave her time to argue, he might never catch her. She *was* a witch after all.

Feeling like a wretch, he grabbed her suddenly by the arm and, giving her no time to protest, positively yelled, '*Close file.*'

As the beautiful paradise of Shangri La dissolved away, Melissa let out the visceral scream of a creature being torn away from its mother's womb.

*   *   *

The path inside the mountain led into a giant labyrinth. Rooms of seven doors each, with six of them leading backwards, and only one leading deeper into the maze.

'Why is it always a labyrinth?' sighed Hecaté. 'Why is there never just a door with a sign on it? Always so difficult. No wonder Tamar hates quests.'

'Does she?' asked Slick. 'I really know very little about her, now I come to think of it.'

'Yes, she is very secretive,' affirmed Hecaté. 'I believe that she fears what will happen if anyone knows too much about her. Her story is quite a tragic one really.'

'She must have been *delighted* then, to have reporters all over her ass,' said Slick.

'Ah, yes, a trying time for us all, it contributed considerably to the recent upheavals in our lives.'

Slick thought about this for a moment and then decided he did not care. 'So what about Cindy?' he asked. 'What's *her* story?' He decided that this was too pointed and added. 'And Denny and everyone, what's everyone's story?'

Hecaté laughed. 'My goodness,' she said. 'Just how long do you think we have here?'

They were pushing on through cavern after cavern always taking what they assumed to be the inner door leading farther into the mountain.

'Not too bloody long I hope,' admitted Slick. 'I never thought this sort of thing could be so boring.'

'No, no one tells you about the boring bits in stories,' she said. 'But they happen all too often.'

'Followed by brief periods of extreme excitement and danger?' asked Slick hopefully.

'Excitement is not all it is cracked up to be,' said Hecaté severely. And not all danger is exciting either. You are, for example, very much mistaken if you believe that you are not in great danger at this very moment.'

Slick did not answer this; he was too busy looking nervously behind him and fighting a strong desire to gnaw on his fingernails.

'You want to know all about us?' resumed Hecaté. 'Starting with Cindy?' she added with just a slight lilt in her voice, which told Slick that he had not fooled her at all.

'You know that she and Finvarra are together?' asked Hecaté, just a little disapprovingly.

'I thought they *might* be,' admitted Slick. 'Only I wasn't sure, I mean they don't seem exactly ... well *she* doesn't seem to ... Oh, I don't know ...'

'*If* Cindy were not as devoted to Finvarra as she might be,' said Hecaté. 'And I personally do *not* know that that is the case. It would not be *you* that she would turn to. I will say no more.' she added in order to forestall any impertinent enquiries.

'I think this might be the last door,' he said, in order to change the subject.

'Why so?' asked Hecaté.

'It's the seventh,' said Slick. 'I just have a feeling.' He shrugged. 'Seven doors to every cave ...'

Slick's feeling turned out to be correct. Beyond the seventh door was a ruined kingdom that had clearly once been magnificent. There were people.

This was not entirely unexpected. If the stories were true, then these were the ancients who had built this kingdom; they were even older than Tamar. Nor were they terribly surprised to see that the men were almost catatonic and seemed very primitive.

'Like cave men,' said Slick in a voice hushed with awe.

'Yes,' whispered back Hecaté, 'it is very sad.'

'But … Tamar, I mean – she's pretty old. Well, I don't mean … but, what I mean is … surely immortality didn't do this on its own?'

'Who knows,' said Hecaté sombrely. 'These are men. They were not supposed to have so many years on the Earth. Perhaps they have not lived for all these centuries. Perhaps they have only existed, learning nothing new, growing inward until their minds turned in on themselves and their hearts froze.'

'Sounds boring,' said Slick. '"Live fast, die young" sounds better to me.'

'You are wise to think so,' said Hecaté, smiling. 'It is the way of men to do just that. The lives of men are but brief candles flickering before our eyes, and this is how it was meant to be.'

'Do you want Jack to do that?' asked Slick with what he believed was great shrewdness.

'I will not hinder his natural path,' said Hecaté serenely. 'Could I be selfish enough to wish him to become like *this*?' She gestured toward the blank eyed ancients, some of whom were drooling, 'Just to have him by my side. When I have strayed so far from wisdom, I too will die.'

Slick was silent.

'Loki was not here,' said Hecaté briskly. 'It is time we returned.'

* * *

Ray was startled out of his usual laid back composure by the terrifying primal scream that heralded the return of Stiles and

Melissa. As Stiles appeared in the computer den clinging on to her tightly, she suddenly appeared to go limp and fell to the floor.

'What's the matter with her?' asked Ray, horrified. They had only been gone a few minutes.

Stiles knelt down beside her with a deep sense of foreboding. Then he straightened up with a grieved look on his face. 'She's dead,' he said quietly.

'N-no,' said Ray. He started to shake.

'I'm sorry,' said Stiles.

'You're *sorry*?' snarled Ray in disbelief. 'You bastard! You were supposed to be looking after her.'

'I know.' he looked Ray straight in the face and, without flinching, told him. 'I'm sorry, I guess I just don't know what the hell to say.'

* * *

The funeral was a private affair, presided over by Hecaté, who considered it her responsibility particularly in the absence of Cindy, who, in other circumstances as her sister witch, would have done this duty. Melissa was cremated according to her wishes, and a small service was held in the garden, by the small lake, or large pond, as you prefer.

It turned out that, if she had a family, no one, not even Ray, knew about it. He spoke for her in shaking voice – no one else was sufficiently acquainted with her to do this task. Fenrir had yet to show his face since the fateful day when he and Denny had taken David to the void. He did not even know that Melissa had died. No one knew where he was, and no one cared very much.

Ray, it seemed had been far fonder of Melissa than anyone had guessed. He had begged Tamar to save her, but she had reluctantly been forced to admit that there was nothing she could do. Hecaté could have brought her back, but it seemed cruel to tell him this, since the price he would have had to pay would have been too high and there seemed little doubt that he would have paid it and then suffered accordingly.

All Tamar could do was take his pain from him, and he was not sure that he wanted her to do this although she offered. It would feel like a betrayal, he said. But Tamar assured him that he would not forget her. He said he would think about it.

The service was, fortunately, more or less over when they were unexpectedly interrupted.

As they stood in a sombre group before the lake contemplating, their own thoughts, three blonde women appeared in the water.

They were standing on the surface of the lake, hands on hips, lips curled in a manner irresistibly reminiscent of teenage harpies. The queen bitches of the school.

Only Tamar failed to react. Everyone else gasped in everything from shock (Slick – who was not used to this sort of thing) to indignation (Ray – who was not used to this sort of thing either but had other concerns on his mind)

The tallest and prettiest of these girls addressed Tamar. 'Woglinde's *very* upset,' she informed her in a tart voice and folded her arms defiantly. This was evidenced by the traces of tears on the face of what was apparently Woglinde.

'*Aren't* you Woglinde?' asked the first speaker, pushing her forward for inspection.

Woglinde nodded obediently and scurried back behind the third girl, who had so far said nothing, but stood there looking as defiant as it is possible to look, without actually having anyone to defy.

'Flosshilde?' said Tamar as if she were not quite sure, although she was. She had a horrible feeling that she knew what this was about and was stalling for time.

But Flosshilde was not to be put off. 'Where is she?' she snapped, looking around in vain for Cindy.

'Who?' asked Tamar with a sinking heart. As if they did not have enough problems.

'The bitch who stole our Rheingold,' Flosshilde said.

'Ah, shit!' said Tamar. 'I *had* to ask,' she added. 'Look, she's not here, but we *will* find her and … Oh my God!' she stopped and slapped herself on the forehead.

'What is it?' asked Denny who recognised a "Eureka" moment when he saw one.

'Water,' said Tamar mysteriously enough pointing a shaking finger at this perfectly innocent element in an accusatory fashion.

'Yes?' asked Denny.

'Rhine maidens,' she added even more inexplicably.

'We worked that much out …' Denny began and then he got it. 'Oh my God,' he repeated. 'I can't believe we went all over the sodding place when the answer was right here all along,'

Their eyes met, shining with excitement, Tamar was bobbing up and down. 'It was so *obvious*,' she said

'Er, does anybody have any idea what they are talking about?' asked Slick.

'Not the slightest clue,' said Stiles dryly. 'But I think Loki's time is up.'

'He's not the only one,' said a voice behind them.

'There!' screeched Woglinde pointing, but everyone had already turned.

Dramatically backlit against the setting sun, Cindy stood still as a statue, and as cold.

'Cindy?' Denny tried and was rewarded with a scornful glance. He frowned, trying to understand.

Cindy turned a savagely cold glare on everyone present in turn until her eyes reached Woglinde. Then she gave a mocking smile. 'Looking for this?' she asked, and held up a small golden ring. The Rhine maidens, as one, howled in fury.

Denny's Wagner came back to him. 'Cindy *don't*!' he called. She ignored him.

'Cindy!' said Tamar warningly.

No one else spoke; there was a sense that the wrong thing said at this point would be disastrous.

'Cindy please,' said Denny. 'Don't do this. The power of the Rheingold will destroy you. It's not worth it. Have you *really* forsaken love?'

Now she looked at him. '*You* ought to know,' she said pointedly, and Denny winced. Then she began to laugh. A bitter, cold laughter that emanated from an entirely empty heart. Everyone shuddered.

'Okay,' snapped Tamar unwisely, 'enough with the Cruella De Ville. Give it up and we'll say no more about it. I know it must have been very tempting, but it's really not a good idea.'

Cindy snorted derisively. '*You*,' she cried furiously. 'What the hell do *you* know about it? When was there ever *anything* you wanted that you couldn't have?' She looked at Denny again just to make sure her point was taken.

'You mean apart from my freedom for five thousand years?' retorted Tamar, stung into sudden anger by the unfairness of this remark.

'Steady,' said Denny putting a restraining arm on her shoulder. Unfortunately, this was the worst thing he could have done. Up until that point there had been a chance, however slim, of reasoning with Cindy. But not now.

'Power lasts longer than love,' she declaimed impressively. 'I hope he's worth it,' she sneered at Tamar. 'Personally, I'd rather have the power. The power of the gods.' and she put on the ring.

'Everybody *down*,' yelled Tamar falling flat on her face and pulling Denny down with her.

Luckily, everyone followed suit immediately as Cindy was enveloped in a bright golden light, which beamed out in all directions like a supernova flattening trees and turning the world white. Even with hands over their heads, the light seared into their eyeballs painfully, and the ground shook.

Then after an eternity of seconds, it was over. Everyone stood up shakily; even Tamar was not quite as steady on her feet as she would have liked.

Cindy treated them all to some more cold laughter.

She looked different now, although it was difficult to put your finger on it. She looked somehow, more beautiful and yet harder, like a perfect statue. The fire of humanity at her heart had flickered out, bounded by an encroaching frost.

'We could take her out,' muttered Denny.

'But we won't,' said Tamar. 'And she knows it. She's counting on it.'

Cindy came forward slowly, smiling triumphantly, an icy, silvery glow surrounded her and her eyes flickered like a blue flame.

She stopped in front of Denny. 'You know,' she said taking him by the chin and forcing him to look her in the eye. 'I wouldn't care now if you died. I could crush you like an insect without a second thought if I had to. But … I still don't want to. I still find you attractive. Strange. She looked reflectively at him for a moment then her face darkened. 'But don't try me,' she added threateningly. Then she vanished in a shower of sparks.

'Ah shit!' said Tamar again.

~ Chapter Thirteen ~

'I SWORE I wasn't going to ask,' said Tamar to Denny as the last sparkle faded, leaving the shell-shocked mourners standing in comparative gloom. She thought about it for a minute. 'And I'm not,' she added firmly.

Denny bit his lip. 'I will tell you if …' he began.

'I don't want to know,' she cut him off. 'Ever.'

They had now lost both Melissa and Cindy from their ranks in one day, but while Melissa's loss was a sad one, at least it was over and done with. The loss of Cindy was a lot more worrying.

'We've lost her,' said Tamar, when Denny suggested trying to help her in some unspecified way. 'She's gone. There's really nothing we can do except be on our guard, because she *will* come after us – especially you,' she added.

'In the meantime,' said Denny, 'we still have Loki to deal with.'

'Gosh,' said Tamar sarcastically. 'I almost forgot.'

'And that's it?' said Slick disbelievingly. 'I thought she was your friend.'

'She was,' said Stiles. '*Was*, being the operative word, or weren't you listening? We'll mourn later. Right now, we have other fish to fry.'

Slick looked mutinous. 'Seems like you don't care,' he muttered.

'We care,' said Tamar. 'We care very much. But we can't help her no matter what we do. She made this decision for herself. Only she can undo it. It's not like alcoholism or something. An intervention's not going to do it, do you understand that?'

'Sounds like you know all about it,' he said.

'I-I've seen this before,' she admitted, 'a long time ago.'

'What happened?' asked Stiles.

'You don't want to know,' said Tamar. 'Look,' she addressed everyone. 'Cindy will be back for us. There's no way of knowing when. It could be years from now, or it could be next week. But she *will* be back. You all need to understand that she's not who she was anymore. When she comes ... well it'll be bad that's all.'

'Vengeance,' muttered Denny remembering what Tamar had said – "Especially for *you*!"

'For now, we have to concentrate only on finding Loki and stopping him,' continued Tamar in a lecturing tone. 'And fortunately I now know exactly how to do that. If I hadn't been so stupid before, we might already have him.'

'All the wrong answers ...' muttered Denny consolingly.

'You said something about the Rhine maidens,' said Stiles encouragingly, as Tamar had stopped with a self-condemnatory frown. 'Where are they anyway?' he added.

'Gone,' said Tamar. The Rhine maidens had slid back into the water at the same moment that Cindy had put on the ring, but only Tamar had had the presence of mind to notice this.

'It doesn't matter,' she added. 'We don't need them.'

Tamar raised her voice so that everyone could hear. 'The fact is,' she said. 'We don't need to find the particular body of water that Loki is looking for.' She pointed to the lake. 'It's in there – somewhere, just as the Rhine is. And all bodies of water come to that. All the waters of the world are a tributary to the one source and all lead to each other. That's how the Rhine maidens got here. If it's water, they can travel within it. To any pool, pond, lake or river that exists. And not only the Rhine maidens, the Lady of the Lake travels the same way, (I *knew* something about that was bothering me.) It's all connected, you see. And we can do it too.'

A flabbergasted silence greeted this pronouncement. The truth was, only Denny believed her. Everyone else was shaking their heads doubtfully.

'You all saw the Rhine maidens,' Denny pointed out.

This was indisputable.

'How will you find it in there?' asked Stiles doubtfully.

'I'll *look* for it,' said Tamar crossly. 'It's like teleporting. It's a different plane. There's no time, so it doesn't matter how long it takes me to find it. It'll still be now when I emerge. This is the quickest way in the long run.' she finished confusingly.

'But you don't know what you're looking for,' pointed out Slick.

'No, but I know what I'm *not* looking for,' said Tamar obscurely.

'Well, I suppose you know what you are doing,' said Hecaté. 'You usually do.'

'But ... I've written a program.' blurted out Ray. 'I mean, I've already found it. Sort of, I think.'

'What do you mean?' asked Denny at the same moment that Stiles chose to say. 'And you're only just telling us this now?'

Ray ignored Stiles. He was still angry with him for one thing and, for another, it was clear that Stiles already knew what he was talking about and Denny did not. He explained briefly how he had made a program for finding the mythical places that were not filed. And how, after he had sent Stiles and Melissa to Shangri La – here he choked a little on his words – he had realised that he could do the same with the place where Loki had reportedly lost his powers, by using the available material on the story to create a file that they could save to mainframe and enter in the same way. Material was in short supply and no names were given, as they already knew, but he was sure he had created a viable file that they could use.

'Bloody hell, that's clever,' said Denny genuinely impressed.

Tamar was nodding in agreement. 'Very impressive,' she said. And under this combined approval, Ray hung his head and went red with pleasure.

Okay,' said Tamar briskly business-like. 'Attack on two fronts. From the files *and* from the water. And let's just hope that Loki hasn't got there already. Now, who fancies a swim?'

'Aren't *you* going that way?' asked Slick.

'Yes, and I think Denny should use the files.'

'I agree,' said Stiles. One each of the most powerful among us. To make sure at least one of you beats Loki to it.'

'I meant,' resumed Tamar looking amused at this summation, 'who's coming with me?'

* * *

Since Stiles had a previously unrevealed and unsuspected aversion to deep water, it was decided that Tamar would take Slick with her and Denny would go with Stiles. Ray would stay behind to research the Tuatha. They still thought it might be helpful if they knew *why* Loki had a grudge against them and seeing if they could find a reference to them in the Norse mythology might give them their answer. So far, no such references had been found, but it had to be admitted that little attention had been paid to this aspect of their research, it had been shunted aside by the more urgent task of finding Loki. As Tamar had said. 'If we find Loki in time, it won't matter anyway.'

Denny had disagreed with this attitude. Details could be important, and Tamar's habit of single-mindedly charging at a problem like a mad hippo at a muddy lake often caused her to miss the bigger picture.

Hecaté was still working on identifying the whereabouts of the Tuatha and Finvarra refused to leave his children. Tamar thought this was wise. She was certain that Cindy would return for them in due course, although what Finvarra could possibly do about it if she did was uncertain at best. Probably nothing. Their best bodyguard, in the event that Cindy tried to take them, would be Tamar herself. Certainly, no one else except perhaps Denny would have a chance of standing up to Cindy now, and Denny would be, at best, an undiplomatic choice. Although, Tamar sensed that the final showdown with Cindy would be Denny's problem in the end. Still, one problem at a time.

Slick was understandably nervous when, at the water's edge, he was given to understand that he just jump in, and Tamar would take care of the rest.

'Look, it's easy,' she said sliding gracefully into the lake with a smile. You won't even get your clothes wet. She demonstrated.

'Okay,' said Slick and clambered inelegantly into the water beside her. He still looked unconvinced standing up to his waist in freezing cold water as his trousers ballooned up with the buoyancy of a hot air balloon. He could feel fish drifting past his knees. He was most definitely very wet. 'Hey…!' he began, but Tamar pushed him down under the water with a firm hand, and whatever he had been about to say was lost in a desperate gurgle. Then everything went dark.

Dawber had begged to go with somebody. He had not done very much to help so far, he said and he wanted to. He was a good fighter – he claimed – and he did not scare easily. Eventually Denny, although somewhat dubiously, agreed to take him through the files with himself and Stiles. He had, so far seen no real evidence that Dawber would be any help whatsoever. However, he had to concede that this may have been because he had, as yet, had no opportunity to show his mettle. He had been, for the most part since his enlightenment, a solitary figure wandering around the house at odd times or keeping to his room and Denny was not entirely sure that he had got his head together yet. Not that he would blame him at all, if he had not, after what he had been through. But they could not afford to have him along if he was going to be a liability.

He felt a little better when Dawber apparently took to the file jumping like an old hand. He was calm and collected as he waited in the disused file that they still used as an access point into mainframe. And frankly, standing in what was quite literally nowhere, on what was patently nothing, could be an unnerving experience even for the veteran file jumper. Stiles was edgy for example; he hated it in here it was like being stuck in the void.

Dawber evidently thought so too. 'Is this like what you guys did to David?' he asked conversationally, before realising that this might not be the most tactful remark.

Denny stared at him in horror. He had completely forgotten about David

'Oh, *shit*!' he said smacking his forehead. 'I completely forgot about that guy. And he might know something too. We were going to question him.'

'I'll go,' offered Stiles. 'It's not as if I'll miss anything what with there being no time in the void.'

Denny nodded gratefully. 'It'd better be you anyway,' he said. 'If anyone can get him to talk …' he stopped. There was no need to elaborate. Stiles gave a shark like grin and cracked his knuckles. Denny could almost feel sorry for David – almost.

He grinned at Dawber. He had been helpful already, and they had not even got there yet. Denny felt a little better about him. 'Ready?' he asked giving him a wink.

'Would it make a difference if I wasn't?' asked Dawber with a short laugh.

'No.' said Denny. 'No one ever is ready for this. That's why we call it improvising.'

'Enough chit chat,' said Stiles. 'I'll see you on the other side. Close files.' And he vanished into the void.

'Close file,' said Denny at the same time. And he and Dawber vanished into mainframe. It was a fine distinction, but by closing files (plural) Stiles bypassed mainframe altogether and ended up outside the network altogether. They had discovered how to do this by a complete accident – well Denny had, and he had ended up in Hell at the time, which was, as Tamar had once told him, and he had to agree, a nice place to live, but you wouldn't want to visit it.

Dawber was less than impressed with mainframe itself. Its immense size, complexity and many layers of existence was disregarded by his brain which simply short circuited the information that it could not handle. To him, as to other humans who had seen this place, (and there were not many) it resembled a tax office, with endless boring corridors painted a uniform shade of yucky brown.

'What now?' he asked.

'We find the file,' said Denny. 'Fortunately, thanks to Ray we should have a good idea where to look.'

'It all looks the same,' said Dawber.

'Only to you,' Denny told him. 'It's this way.' He set off down a corridor at a fast-paced stride.

How he could be so certain was a mystery to Dawber, but he was learning fast – you don't argue with Denny.

Slick was equally nonplussed at this moment. As far as he was concerned, the underwater pathways all looked the same. Dark, with things floating in them, nasty sinister things. But Tamar forged ahead as if she knew exactly where she was going. She was trying different locations, always drawn by the magic in the waters. At least, that what she said. As far as Slick was concerned, they could have been going in circles and he would not have known the difference.

It was a decidedly odd experience. They were not exactly moving, not as Slick understood the term. It was more as if they were still and all the lakes and rivers and even seas of the world were moving past them like a slide show and yet were all in the same place at the same time, it was as Tamar had said; all the waters of the world were one. And even that was an inadequate description for the experience. He bitterly regretted that he would never be able to describe what it had been like to anyone. There just were not words. But he was most relieved that he could breathe all right.

Tamar herself looked like a mermaid. Actually, she looked nothing like a real mermaid – Slick had never seen any mermaids, and if he had, he would pray never to see one again. But she looked almost ethereal, like a part of the water. It was more than mere camouflage, at odd moments she seemed almost transparent, particularly her hair, which streamed behind her like an opposing current in a tranquil tide pool. Slick was fascinated.

Suddenly she darted forward grabbing Slick by the wrist and dragging him to the surface of what turned out to be an underground lake. As she emerged, her normal appearance reasserted itself, and she shot out of the water at a velocity that staggered Slick and (as she was still gripping him tightly) left him breathless as he followed in her wake.

'This is it,' she announced. She looked around for signs of company. There were none. No one had been here for centuries.

'I think we made it,' she said.

Denny and Dawber were coming to the same conclusion. The underground lake seemed never to have been touched. It would be a few minutes before Denny was to realise why.

'There's no one here,' said Dawber unnecessarily.

Denny frowned; something was wrong.

I guess we got here before him?' asked Dawber uncertainly.

'Before anyone,' said Denny as the truth hit him. 'Damn, damn, damn, damn, *damn*!'

~ Chapter Fourteen ~

STILES HATED THE void. It was not dark, and it was not light. It was not hot, cold, or temperate. It was not anything. Still, he reasoned, after a week or so here, which would have seemed far longer, eternity being what it is, David ought to be feeling quite cooperative by now.

After dragging an unresisting David back to the disused file, Stiles proceeded without preamble to the interrogation. He opened with a fist to the face, a popular gambit and usually very effective. It did not seem to have much effect on David, however, who was on the verge of a nervous breakdown anyway.

'Tell me what I want to know,' offered Stiles, changing tack and being quite kindly – for him. 'And I won't have to send you back to the void.'

David gave him a hunted look. 'Policeman!' he shrieked and began to laugh hysterically.

Stiles shrugged. He was not having any nonsense from this character; he had seen these tactics before.

'Okay, if that's the way you want it,' he said calmly.

David stopped laughing at once. A cunning look came into his eyes, which Stiles did not fail to note.

'But do you really know what you want to know?' he asked obscurely.

But Stiles had been around far too long to fall for this one. David had given him an opening here that he did not intend to waste.

'Just tell me *exactly* what the hell is going on, *all* of it mind, or I send you back into the void.' he said.

David narrowed his eyes. He had clearly not expected this. 'You won't like it,' he hedged.

'I never do,' said Stiles imperturbably.

'It'll take a long time.'

'I've got all day,' said Stiles. This was true in a manner of speaking.

David licked his lips nervously. He looked about him in the manner of a trapped animal, but suddenly Stiles was not buying it. He had realised that David was acting. He *wanted* to talk, he probably always had. All this had very likely been unnecessary. He ostentatiously stifled a yawn, and David changed his demeanour instantly; he capered – there really was no other word for his manoeuvrings – like an anxious puppy.

'No no,' he said. 'You need to hear this. It's important.'

Stiles gave him a sceptical look. 'So tell me,' he suggested indifferently. 'That is, if you really have anything worth hearing.'

David lost his temper. 'You certainly thought I did a minute ago,' he snapped. 'Either you want to hear this or you don't.'

'I said I did, didn't I?' said Stiles as if he did not care one way or another. He was now aware that David was desperate to tell his story and nothing he did or said was going to make a difference in the end. But a studied indifference would probably speed things up. It was about keeping the balance of power in his hands. He wanted to hear David's story just as much as David could want to tell it. But he had no intention of letting David know this. If he did, David could continue to procrastinate for hours.

David told him his story, and it was quite a tale too. By the end of it, Stiles was as staggered, shocked and dismayed as he had ever been in his life. How could they have got it all so wrong?

* * *

Ray was undergoing a similar reversal of his previous opinions, having finally found a reference to the Tuatha in the Norse legends. It was not what he or anyone had expected. And it changed everything. In fact, everything was far worse than they had thought.

He had cross-referenced the Celtic legends with the Norse and had finally formed the strong opinion that the Tuatha *had* appeared in the Norse legends – as Giants. This opinion was bolstered by the fact that the Tuatha were also frequently referred to as "Giants" in the Celtic legends.

Having made this determination and having looked into the role of the Giants in the Norse legends Ray was forced to admit that they had almost certainly made a terrible mistake. In fact, they had been wrong on almost every count.

* * *

'What's wrong?' Dawber quite naturally wanted to know.

'We're in the sodding *past*!' snapped Denny.

'What?' how do you know?'

But Denny could not explain how he knew – he just knew. 'Call it a hunch,' he said sourly.

'So …?'

'*So*, Ray sent us to the place where Loki hid from Odin – the exact place, and time, unfortunately.' He rubbed his head wearily. 'Oh, it's not his fault. I should have seen this coming.'

'Why unfortunately?' asked Dawber. 'I mean we could just grab Loki now and …'

'No, no, no, no, *no*!' screeched Denny. He calmed down a little. 'Look,' he said. 'I know it might *seem* like a good idea. But we can't. We can't risk changing the past. You'll just have to trust me on this. The sooner we get out of here the better. In fact. Anything we do could … Oops, company. Let's go.'

'But …'

'Close file,' said Denny firmly.

'Oh, okay then.'

* * *

Tamar was not really having better luck although she *was* in the right time.

'So where the hell is Loki?' asked Slick eventually. 'Could we have missed him?'

'We don't know exactly when he's going to turn up,' said Tamar testily. 'I don't care about that. He'll get here eventually. I'm certain he hasn't been here yet. But where the hell is Denny? He should have been here by now.'

'Maybe he's been and gone … what the hell am I talking about? Sorry,' he added as Tamar gave him a look. Not any particular kind of look, just a look. It made his skin crawl.

Then Tamar suddenly cried. 'Look out, company.' All thoughts of Denny's apparent abdication temporarily forgotten.

Slick was dragged unceremoniously back under the water. The tall, cadaverous figure that approached the water rubbing his hands in gleeful expectation could surely not be Loki, he thought. He had somehow been expecting something more – more impressive. How could that bag of bones be Loki? It *couldn't* be.

It was.

'Stand guard Fulk.' said Loki to the hairy creature trotting along beside him. There was a whine, like that of a dog that scents danger. Fulk looked hard at the water, then sniffed.

Loki lost patience. 'Oh for Odin's sake Fulk,' he snapped. 'Just keep watch – over there.' he pointed to the cave entrance.

Fulk shambled away muttering, and Tamar let out a silent sigh of relief.

She looked at Slick who nodded. 'Close one,' he mouthed.

Loki then reached into his tattered robe and brought out a golden goblet encrusted with jewels and frankly in the worst possible taste (all gods have very bad taste). His eyes were gleaming with barely suppressed excitement. Tamar caught her breath and metaphorically squared her shoulders. As Loki dipped the goblet into the water, she snatched it from his hand

and rose out of the water in one smooth vertical movement scattering water in all directions. It was an impressive move but Loki was too shocked to appreciate it properly.

He recovered fast and dived at Tamar who moved easily out of his way. 'Ah, ah, ah,' she said shaking her head in derision, 'naughty, naughty.'

Then without warning Fulk dived into the water and came up as a giant wolf with a struggling Slick clamped tightly in his considerable jaws.

Tamar stared in horror and Loki gave a satisfied smile and held his hand out for the goblet. It was stalemate. Tamar could have howled with frustration. Denny would never have let it happen to him.

'Don't give it to him,' said Slick through pain clenched jaws. 'I'd rather die than be responsible.'

'He means it,' thought Tamar, looking at him. 'What a pity it doesn't work that way.' Noble sacrifices were all very well, but in the final analysis, no one ever won by allowing the (fairly) innocent to die. She would not be complicit in murder. It was only a short step from there to doing murder yourself. No excuses were good enough – ever! And she would not take even the first steps on that slippery slope. Not again (it had taken all Denny's love to pull her back the last time.) They would just have to find another way.

Besides, she owed him.

She looked at Slick sadly and shook her head. Then she threw the goblet high in the air and both Loki and Fulk leapt to catch it. Tamar grabbed Slick as he fell, and teleported away.

Round one to Loki.

Part Three

RAGNOROC

~ Chapter Fifteen ~

'WHAT THE BLOODY hell is going on?' snapped Denny, on arriving back in the disused file and seeing Stiles and David unexpectedly head to head in, apparently, quite friendly conference. He was feeling bad tempered and frustrated enough already, thanks to the abortive trip to Loki's lake.

'You're back rather soon,' said Stiles heavily. 'I guess it didn't go well.'

'Wrong time period.' said Denny curtly. 'I guess it was a risk. What's going on here?' he repeated.

Stiles gave him a wan smile. 'Sit down mate. I've got some bad news.'

Denny started in shock. Not that Stiles had bad news – was there ever any other kind? No, it was the smile. Stiles did not do the defeated thing. And he rarely gave anyone a smile of any kind, and when he did it was always a shark-like grin, never *this*. Suddenly Denny was frightened although he did not yet know why. He just knew that something was very, very wrong.

'It's Tam, isn't it?' he blurted out in an excess of terror. What else could have pasted that bereavement councillor expression on Stiles's face?

'No.' said Stiles shortly, and waves of relief washed over Denny. Now he did sit down. Unfortunately, there was nothing to sit down on, but that never bothered Denny. He just sat on nothing – he never even noticed.

'What is it then?' he said partly angry that he had been so badly frightened and partly relieved that it had been unfounded.

'Ragnoroc.' said David lugubriously. Stiles reached out and, almost absent-mindedly, smacked him across the head. 'You keep it shut,' he said casually.

'It seems that our mate here *was* spying on Fenrir. On Odin's orders,' said Stiles.

Denny frowned trying to work this out. 'But I thought ...' he began.

'We all just took Fenrir's word for it,' interrupted Stiles with a dry humourless laugh. 'Even *me*,' he added with a touch of incredulity.

'And *you* never take anyone's word for anything,' supplied Denny. 'Get on with it. What's Fenrir up to?'

'Working for Loki,' said Stiles baldly. 'Everything he told us was a lie.' His voice was shaking with fury. 'I blame myself. I'm supposed to be the one who questions everything, and I didn't and now...' He trailed off to pull himself together.

'Abridged version, Fenrir is Loki's son.' he continued in a calmer voice. He *was* sent to earth by Odin – that part was true – but it was as a *punishment*. Just as Loki was imprisoned, his son was banished – his memories stripped, and his identity changed. But when Loki escaped, Fenrir remembered. Odin knew it would happen, so as soon as Loki was discovered missing, he sent David and Brynhilde – that's a Valkyrie – to watch him – Fenrir that is. She's still at the agency. Valerie ... Something, ha!' he stopped to look at David for confirmation at this point, who nodded silently.

'Odin thought that Fenrir might lead him to Loki before it was too late,' Stiles rushed on. 'That's why he was having him watched. But he was too clever for that. If he *is* in contact with Loki – and I think we can assume he is – he never let anyone catch him at it. The awful thing is, all the clues were there, but we never thought to look for them,' he added despondently.

'We could easily have found out that Fenrir was Loki's son. Tamar knew, she even *said*, that Odin was interested in genetic manipulation. That alone could have told us that David was working for him all along, not spying for Loki as we assumed. All those experiments on Hanks forest creatures – that was Odin.'

'We didn't know what to look *for*,' said Denny reassuringly. 'How could we? So, let me get this straight. David was working for Odin – spying on Fenrir who was really working for Loki who is going to get his powers back and destroy the Tuatha thus destroying the world in the process. We aren't that much worse off than before really. We knew most of this already, and it's not as if we really trusted Fenrir …' He trailed off at the look on Stiles's face. 'I'm wrong, aren't I?' he said.

'We missed the biggest clue of all,' said Stiles. 'All because we believed Fenrir's version and never thought to look up Loki and find out his story. Odin didn't send his servants after Loki to protect *us* from some fictional battle. He was after saving his *own* skin. If Loki was *really* going to battle the Tuatha, Odin couldn't have been more delighted. But that's *not* what he's up to at all. Loki's here to *lead* the Tuatha in the fight against the Gods on Valhalla at Ragnoroc. As we'd have known if we'd bothered to find out anything about Loki,' he added in bitter recrimination. 'Loki is *Tuatha* – or as the Norse legends would have it – a giant. He isn't a god at all. He was adopted by Odin as a brother and then he betrayed him. It's all in the Edda, if you care to look.' He shook his head wearily.

'Ragnoroc?' echoed Denny in wonderment.

'The twilight of the gods,' supplied David helpfully.

'I know what it is,' snapped Denny. 'How could we have been so blind?'

'You didn't *want* to see,' said David. 'You wanted to be heroes – save the world – and you never considered that maybe none of this had anything to do with you.'

'It has now,' said Denny decisively. It became our business when Fenrir decided to get Tamar involved. 'Why did he?' he added in puzzlement.

David shrugged. 'I was never able to work that out myself,' he admitted.

Denny smacked his forehead. '*Tamar!*' he gasped. 'She doesn't know what's going on, and she's gone after Loki.'

'Well, maybe she'll be able to stop him.' said Dawber diffidently.

'How can she stop him?' snapped Stiles, giving him a withering look. 'She doesn't know what it is she's trying to stop.'

Denny groaned. 'We have to warn her.'

'But, if she stops Loki from retaking his powers,' persisted Dawber, 'which is what she's trying to do, isn't it? Won't that stop him just the same, no matter what he's up to?'

'He's *Tuatha!*' said Denny. 'You don't know what that means,' he acknowledged. 'She doesn't know what she's dealing with – she won't stop him. She isn't invincible you know? She just acts like she is. And if she doesn't know his powers, she can't fight them. The Tuatha have powers over the mind. It's possible to fight it, but you have to be *ready* for it, and she doesn't know! D'you see? She doesn't *know*!'

'She'll never see it coming,' agreed Stiles gloomily.

'See what?' asked Dawber.

'Whatever it is he decides to do,' said Denny.

'But he doesn't *have* his powers,' argued Dawber, feeling they were taking far too black a view of things. 'Not yet at least. I mean isn't that the whole point, to stop him from getting them back?'

Denny and Stiles looked at each other and laughed derisively.

'And if you believe that, you'll believe anything,' snorted Stiles.

'I don't understand,' said Dawber plaintively. 'What's going on? Does he have his powers or doesn't he? I don't *understand*!'

Stiles just patted him on the shoulder. 'Let's just say, things are never quite that simple.' he said.

* * *

'Right, let's get after him,' said Tamar reappearing in the cavern with a dripping wet and very shaken Slick.

Slick just stared at her.

'What?' she said, laughing. 'You didn't think that was the end of it did you? Just because I gave him the goblet doesn't mean I'm giving up. Think what's at stake.'

'You saved my life,' said Slick, patently ignoring this instruction. 'You didn't have to. It could all have been over by now if you ...'

'Oh shut up,' she said.

'We don't know which way he went,' said Slick, chastened.

'No. shut *up*. I'm concentrating.' She closed her eyes then opened them again in frustration. 'I can't sense him at all,' she said. 'Even in here. It's very strange. It's like he was never here at all. The only other time I had this feeling was when I was trying to find the queen of the Sidhe.'

'What does that mean then?' said Slick.

'It means that his powers are a bit more formidable than I anticipated,' she said, 'if he can block his aura like that.'

'Footprints?' said Slick pointing at the muddy ground.

'Ah, the old fashioned way,' said Tamar laughing. 'Well done,' she added.

'Why would he have walked, though?' asked Slick, 'if he's got all these powers now?'

'Loki can't teleport,' said Tamar. 'He never could. I don't know why.'

'He can become invisible, though,' she added. 'Or turn himself into a tiger or something, so watch out for yourself.'

'Or rather for an invisible tiger,' said Slick, making Tamar wonder if he were channelling Denny. That was the sort of thing he would say.

She gave him a bright smile. 'I wish Denny were here,' she thought, 'or Jack – both of them really – and Hecaté.' She did not allow herself to think about Cindy; there was no point.

They followed the footprints up a narrow pathway that burst suddenly into bright light. 'Ow!' complained Slick shielding his eyes.

Tamar merely narrowed hers in deep suspicion. 'Hmm!' she said.

'What,' asked Slick slowly opening one eye and taking in the scene. '… the hell is this place?' he finished, opening the other eye the better to stare in bewilderment at the bright snow capped mountains and clear aquamarine lakes and grass the colour of fresh parsley. It reminded Tamar of the Faerie realm, too pretty to be real. But there was breathable air, crystal clear and icy cold. A faint breeze stirred the grass and the colours were real, but too bright and fresh. Like the world was brand new.

Had they gone back in time?

'Freshly minted,' said Slick echoing her thoughts. 'It looks like a holiday brochure. You know, come and visit lovely Sweden – we haven't edited the photos – *much*.'

'Asgard.' said Tamar realising the truth. 'How the hell did we end up here? And *why*? The Tuatha aren't *here*, surely? What's he up to now?'

'Maybe he forgot something,' said Slick and immediately wished he had not. *What a stupid thing to say.*

'Maybe,' said Tamar uncertainly. And Slick realised with a cold, sick horror that she did not understand. She did not know what to do. *Gulp.*

Tamar swallowed her uncertainty and showed a confident face to Slick that was so convincing that he almost wondered if he had imagined her momentary confusion.

'He went that way,' she said positively pointing to the farthest and highest mountain in the distance. 'Valhalla.'

Her brow furrowed again for a moment, as if she were trying to remember something or work something out. Then she turned to Slick with another bright smile. 'Come on then,' she beckoned. 'Let's get the swine.'

Slick hung back unwillingly. 'Shouldn't we go back for the others?' he said nervously. He had not expected this, although he realised, on reflection, that maybe he should have. It was always like this with Tamar. Nothing went to plan, everything was improvised on the spot. He took some small comfort in the fact that Tamar and her friends had a far better track record that his own (former) colleagues at this sort of thing, and in thhe fact that, in his own personal experience of her slap dash, take it as it comes, make it up as you go methods, he had never actually seen her fail. He had to take comfort in these things, as she said. 'We can't go back. There's no time.

'No time for what?' he wondered. It was not as if they had the faintest idea what Loki's timetable actually was.

'He isn't going to be hanging about now that he's got his powers back,' said Tamar, once again uncannily reading his mind. 'Besides, if we go back now, we'll lose his trail. By the time we get back here, he could have gone *anywhere*. We have to keep after him.'

This made sense Slick silently conceded. But for some reason he would have felt better had Denny been with them, or even that grumpy sod of a policeman would have been better than nothing. Slick was acutely aware that he had no control over Tamar; he might as well try to hold back a hurricane. At least if her husband were here she would *listen* to him, and her apparent respect for the policeman – Stiles that was his name, Jack Stiles – meant that she might even listen to him too, although he was less certain about that one. Either way the backup would be very welcome.

'It's' only one measly demi-god,' said Tamar contemptuously, answering his thoughts as if he had put them into words. 'I can handle Loki. Just don't let his muscle get hold of you this time.'

'How *do* you do that?' asked Slick. 'I never said a word.'

'Women's intuition,' said Tamar and strode off toward Valhalla.

* * *

'Actually, I reckon it *is* our business,' said Ray. 'According to the legends, after Ragnoroc, when Asgard has been taken by the giants they will then turn their attention to Midgard (Earth).

Supposedly Fenrir is going to eat the sun and turn the world dark – end of world.' He banged his hands together emphatically.

Tamar's walking right into bloody Ragnoroc,' Denny had said. 'It's none of our bloody business what happens to a bunch of mouldy old gods, but we have to get Tamar and Whatisname out of there before it all kicks off. Anything could happen to them. Even Tamar's not ready for this.' He was chewing his bottom lip nervously as he spoke.

Now, after Ray's words, he rounded on David. 'You forgot to mention that little detail did you?' he snarled. 'Just slipped your mind I suppose?'

'I suppose it did,' drawled David insolently. 'If Asgard *is* destroyed after all, it can't matter to me what becomes of Midgard afterwards. I'll be dead.'

'You son of a bitch,' said Stiles, but without much venom really. It was not as if this attitude was a surprise.'

'Who *are* you anyway, really?' asked Ray suddenly. 'David's not a very Norse name … Oh my God – David – Vidar. You're Vidar.'

David did not deny it.

'Then Odin is your father?'

'Odin is *everybody's* father,' said Vidar, 'at least in Valhalla anyway. Family relationships don't mean much up there. Why do you think they call him the "Allfather", because he's so benevolent?' He gave an amused snort.

'Where's Brynhilde?' said Denny suddenly and apparently irrelevantly.'

'Why?' asked Vidar.

'Because if we're going to fight Loki and a lot of Giants at Ragnoroc,' said Denny grimly. 'We're going to need all the help we can get.'

And with that, the decision was made. The die cast.

'I hope we aren't all going to regret this,' said Stiles, wondering vaguely if a machine gun would work on a Giant.

* * *

Cindy was no longer angry. She was no longer anything much, apart from deeply ambitious. The god inside longed for nothing more than power and glory. But past experience had taught her that, intoxicating as this power was compared to her witchly powers, it was still not enough to go up against Tamar – or Denny for that matter. She had seen them defeat gods before. She must not allow herself to get swept away by this feeling of invincibility that filled her as other poor mortals who had suddenly gained great power had done. She knew, better than anyone, what she would have to face in the quest for power and control.

Sadly, if Tamar were to be defeated, Cindy knew that she could not do it alone.

But she *was* alone, and she had no desire for company, no wish to share the prize when it finally came. Time was on her side now, though. She could afford to wait for many years if necessary before putting any plan into action. Now that she too was immortal. A long-term plan had not helped others, though. The Faerie Queen had had a long-term plan, as had Askphrit and they had fallen when faced with the final hurdle. But they had underestimated what they were up against. She would not. Had she not lived with her enemies, fought alongside them? Did she not know what they were capable of, what they were most likely to do? So, that was one advantage, but the fact remained that her powers were not strong enough. She needed an ally, however distasteful this idea might be. But need it be?

There was one whom it might not be so distasteful to ally herself with. Someone who she could train to her will. Of course, it would mean tipping her hand to her enemies. They would know she had him with her, but might they not see it as a natural thing? As evidence of some remaining humanity within her rather than part of a design? Yes, on balance, she thought they probably would. Their greatest weakness, in Cindy's opinion, was that they always saw what they wanted to see, believed what they wanted to believe. It was a very human reaction after all. And they would all want to believe that she was still human inside, like them. She imagined that they had some vague idea about *saving* her. The idea made her want to laugh out loud. *Save* me? What arrogance! As if I ever needed any of them.

She stirred the water gently – it was nice to know that she could still scry; her remote vision, being a new power, was still difficult to control, but you knew where you were with scrying – and gazed into its depths.

All was quiet and still. With her increased senses, she could make out the shadowy figures at the edges of the water and hear the distant murmuring of people in other parts of the house beyond her vision. *He* was there; she could not see him, but she could hear him, shouting orders as usual. In the old days, her heart would have flipped over at the sound but no more. Now she listened intently and dispassionately. They were leaving soon, she gathered. Off on some ridiculous, pointless quest. Blundering in where they had not been asked to go. As soon as they were gone, she knew what she had to do.

She drew back and surveyed the forge where she had made the ring. No one had been here in centuries, yet the place had seemed curiously untouched by time, like the castle in the Sleeping Beauty. Even the mould in which the ring had been cast was still there, just waiting for her. She would awaken this place. Build on its ruins a citadel, a palace fit for a god.

Would they never leave? She paced impatiently and then took hold of herself. What was there to be impatient about? She had all the time in the world.

~ Chapter Sixteen ~

'I DON'T THINK he came this way at all,' stated Slick morosely sitting down on a handy promontory and pulling up grass. They were about halfway up the mountain with no sign of Loki anywhere. 'I think we've been played.' he stared challengingly at her. 'What do *you* think?'

Tamar did not answer.

'I mean, why would he return to Valhalla anyway?' continued Slick mercilessly. 'It doesn't make sense. The Tuatha aren't here, are they? They're on Earth. Aren't they?'

'*None* of this makes sense,' said Tamar, 'but, since we're here anyway. I'm going on. I want to see Odin. I think it's about time we got some answers.'

Slick felt his mouth go dry. '*Odin*?' he rasped. 'You want to go and see Odin? The King of the gods ... Actually Odin himself.'

'Yes, Odin *himself*,' she replied with heavy sarcasm. 'Oh, untwist your knickers, he's only a god. You didn't get this bent out of shape about Loki. Odin's no different really. He won't do anything to you. I think he knows what's really going on here and I intend to make him tell me.'

'You intend to *make* him tell you?' asked Slick incredulously.

Tamar looked pityingly at him. 'You haven't really got the hang of this yet have you?' she said. 'Odin's only a god. Local deities, minimal powers when compared with say a Djinn. Don't expect too much or you'll be disappointed when you meet him. He's just an old man. He's never been able to stand up to *me* anyway.'

'You've met him before?'

'You *know* I have.'

'Oh, right yeah, yeah. I remember now.'

'You didn't really believe it, did you?'

'It's not that exactly, it's just … Well, it's all a bit hard to take in really.'

'I know what you mean,' said Tamar understandingly. 'It gets easier, okay?'

'Okay.'

'I think I just worked something out,' said Slick. 'Fenrir said that Loki's powers could only be *reached* through a place on Earth. He didn't say that they were *on* Earth though. I reckon that place was a sort of separate dimension, like purgatory. You know, you can only enter from Earth and only exit into Asgard. One way doors type of thing.'

'And that's why he had to go to Earth to get in,' said Tamar. 'Damn clever. I wish I'd thought of that. You're probably right.'

'It's just a theory,' said Slick modestly. 'We've no proof.'

'It makes sense though. But we're still going to see Odin,' she added to Slick's dismay. 'There are other unanswered questions I want answering.'

'Like what?'

'Like what Loki's got against the Tuatha for one thing. That never made sense to me. And besides, Loki set this trap on purpose, he *wants* us to go to Valhalla, and I want to know why.'

'But if it's a trap …' began Slick alarmed.

'It's not a trap when you *know* it's a trap,' asserted Tamar. 'Besides, I told you, I can handle Odin.'

Slick sighed in resignation. He was learning, as Denny had before him, that there was no use in arguing with Tamar. She never argued back; she just did what she wanted to anyway.

'No more women for you mate,' he told himself. 'If I get out of this one alive, I'm becoming a hermit.'

Then he looked up and saw Valhalla looming above him. The mightiest citadel ever created. They had arrived. His knees began to shake. Tamar was hammering on the immense door like the bailiffs at his neighbour's flat, after he had run up a vast internet shopping bill. For some reason, this did not make him feel any calmer.

* * *

Vidar, under pain of extreme pain (Denny had told him that Stiles would sing until he agreed) had contacted Brynhilde AKA Valerie Byrnehil.

Brynhilde had been deeply suspicious at first, but had eventually been won around by Denny's argument. "We've got to help Odin to help ourselves." This selfish point of view was one that she could identify with having lived among the gods, and she had agreed to take them into the heart of Valhalla where all the action was going to be.

This was not exactly what Denny had had in mind. He had been hoping that they could find Loki and stop him before it got to that. But it turned out that Brynhilde had no idea where Loki was, only where he was going.

'Ve haf lost him,' she said, 'he alvays vas von trickster. Von minute there, und then gone. Poof!' She indicated that he was always disappearing.

'How will you get us into Valhalla?' asked Stiles, wondering why they did not just use mainframe.

'Ve shall ride of course,' she said and let out a piercing whistle.

Immediately there was a sound of thunder in the air. Every head turned upwards and saw only the ceiling; there was a dash to the window, which Denny won and he saw, they all saw…

seven flying horses, steered by leather clad, golden braided maidens brandishing swords and singing a stirring but incomprehensible warrior song.

'The Valkyries!' breathed Ray in awe. 'Now I've seen everything.'

'Not quite everything,' said Denny amused.

The Valkyries trotted into the yard and, from this distance, they looked quite normal (apart from their attire of course) as did their horses. Brynhilde went to meet them, and an argument seemed to be developing.

'But zey are not *dead* Brynhilde.' Denny heard as he crept closer.

'Und not all of zem are varriors either,' said another, her lip curling.

'Zey vill all be both before zis day is over,' Brynhilde assured her.

'Ve carry the slain,' asserted one in a stubborn voice. 'These are *alive*.'

'Are ve going to haf a philosophical discussion now?' snapped Brynhilde, losing patience.

'No, Brynhilde,' she was assured by the wide-eyed Valkyrie who looked as if she were not sure what this meant. 'I just meant zat ze slain are much lighter than ze living, I am not sure zat ze 'orses vill cope. Although zeze varriors *are* very thin,' she directed a sneering look at Denny.

'Size doesn't matter,' said Denny with a sunny smile.

'It matters to my 'orse,' snapped the Valkyrie.

'Why don't we just use the mainframe?' hissed Stiles in Denny's private ear.

'Do *you* want to offend them?' said Denny jerking a finger at the buxom Brynhilde, who was standing, hands on hips in a manner strongly reminiscent of a pissed off P.E. teacher.

'I see what you mean,' said Stiles.

'We need their help, I think.'

'Not as much as they need ours,' Stiles pointed out.

'They can take us straight to Odin, no messing. We don't have time to piss about in mainframe really. Not this time.'

'You vill ride vis me,' ordered Brynhilde bossily, taking Denny firmly by the arm.

Stiles smothered a laugh. What was it with Denny anyway? He was turning into Captain Kirk or something. It was that little boy lost thing, he thought without a trace of envy. No woman was safe. No, that was not true – ordinary women still tended to look straight through him, it was only magical women who went for Denny (except for his Hecaté, of course who tended to treat Denny as a favourite nephew. He gave her an affectionate look; she was also looking amused he noticed.) Cindy was a case in point; the thought cast a shadow over the bright afternoon. What would become of her now?

There was no time to worry about that now. He dismissed the thought as he was helped onto the back of a rather large looking horse, now that he came to see it up close. It twitched its flanks as he mounted behind the sneering Valkyrie and took off almost before he had settled down. He grabbed helplessly at the Valkyrie's waist with a muttered apology for this familiarity, but the Valkyrie ignored him as if she were used to this happening.

He could see Brynhilde with Denny riding behind her; they were up in the lead, of course. It was difficult to tell, but it seemed as if Denny was enjoying the ride. He always did like going fast with the wind in his hair. Stiles had to keep reminding himself not to look down. Behind him, he heard a whoop of joy that sounded like it might have come from Ray. Christ – was he the only one *not* enjoying this?

Hecaté, with customary grace, had leapt lightly onto the proffered horse as if she had been doing it all her life. She waved reassuringly at him as they passed. Stiles gave her a strangled grin and held on for dear life.

Denny was finding the whole experience exhilarating. A devotee of fast cars and motorbikes, this was, for him, the ultimate joyride. And hey, to ride with the Valkyries, that would be one to tell the grandchildren.

'Da, da, da, da, daa. Da, da, da, da daa.'*

*[This, in case it is not clear, is a vain attempt to represent Denny humming "The Ride Of The Valkyries" By Wagner.]

'I hate zat song,' Brynhilde admonished him.

'How about Stairway to Heaven?' asked Denny cheekily.

'How does zat go?'

Denny rolled his eyes. 'You've never heard "Stairway to Heaven"?' he said disbelievingly, and started to hum the opening bars.

* * *

'Well. It's about time you arrived. Cutting it a bit fine, aren't you? Do you know how many strings I had to pull to get you here?'

Tamar gave Odin a neutral look. The one that made Slick very nervous. 'None?' she suggested.

Odin glared at the handmaidens that had ushered Tamar and Slick into the grand throne room where Odin had been awaiting them. It was a monument to pure tastelessness, Slick noted even through his terror. Golden walls, the whole bit. The handmaidens scattered, and Odin resumed his benign expression, as if replacing a mask, and tried hard to pretend that he was unaware of the raven on his left shoulder pecking determinedly at his ear.

'Ha! Well you're just in time anyway. Er, it's just the two of you then?' he asked, looking over Slick's shoulder in a distracted way.

'Is that a problem?' said Tamar menacingly.

Slick frowned in puzzlement. Odin was talking as if he had been expecting them.

'No, not really, as long as *you're* here.' said Odin. 'It's just that I heard that you travel in a pack these days. Is this your husband that I've been hearing about?'

'No.'

Behind her Slick blushed bright red, which did not escape Odin's notice.

'Oh well, I won't say a word,' Odin told her conspiratorially and gave her a huge wink.

Tamar just gave him a blank stare. She was waiting for the other shoe to drop. Something funny was going on here. She signed to Slick to say nothing. Let them talk, Stiles always said. Never let them know that you have no idea what's going on. That way, they'll tell you everything you want to know, and more besides.

'Cold as a mountain top,' muttered Odin, looking away from the stare.

'Anyway,' he resumed. 'Lots to do, Loki will be here soon, and Ragnoroc cannot be far behind eh? What's the plan?'

'Er?'

'Well, well, you never were much of a one for the forward planning I suppose. You *can* help us though, can't you? I mean I *had* hoped that you would stop Loki before it came to this, but I suppose you can't fight mythology. As soon as Loki escaped, we knew that he would gather the Giants for Ragnoroc. Is something wrong?'

Tamar put her face straight. 'No, nothing.'

'What a pity you didn't sort out Fenrir when you had the chance. But I suppose you know what you're doing. I mean, ha, ha, you certainly aren't going to let him get away with it are you?'

'Certainly not,' said Tamar firmly, without any idea what she was agreeing to.

'I knew you'd come, even though you don't like me much.' He held up a hand to silence her protests, even though she had not opened her mouth. 'No, no,' he said. 'I always knew you weren't keen on me. I can't say I blame you really. I'm a bastard. I know it. But after all, if Loki wins its curtains for Midgard too, once Fenrir swallows the sun. – Damn the thing.' This last was aimed at the raven; he had finally given up his pretence at indifference and he grabbed the raven, which squawked indignantly, waking the other raven, sending them both flapping agitatedly around the hall.

'Midgard?' interjected Slick, swallowing a snort of laughter.

'Earth,' said Tamar. 'Where's Thor?' she asked Odin. She had adjusted to the new situation quickly as she always did.

So, she had been lied to and tricked, played for a fool and generally messed about. So, she had reached this point by an entirely spurious route. So, there were still a lot of unanswered questions. So, what else was new? Tamar, quick thinking and impulsive, always faced the situation in front of her and dealt with it. The past was irrelevant. The fact was, that here and now, Loki was on his way to Valhalla with the "Giants" (presumably the Tuatha – oh, she *had* been fooled) and Fenrir (who had clearly been lying from the start) and she had to find a way to deal with it or it was, as Odin so eloquently put it "curtains" for the Earth.

'Thor?' echoed Odin. 'He's upstairs, polishing his hammer, ready for battle you know.'

'Get him,' she ordered. She did not really want to see Thor, who was uncomfortably like Hogswill the Hairy backed – a drunken Viking that she had been enslaved to and whom she had no desire to be reminded of. But she needed time to think.

'I shall send for …' Odin raised his head, listening. 'They're here!' he ran to the window in a panic.

There was a thunderous sound outside, getting closer. Bloodcurdling shouts filled the air. 'Ah, it's only the Valkyries,' said Odin in a relieved tone. 'What on Asgard is that they are singing?'

Tamar shoved him aside and looked. A broad smile spread over her face. 'It's Denny,' she said.

'What?' said Slick beside her now and straining his eyes to see. 'Even *you* can't possibly see that from this distance,'

'No,' Tamar grinned in delight. 'But I can hear. Only Denny could get the Valkyries singing "Stairway to Heaven".'

~ Chapter Seventeen ~

'TAMAR!' DENNY RAN toward her and crushed her in his arms. 'Thank God!'

Tamar returned the embrace laughing as she did so. 'When are you going to learn,' she said into his hair, 'that you don't need to worry about me?'

He held her away from him and gave her a baffled look. 'Never,' he said.

And Tamar felt suddenly as if she were being drowned in golden sunshine.

Slick nudged Ray and pointed to the look on her face. 'Looks like a bad case of the warm and fuzzies,' he said.

The hall was now fairly full. There were the Valkyries of course, standing in formation like rock n' roll cheerleaders. Vidar had gone to kneel before Odin, leaving Ray and Dawber wondering if they should be doing the same.

Slick had no such qualms. Watching Tamar bossing Odin about like a naughty schoolboy had greatly diminished the awe of his presence, and such a thought never even occurred to

Stiles. Hecaté considered herself at least his equal, and Denny, as yet, had not even noticed him.

'You have done well,' Odin was heard to say to Vidar, drawing a derisive snort from Denny.

'And you must be the husband?' said Odin, looking up in surprise at this noise.

'Introductions later,' said Denny, '*if* we're all still alive. Loki's right behind us.' he looked questioningly at Tamar who nodded to indicate that she knew all about it.

'Right,' he said, apparently *apropos* of nothing. 'Got any ideas?' he asked her.

'Fight,' said Tamar succinctly.

'WE *WILL* FIGHT!' came a thunderous voice that shook the room. Everyone turned to see a massive figure standing in the doorway swinging a massive hammer.

'Hello Thor,' said Tamar without enthusiasm.

'Djinn,' he acknowledged her with a dismissive grunt. Denny went red with fury at this, but Tamar restrained him. 'He doesn't know any better,' she said placatingly.

'Father,' he nodded brusquely at Odin

'See?' said Tamar. 'The same to everyone. He doesn't mean anything by it.'

Now the other gods were filing into the hall in a silent procession. One by one, as the visitors watched in fascination, they stood before Odin, bowed and moved on to stand together on the other side of the throne.

When this was over, Thor addressed them. 'BATTLE!' he bellowed.

And the reply came back. 'BATTLE!'

'BATTLE!' repeated Thor even louder than before, brandishing his hammer wildly.

'BATTLE' returned the assembled gods banging their weapons on the floor. 'BATTLE, BATTLE, BATTLE, BATTLE ...' they chanted in rhythm with the banging.

'Oh brother!' said Denny, as the noise rose to a crescendo.

Then the skies over Asgard flickered as if a bird had flown across the sun, and then went dark. The noise ceased abruptly as if all sound, as well as light, had been sucked from the world, and Valhalla stood in a vacuum of silence and darkness. No one moved, even the pennants on the battlements stopped fluttering. The whole world was frozen in a moment of time that simultaneously lasted forever and went by in instant.

'Oh, no,' breathed Tamar. She alone had seen this before – long ago. She alone knew what it meant. And she thought of the collective power of the Tuatha and their magical hosts, gathered outside the doors of Valhalla.

The light over Asgard would never shine again. It was over.

There was more than Loki behind this; he was only the instrument. This was destiny, unstoppable and inexorable. The time of the Norse gods had finally come. They had cheated their fate long enough.

So, it had been for the Greek gods. Long ago, she had seen this darkness fall over Mount Olympus. The file was being erased, and they were all stuck inside.

She became aware of the sounds of battle going on all around her, overlaying the stillness and silence. She saw herself fighting desperately for her life, while she stood calmly by and watched in a detached way

'Of *course*,' she realised, both were true. That this battle would go on forever for the participants, but also, that nothing would ever happen here again. With a kind of cold horror, she understood that she was watching, from the inside, a file of mythology becoming a disused file. A file containing a thing that had never happened. In a distant kind of way, she remembered explaining this phenomenon to Denny shortly after they had first met. It had not seemed so bad then. But then she had not been the one being erased forever.

How had she escaped before? She did not know, could not remember, but she dimly understood that in those days, as a Djinn, she had been a file all by herself. That was no longer true; she had joined the world – because of Denny. There would be no escape this time.

'So, how it that she could see what was happening, as an observer as well as a participant? She was not supposed to *be* here. But then, neither were Denny and her friends.

That was a point, why *were* they here? Superficially, they were here because Loki had manipulated things, through Fenrir, in order to draw them into Ragnoroc. Odin might have also been behind some of it. They undoubtedly had their reasons, or *thought* they did. Loki had certainly never liked Tamar much. Dragging her into the Twilight of the gods might have only been his idea of a joke. He had had a twisted sense of humour at the best of times, and several thousand years of torture had probably twisted it even further.

The truth was, though, that the file clerks in mainframe were behind this.

The Norse Gods had escaped their fate the first time around. While the Greeks, Egyptians, Mayans etc were all discarding their old belief systems, and their gods were relegated to the ignominy of the deleted files of fiction, the Norse gods had managed to hang on somehow. Ragnoroc had been averted the first time around, and the gods of Asgard had been a thorn in the side of the tidy minded clerks ever since. Much like the Djinn had once been.

So, had the clerks finally had enough of Tamar and Denny messing around with things that did not concern them and decided to finish them off once and for all? The idea had a certain poetic justice about it, she had to admit. Their own predilection for intervening in things that were not their business, used against them. And the clerks would know that they would not be able to resist interfering in this one.

But while she could admire, in the abstract, the genius of the plot against them, it did not mean she was going to put up with it.

But what could she do?

She was part of the file now; she had no control over events from the outside. Asgard was no longer real, the events taking place before her very eyes had no relevance, no meaning, they were no longer real. Fenrir could eat the sun if he liked, there was no point in stopping it. It was not the real sun anyway. Outside, the world was going on as normal.

But what if she *did* stop it?

Tamar stood in the empty file looking at on at the battle taking place within, as if she were watching an old newsreel of something that had happened long ago, and could no longer be changed. She was there, and also here, watching herself. She wondered idly what that other self was thinking. She felt as if she ought to be able to remember, as if she were watching events that she had taken part in long ago from a distance of many years. But that other self was not real now, any more than any of this was real. It had never happened. That was the point.

If she closed her eyes, she would find herself in an empty file, alone? And then she could leave, because she was real; she could close the file and return to mainframe, leaving her unreal self behind. Or she could remain, wandering through the battle like a ghost for the rest of eternity. Some choice!'

She saw Stiles and Denny fighting back to back, they looked grimly happy – the joy of battle. Were they still real? Or were they a part of the unreal world now? Could she get them back? Or were they, like her, watching the battle from some unknown vantage point, as well as participating? Was this happening to all of them? For the first time in her long life, Tamar was tormented by an agony of indecision. Tears of frustration formed in her eyes.

She did not know what to *do*!

'*If you want to, I can save you,*' Denny had sung that to her. Startled by the clarity of the memory, she blinked the tears from her eyes. '*I can take you away from here,*'

'Denny?' she whispered.

Denny *was* real. They were *all* real, of course they were, how stupid! 'It's not over yet!' she told herself. At least, she counted on her fingers, six people – seven if she included herself, were still real, and the others … well, it was not too late for them either. Ragnoroc was about to be cancelled all over again.

'Sorry guys,' she said silently to the clerks in mainframe. 'I'm the fly in your ointment – again.' She closed her eyes. 'Close file,' she said firmly.

~ Chapter Eighteen ~

THE NOISE WAS incredible. Thor's hammer crashed with a thunder that shook the surrounding mountains causing great tracts of ice to shatter and slide down the mountainsides, the sound of their falling lost in the tumult. The darkened skies were filled with flashes of lightning, so bright they seemed more like exploding suns.

Battle cries and the screams of the dying, the clash of sword, spear and battle axe fused together in a single deafening wall of sound.

It was like being in the middle of an earthquake in a thunderstorm after a meteor strike during a nuclear war. And that was just the background noise – the special effects so to speak going on behind the action.

It was impossible to stand. The ground was continually moving under the feet, splitting and tilting the unwary into great crevasses that opened as the ground fell away from under them.

Denny, although fighting like a maniac, yet felt strangely detached. His presence here, he knew, was totally irrelevant. He would fight, but he could not win, could not change the outcome. One lonely warrior, however valiant, however good, could not single-handedly win a war between hundreds of opposing combatants. Nor could seven, he added to himself, acknowledging the others, they were simply too few. And even had they been a hundred – or a thousand, there was an inevitability about the conclusion that could not be avoided. The time for Ragnoroc had come, had been decided upon elsewhere and there was no stopping it. They would die here, victims of their own hubris, lost in a mythology that they had no part in, and Ragnoroc would be an established fact. Something that had happened, that could not be changed. It felt as if it already was.

'The only way to win a war is not to hold it.' these words dropped into Denny's head from a place of silence, sharp and clear against the tremendous clamour all around him. And yet he heard them through his ears in the ordinary way, which should have been impossible given the decibel level assaulting his senses.

'Finally losing my mind,' he muttered, deftly decapitating a giant that had incautiously come too close to his swinging broadsword, which was actually the Athame wearing a cunning disguise. 'Bloody hearing things now.'

Stiles was in trouble, and despite his conviction that they were all going to die anyway, Denny's instincts took over, and he leapt into the fray to help him out. They were fighting back to back when Denny felt a sudden vacuum close to him an empty space that had been filled with noise, blood and confusion. Then the whole world went dark.

'Funny, I don't *feel* dead,' he told the empty space. 'Christ, now I'm *talking* to myself,' he added.

'The only way to win a war is not to hold it. Go back.'

'Who *said* that?' snapped Denny. 'I know that voice.'

'Damn,' came the voice. There was a crackling sound and, 'is this thing on?' Then dead silence.

'Hello?' said Denny uncertainly. 'Is anybody there?' He felt a fool. Like a man at the wrong end of a séance. Surely, it was the living who said things like that to the dead, not the other way around.

But now he was certain that he was not dead, but somehow in a file in mainframe, and somebody was trying to contact him.

'Hello?' he tried again.

'Crackle crackle hiss ... 've to go back.'

'What?'

'... go back, damn! Wait ... min...te ... tryi... fix... blast... thing... stan... by... *hell*.'

'*Clive*?' asked Denny suddenly recognising the broken voice.

'Of course ... stupi... boy,' came the voice. 'Other... tried to fit you up. Felt oblig... help. Owe you one ... can ... hear me?'

'Sort of,' said Denny. 'You're breaking up terribly.'

'Unauthoris... tra...mission... bad quality... sorry crackle, crackle beeeeep! Is that better?'

'Yes, where are you?'

'Better you don't know. Now, I haven't got long before they find me, so listen carefully...'

Denny listened.

'A deleted file?' thought Denny. It made sense (the file was definitely empty) as did everything else Clive had told him, except the part about going back. Why go back? There was clearly no point. Unless he had meant something else.

Not that you could rely on Clive, he often edited the truth, as Denny knew to his cost. The problem was you could never be sure of him. One minute he was asking for your help, the next saving your life, and the next telling you blatant lies for his own unfathomable purposes.

But this time, he had left Denny in a real dilemma. He could escape right now and leave everyone else to their fate. Or he could stay here and ... leave everybody to their fate, come to think of it. Not really a dilemma then.

There had to be a third choice. One that Clive had left deliberately vague, in order to cover his own back perhaps with the other clerks, those who had set them up – or so Clive averred.

'The only way to win a war is not to hold it. Go back.'

Denny closed his eyes. 'Close file,' he said.

'You took your time didn't you? We have work to do, you know.'

'Tamar?'

* * *

One minute Stiles was fighting back to back with Denny and the next, he felt a cold wind, a rushing of empty air behind him and then everything went dark.

'Jack'll never go for it,' said Denny. 'Not if he thinks he's leaving us behind.'

'It doesn't matter,' said Tamar, 'just so long as I have you.'

'Tamar!'

'Oh calm down, I don't mean I'm leaving them behind. I just mean that my little plan for sorting this out will work better with your help.'

'What little plan? Actually, look, go back to the beginning. What the hell is going on? How did *you* get out anyway, was it Clive?'

'No, I got out by myself, but because I did, it gave Clive the chance to get us all out. Without them knowing it was him.'

'Why didn't he just *say* that then?' said Denny, exasperated.

'Because, then they might find out it was him. It's all to do with free will and all that. Denny, you *know* this stuff. He isn't supposed to help us really. And from now on, it's up to us. He'll give the others the chance to leave, but it's got to be *their* decision. But, like I said, it doesn't matter anyway. There are no restrictions on *us* helping them out.'

'Okay,' said Denny falling in with the new situation with the ease of long practice. 'So what *is* this great plan?'

'Sarky!' said Tamar but without rancour. 'You must have noticed where we are,' she added inconsequentially.

'Mainframe, so what? It's what I expected.'

'Me too. That's why I need you.' She gave him a sidelong glance of pure delighted wickedness, which he found deliciously irresistible. 'Come on Super-Geek,' she said. 'Let's Hack!'

'Hack what?'

'Everything!'

* * *

Stiles knew exactly where he was, but he had not the faintest idea what to do about it. He had spent enough time in deleted files to recognise the peculiar emptiness that surrounded him, and his investigative brain soon put together the pieces and deduced that this was the deleted file of the Norse Gods and all their history. So, it was all over, was it? Well, that was what Ragnoroc was all about he supposed. But until this moment of revelation, he had seen nothing inevitable about it. A typically human failing this. Few people truly believe in the inevitability of a preordained destiny. The belief in free will and the ability to effect change is too deeply ingrained in the human psyche. An "it's not over till it's over" attitude that precludes the possibility that something One is currently experiencing might have been over and done with long ago. If people knew the true nature of time and destiny, they would not see the world in such simple terms. But then again, what would be the point of living in such a world?

Stiles had had the advantage of experiencing a different view of the world than most. He had seen eternity, and it did not frighten him. But that did not mean that he was ready to accept it without a fight. The thing about humans is that when faced with the inevitable, they invariably set about trying to change it. It was one of the things about humanity that drove the clerks mad because, occasionally, when humans took this attitude, the inevitable could suddenly become very uncertain indeed. This made things very untidy and caused a lot of unpaid overtime.

Tamar *never* accepted the inevitable (at least, not if she did not agree with it) even though, with all she knew about the universe, she ought to have known better. And Stiles had learned, through her, that although the flow of the universe was a pattern of preordained events – unchanging and unchangeable – marching inexorably toward their unavoidable conclusion, yet through sheer force of will, the inevitable could become the un-inevitable. He had seen her force a path through destiny and out the other side many times. In other words, humans were right, free will counts and nothing is inevitable really. Even when it's over.

With all this in mind, Stiles shrugged his shoulders and turned back to the battle.

* * *

'There's no point in going back through time,' Tamar explained. 'Not this time. Because it's not there, all the history of the Norse gods is now part of the same deleted file. It's no longer a part of history. And that includes *our* interactions with them, like me meeting Loki. If we want to change what's happened, the only thing we can do is crash the system.'

'They'll make us fix it afterwards,' said Denny gloomily. 'It'll take a hundred years.'

'Well, we're going to have to reprogramme anyway,' said Tamar blithely; apparently unaware of what she was suggesting.

'Reprogramme *mainframe*?' said Denny aghast. 'The whole *universe*?'

Then he shrugged. 'Sounds like a challenge.'

Tamar grinned. 'I knew you'd say that,' she said. 'So, come on then tech-head, how do we do it?'

'I think I preferred "Super-Geek",' said Denny. 'We could try a virus,' he added thoughtfully.

'Got one in your pocket?'

'I'd need to write one,' he said. 'It'd need to be pretty bad to crash the whole of mainframe. Do we really need to crash the whole system?'

'You tell me, brainiac. We need to be able to get into the Ragnoroc file and change it. Which we can't do since it's already been deleted. Is this too complicated for you?'

'It's just a bit metaphysical. I can cope,' he said pulling a wry face. 'So, we need to be able to go in to a file that's already been deleted.' He thrust his hands into his pockets and slouched languidly. 'We need to somehow open this file *before* it was deleted – even though it already is.' He sighed and straightened up. 'We need to crash the system.' he said decisively.

'Can't we just find the file on the hard drive and, oh I don't know retrieve it or something?' asked Tamar. 'Deleted files *can* be retrieved can't they?' Crashing mainframe suddenly seemed *too* drastic, even though it had been her idea in the first place.

'Cold feet?' asked Denny raising an eyebrow. 'Okay, yes we *could* just retrieve the file – *if* we could get into the hard drive, which, we're going to have to do anyway if we want to crash it, and it won't be easy. I mean there *is* security. They aren't just going to *give* us access. But if we simply go in and retrieve the file what would we get?' He answered his own question. 'Nothing, a deleted file. Big deal. You said it yourself. We need to get into the file *before* it was deleted in the first place. It's not in the history files. We can't find it that way. We need to crash the system and restart it. That way, *every* file that belongs to the Norse gods will be rebooted from the start. Well, in fact, every file in mainframe will. But we needn't concern ourselves with the rest of them, actually. They'll just run the way they did before – or rather *continue* to run, the way they did before. We won't actually have to reprogramme mainframe, after all. It's not as bad as I first thought.'

Sensing that Tamar was still uncertain, he felt compelled to explain. 'You see, a program file isn't like a tape that rewinds and starts from the beginning, there is no beginning, not in a traditional sense. Just like a picture has no beginning, it's just pixels. A file is just data, a web of interconnected code.'

Tamar's blank look was not encouraging. Denny tried again.

'What I'm saying,' he sighed, 'is that it's not going to be like starting again from the beginning of time. There is no time in mainframe anyway, and time doesn't actually have a beginning as such. It's like a big ocean ...' he halted realising he was getting off the point. 'Look, when mainframe reboots, all the program files will just come back on line. As long as we don't go in and actually, rewrite the code. The files will just be ... Well, it'll just *be*, basically. (We had certainly better hope so anyway). The clerks might have a *bit* of sorting out to do; some of the data might be corrupted in the crash. But it'll serve them right if they do. Anyway, once they restart *et tout voila*, we can retrieve the file we want *before* it gets erased and do what we want with it. And the best part is, they'll never know what happened. After mainframe reboots, apart from the one file we change, it'll be like it never happened.'

'I'm just going to have to take your word for it, aren't I?'

'This was *your* idea in the first place. You *knew* we would have to do this. *You* told *me*.'

'I know.'

'So what are you talking about then?'

'Nothing. I guess I just hoped there might be another way.'

Denny nodded understandingly. This was a like changing history in a big way – you never knew what it might do to your own destiny, not to mention that of countless billions of other people. But he was confident that he knew what he was doing. He knew and understood mainframe these days far better than she did. Far better than anyone – even the clerks that ran it; they only knew their own little departments but Denny knew a lot more. On top of which, he was pretty certain that something like this had probably been done before, perhaps many times. After all, how would anyone know?

'You know where mainframe central control is, don't you?' he said, thus taking the decision out of her hands.

'Yes, I've been there. It's awesome actually, like talking to God.' She was biting her lip – a bad sign.

'How are we going to get in?'

'Well actually, getting in won't be a problem,' said Tamar holding up the access card that she had stolen on a previous excursion to mainframe. 'I never leave home without it,' she said. 'Well, you never know,' she defended herself, as Denny started to laugh.

'You're wonderful,' he told her.

'Are you sure that crashing the system won't cause a lot of damage?' she said suddenly, cutting across his merriment.

'Trust me,' he said reassuringly, slouching back against the wall and grinning. 'I can do this. Take me to see God.'

~ Chapter Nineteen ~

THERE WAS ACTUALLY nothing altruistic at all about Clive's rescue mission. He was merely running damage control.

As soon as he had realised that Tamar had somehow escaped from the file, he knew that, sooner or later, she would cause a whole lot of trouble in mainframe in order to get her friends out too. The other clerks would never see it that way, of course. Their understanding of human behaviour was non-existent, and Clive just did not have time to waste trying to convince them.

But if he managed to get all her friends safely out of the file, all fit and ready to fight another day, then Clive hoped that would satisfy her enough to persuade her to leave the rest well enough alone. (You can see that Clive did not understand Tamar very well either if he thought that.)

The problem was, they had to be brought out in the same order that they had arrived. Only the one who had arrived with Tamar, before the battle began and the files merged ready for deletion, was an inconstant factor. He would have to come out last.

Denny first then. *He* had been no problem. He had cottoned on immediately and left like a good boy – back into the loving arms of his sweetheart all happy ever after. But the man Stiles had gone and buggered it all up. The bloody hero type, Clive dubbed him and cursed him up and down. He had only gone and rejoined the battle. *Why?*

Clive seriously doubted that Tamar would be satisfied with only Denny's release. She would want them all. It was a concept that Clive did not personally relate too, but he understood it in an abstract way. He had observed enough of it among Tamar and her friends. Loyalty.

Well, he had done all he could. The man Stiles had ruined his perfect plan, and now Tamar and her sidekick were running loose in mainframe somewhere, doing God knows what. And, heaven knew, *she* was bad enough on her own. Clive gnawed at his nails and prayed to the Processor that they were not going to do anything stupid.

* * *

'You know, you'd think I'd get used to this,' said Denny sitting on a cloud and looking distinctly uncomfortable.

'I mean, let's face it, it's a bit disappointing really, isn't it? At least it is for me.'

'Disappointing?' Tamar was nonplussed.

'When people think about talking to God, I seriously doubt that this is what *anyone* has in mind,' he explained. 'It's not very... glorious, is it?'

'It's not really *God*,' said Tamar.

'I know that. It's just ... you know it's getting hard to believe in anything anymore.'

'What, you mean like "Truth, Justice and the American Way?' said Tamar and went off into peals of derisive laughter.

Despite himself, Denny grinned. 'Not exactly,' he said. Then he sighed. 'I just mean that ... maybe people – humans – are better off not knowing this stuff. I mean look at this place. If people knew ...' He gestured futilely.'

We don't need to *believe* in stuff,' said Tamar. 'We know the *truth*.'

'Maybe that's what I mean. Maybe we aren't supposed to know this much about it all. Maybe we aren't supposed to know how it all really works. Maybe humans are supposed to have an unsubstantiated faith in the unseen and the intangible. Maybe we need that. The reality is a bit of a disappointment.'

'Stop saying "maybe". The word is starting to lose all meaning,' was all Tamar could come up with after this diatribe.

Denny nodded. She was not human; she did not understand. But then again, he was not entirely human himself anymore.

'The *search* for the truth is the important thing to most people,' she said suddenly, proving him entirely wrong. She *did* understand – at least partly. 'But let's face it,' she continued. 'We aren't most people.'

'So, how long do we have to wait?' said Denny abruptly changing the subject.

'Wait?' said Tamar. 'We don't have to wait at all. Just ask.'

'God?' said Denny tentatively, feeling a fool for the second time that day. Talking to no one can have that effect.

'Yes?' came a sing song voice out of nowhere.

'Am *I* a disappointment?' said Tamar suddenly.

'What?' no of course not. Where did that come from?'

'I *was* the intangible, the unseen, a mere focus of belief – until you actually *met* me.'

'That's different. Look is this the right time for this conversation?'

'I just wanted to know. It's all right. Go on.'

Denny shook his head. 'Er … God?'

'Yes,' said the voice patiently, and Denny had the impression that it could go on doing this all day.

'Set up interface,' said Denny and crossed his fingers.

'Initialising,' said the voice of God. This was what Denny had hoped. The security here was a joke in some ways. Because Tamar had an access card for central control, mainframe assumed that they were authorised users. Apparently, it had not occurred to the programmers that an access card might be stolen, and no security protocols had been put in place against this eventuality. Once you were in, you were in. No more questions were asked. Not even a password.

Denny would have been ashamed to have been the author of such a weak programme.

'Choose interface mode,' said "God."

Denny hesitated.

'Choose interface mode,' repeated the voice.

Denny gave Tamar a panicked look. 'I don't know what that means,' he admitted.

But the system was far too patient and helpful for its own good. 'Modes for interface are: keyboard, manual interface, voice control interface, automatic interface. Please choose interface mode,' the song-song voice rang out.

'Automatic interface,' said Denny rashly.

The point of establishing an interface was to search the database for the files they wanted in order to save time later. Knowing the file numbers would be a big advantage – one that had been somewhat lacking in previous adventures, where they had been forced to use the tiger tail approach in searching for files,* and wasted a lot of time. Once this was done Denny would use the interface to shut down the system from the inside. No viruses needed. *He* would be the virus.

*[So called, by hunters, because it refers to the process of finding a tiger by wandering around until you step on its tail. Then you *know* you've found it.]

He had known that he would have to "get inside" mainframe in order to accomplish this and once inside, he would (hopefully) be able to find the shutdown command used to make mainframe to shut down and reboot. What he had not bargained on, was how literal this operation would be.

Before Tamar's horrified eyes, Denny literally dissolved into millions of particles of light. If you had the eyesight to see it, and Tamar did, you could see the data stream. The particles were actually tiny pieces of binary code. Then he vanished.

It was a bit like seeing a nanobe swarm disintegrate. Of course, all human beings were nothing more than a swarm of cells and in here, in mainframe, a swarm of data. But it was still horrifying to see it separate like that.

'Denny?'

'Yes, I'm here.' It was Denny's voice and yet it was not.

'Where are you?'

'Can't you see me? I'm right here. Oh, hang on a minute.' he sounded perfectly calm which was a relief.

A three dimensional image of Denny appeared before her eyes. It was pretty convincing. To the casual eye, it might have seemed as if Denny had simply rematerialised. It was made up of data, just as the real Denny was inside mainframe. But, looking closely, it was possible to see that it was no more than a holographic image, swirling data patterns. The real Denny was far away.

'Are you all right?'

The image managed a wooden smile. 'I'm fine, really. I'm inside.'

'You *are* mainframe?'

'No, I'm more like ... like a ghost in the machine, but I can see *everything* from here. *Do* anything!' the slightly mechanical voice sounded excited. 'I never knew. I never expected *this*. To be *inside* mainframe, I can control the universe from here if I want. And, Oh God, it's so beautiful. To see the whole universe as data. To know everything. I know *everything* Tamar, *everything*! Ask me anything.'

'Don't let it go to your head,' said Tamar dryly.

'Killjoy,' said Denny laughing. But Tamar was relieved. That was her Denny all right. Apparently not even becoming instant ruler of the universe could disturb his equilibrium for long.

Denny was more awed by the incredible power of mainframe itself than he was impressed by his own ascent into omnipotence. Now this – *this* was something to believe in.

The saying goes "power corrupts and absolute power corrupts absolutely" but Denny was not the corruptible type. Self-effacing all his life, he had taken to power, apparently with the same calm equanimity with which he seemed to accept everything from blistering disaster to falling in love, but actually, underneath it all, with a kind of wondering disbelief, and with the certainty that he did not deserve it and that, if he abused it, it would disappear as mysteriously as it had appeared.

It never occurred to him that true power is earned and that he had earned this power too, which seemed as if it had simply fallen into his lap. Earned it through years of blood, sweat and tears; that the steps that had led him here had also trained him to handle this kind of power without losing his head. That, through the earning, he had acquired not only power, but self-control.

A self-control that was now second nature to Denny. Without ever thinking about it consciously, he had never really considered his power as his own, to wilfully wield as he chose.

He certainly did not consider this new power (which he did not even realise he had earned and fully deserved) as his own. The idea of abusing it would never even occur to him. He felt blessed but undeserving – as he always had.

'I found something.' Denny's voice broke through the reverie that she had fallen into. She had been sitting on a cloud, just waiting, for about half an hour.

'What?' she could tell it was not the files he was supposed to be looking for.

'Us – our files I mean.'

'Oh!' She was shocked. Somehow, she had not thought of this.

'Thing is, I could ...' he seemed to hesitate. 'That ordinary life you wanted? You can have it. I mean if you want to. Just say the word.'

'You're *kidding*.'

'Do I *look* like I'm kidding?'

Tamar looked at the hologram of Denny, with its unresponsive features and decided not to go there. 'Will... would we still be together?'

'If that's what you want. I can rewrite them any way you like. And it wouldn't be like that time that Askphrit futzed with our destinies. There wouldn't be any alternative lives out there. It would just be the way it is. The way it had always been.'

'You know I always wondered about that.' said Tamar with skilful evasion. 'I mean, Askphrit changed our destinies. He could have made them anything he wanted surely. So why did he … I mean why were we still together, even in his messed up version? You'd think he'd have separated us. You know, divide and conquer and all that. I mean he really hated us.'

'I don't know, maybe it didn't occur to him, or maybe he couldn't. Perhaps you can't fight destiny that way. Maybe we were meant to be together. Yeah, I'd like to think that.'

'You soppy sod,' she said nevertheless sounding pleased.

'You know what I think, though.' she continued, referring back to the question in hand before he could ask again. 'I think that in some way, we would *know*. If we *were* ordinary people we'd always feel like something was wrong, something was missing. But we wouldn't know what it was. That would be terrible. We'd probably spend our whole lives feeling vaguely unsatisfied, without ever knowing why. That would be just awful.' She let out a sigh. 'It might *seem* like a good idea, but we have to face the facts … *I* have to face the facts. You and I, we *aren't* ordinary Denny. We aren't *meant* to be ordinary. We aren't meant to *have* an ordinary life. No, don't change it. I don't want to always be wondering who I really am.'

'Been there, done that,' agreed Denny with a tinny laugh. 'Admit it. You don't really *want* to be ordinary,' he added astutely.

'No, I suppose I don't. Do you?'

'Me?' Denny sounded surprised. 'I never did.'

'But you would have done it anyway,' Tamar realised, 'for me.'

'You might do something about the reporters, though,' she said lightly. 'As long as you're in there, you know – whatever.'

'Anything but ordinary,' said Denny, after another interminable wait. 'Agreed?'

'Yes.' said Tamar, slightly wrong footed. Hadn't they settled this?

'We'd rather be *dead* than be ordinary, right?'

'Right,' said Tamar uncertainly. She was not at all sure, now that she thought about it that there was all that much difference between "ordinary" and "dead".

'Good,' he said gleefully. 'After all, if I *were* ordinary. I couldn't do *this*!'

And the universe switched off.

'Should have had a drum roll,' he said to the ensuing darkness.

~ Chapter Twenty ~

IN THE BEGINNING, there was the word, and the word was "startup".

The word blinked in the darkness at Denny as main power was restored.

Where did mainframe draw its power from? Denny wondered. It had never occurred to him before to wonder about this. But in the stillness and darkness of a dead universe, Denny was finally aware of something else, something bigger out there. It never ends, he realised. There's always something else, something further out. Mainframe was only a small component in a much larger system. The thought was strangely comforting. Particularly in light of what he had just done. The magnitude of which was just beginning to hit him.

'Talk about the end of the world,' he thought with a terrified awe. Then, for the first time in a long, long time, Denny did what he had never thought to do again, since he had met Tamar. He panicked.

'What the hell have I done? We've really gone too far this time.'

'Ohgodohgodohgodohgodohgodohgod!'

Time is not linear, nor is it circular. Time is like a great sea. All of time moves within the confines of mainframe as the sea moves within the seabed. Parts of it escape to lap upon the shores, and within its confines, it flows in all directions. But the most part of it remains within the confines set for it. You can dive into the sea at any point, as long as you have a jumping off place (otherwise known as file access)

This is what Denny had learned from mainframe.

But from the moment he had hit the shutdown command, time had ceased to exist. He had been linked to mainframe and then he had been suddenly disconnected as the power died. And now, he was lost in a vast sea of nothing at all. The void – the *real* void – not the dead spaces between data, like the spaces between the walls in houses, where they had shoved David/Vidar to think about his crimes. Nor was it like the emptiness inside a disused file. A file was a solid thing; it existed, and beyond its confines, life went on. The emptiness was only inside. But here, there was no "here" and there never had been. It had no confines, infinite space, infinite nothing, forever and never, everywhere and nowhere.

No wonder Denny was panicking. He knew now that he, everyone, and everything else had always been linked to the mainframe. He felt as if he had been cut adrift. He was floating free from reality. Even death was not so final.

He forced himself to calm down. There had to be *something* out there. He faced the proof of this:

STARTUP>

It blinked impassively at him, which made him feel better. A link back to reality.

He made the connection; he would never know how, with no physical body, he was able to touch the words, but the moment he did, he felt the life force of the universe flow back. The words changed.

BOOT OPTIONS>

BRING SYSTEMS ONLINE MANUALLY (SAFE MODE)

There were no other options; it must be because he had hit the shutdown command without saving the system. But that had been the point hadn't it? He had been right the first time. This *was* going to take a hundred years.

Or maybe not.

Denny was fairly certain that the files were intact. That bringing all the systems on in safe mode one by one was unnecessary. The system was just being cautious.

Well, to hell with that. He had already pretty much thrown caution to the winds in shutting down mainframe in the first place. And there was no way he was spending any more time in this creepy place than he had to. Although connected to mainframe again, he could still feel the tug of the infinite just waiting for his control to falter to hurl him away into the void.

The files would reset – he was certain of it. He made his decision and hit escape.

Everything went black for the longest few seconds of Denny's life. And then the screen buzzed and cleared.

WELCOME TO MAINFRAME>>

SYSTEM STARTUP>

MANUAL REBOOT>

Damn the thing! He did not want to have to … then he realised what he was seeing. This was actually pretty perfect. Systems were online, ready for startup and the *files* were awaiting a manual reboot.

'I don't know why it can't just *say* that,' he grumbled.

Well, he knew which file he wanted to reboot first.

System startup provided another shortcut.

REBOOT FILES>>

MANUAL> (RECOMMENDED)

AUTOMATIC>

Denny booted up the file he wanted and then hit escape. The screen reset.

To hell with recommendations, he decided. Boot the rest up automatically.

There were a few tense minutes as the files booted up; all the while, the screen was flashing:

SCANNING FOR ERRORS ON YOUR HARD DRIVE …

Then finally:

WELCOME TO MAINFRAME>>

Which File?

Denny heaved a prodigious sigh of relief. He had done it.

~ Chapter Twenty One ~

'DO WHAT?' said Tamar.

'Denny held up a small silver disc and grinned.

'What's that?'

'File A7790/500595B12. Also known as the Ragnoroc files.'

'You've *done* it? But you were only gone – well, you *weren't* gone, at least …'

Denny grinned. 'Bit of an unforeseen side effect,' he told her. 'When mainframe rebooted … well, let's just say that this wasn't the only deleted file that suddenly reset.'

Tamar's hand flew to her mouth. 'Oh, no!'

'Right. Let's get out of here before they catch us.'

'But the deleted files …?'

'Not our problem,' said Denny with unusual callousness.

'But Denny …'

'Serves the sods right,' said Denny. 'They tried to delete *us*.'

'I know, but …'

'Look,' Denny relented, 'the deleted files aren't actually running. There are no Meittlepolyattlepusses roaming around out there, I only reran the current files. All the clerks will have to do is delete them again. 'It's all right really. Just a bit of extra work for them, you can't say they didn't ask for it. But they can't delete *this* one because I have a copy. All we have to do is upload it again. Which was pretty much the plan all along wasn't it?'

'Was it?'

'Well, how did you *think* we were going to do this?'

'I don't know. *You're* the genius.'

'I'm flattered, really. But this was *your* mad idea in the first place.'

'But only *you* could have pulled it off.'

'We haven't pulled anything off yet,' he reminded her. 'We need to get to a console – any console, and upload this disc into the mainframe. Then it's up to you. What exactly did you have in mind anyway?'

'We're going to rewrite a bit of recent history,' she told him. 'What's a Meittlepolyattlepuss?'

'Something that never existed,' said Denny. 'Like an honest politician.'

* * *

The house was eerily silent. Only Finvarra and the boys were left, and they were upstairs in another wing somewhere.

'This *has* to work,' said Tamar. 'We have to get them back. I can't stand the quiet.'

'It'll work,' Denny assured her. Neither of them mentioned Cindy, who would not be coming back, no matter whether this worked or not.

Not that Denny had not considered trying to fix the Cindy situation when he had been in mainframe. He had, within these files the fate of the Rheingold of course, as part of the Norse legends. But Denny finally decided that he did not have the right. Cindy's fate was her own business. Hadn't he done enough to her?

'Okay,' we're ready,' said Denny. They grasped hands and looked at each other – memories flooding into their minds of the first time they had done this together. Tamar leaned forward with an enigmatic smile on her face. And pressed "Enter"

'Beam me up Scotty,' they said together as they de-materialised.

* * *

'Stand guard Fulk,' said Loki to the hairy creature trotting along beside him. There was a whine, as of a dog that scents danger. Fulk looked hard at the water, then sniffed. Loki lost patience. 'Oh for Odin's sake Fulk,' he snapped. 'Just keep watch – over there.' he pointed to the cave entrance. Fulk shambled away muttering.

Loki then reached into his tattered robe and brought out a golden goblet encrusted with jewels. His eyes were gleaming with barely suppressed excitement. Under the water, Tamar caught her breath and metaphorically squared her shoulders. As Loki dipped the goblet into the water, she snatched it from his hand and rose out of the water in one smooth vertical movement scattering water in all directions. It was an impressive move, but Loki was too shocked to appreciate it properly.

He recovered fast and dived at Tamar who moved easily out of his way. 'Ah, ah, ah,' she said shaking her head in derision, 'naughty, naughty.'

Then, without warning, Fulk dived into the water and came up again, struggling ineffectually against the iron grip in which he was held by a grinning Denny.

'What?' said Loki.

'I *knew* Denny wouldn't let himself get caught out,' thought Tamar with satisfaction.

* * *

'Well. It's about time you arrived. Cutting it a bit fine aren't you? Do you know how many strings I had to pull to get you here?'

Tamar shrugged. 'Cutting it a bit fine for what?' she asked.

'Ragnoroc. Loki will be here soon, we have … what's that?'

Denny had come forward and dropped a struggling sack onto the floor at Odin's feet.

'It's Loki,' said Tamar, reaching down and slitting the sack open.

'He's *your* problem now. We're going home.'

'No Ragnoroc?' said Odin thunderstruck.

'No.'

Odin's face creased into a mammoth grin. 'Thor *will* be disappointed,' he said.

Tamar grinned back suddenly. 'Hand Loki over to him for a while,' she said. 'That ought to ease his disappointment.'

Odin laughed infectiously.

Really, he seemed almost human when he was like this, thought Tamar.

'It will indeed,' he said.

'No!' wailed Loki from his awkward position at Odin's feet. Denny had bound him hand and foot, chains *and* manacles, as stipulated by Tamar. 'He deserves it,' she had said.

He was ignored. 'Just the two of you is it?' asked Odin amiably. 'I had heard that you travel in a pack these days.'

Tamar smiled. 'Sometimes,' she said.

'And this must be the husband that I've been hearing about.'

'That's right.'

'Got a name has he?' said Odin, a faint reprimand in his tone.

'Denny Sanger,' said Denny holding out a hand.

'My goodness,' said Odin returning the handshake. 'Well, I'm really most grateful to both of you – thought our time was up this time.'

'We're happy to help,' said Denny suppressing a grin.

'Vat am I to do vis zis?' asked a handmaiden, holding out a leash with a large wolf attached to one end of it. 'I vound it tied up in ze entrance vay und it is makink vun mess of ze floor.'

'Oh, sorry,' said Denny, 'I left him there. 'He's all right though. He won't be giving you any more trouble. I think I've got him pretty well trained now.' This was apparently the case.

Fulk was cowering abjectly, his nose was down to the floor, his ears lay flat against his head, and he was shaking convulsively. He let out an ingratiating whine when Denny spoke.

'But not house trained apparently,' said Odin with another laugh. 'Freya will not be amused. Look he just did it on the rug.'

'Perhaps you can keep him outside,' said Denny.

'He's nervous,' said Tamar. 'You terrified him, you great bully.'

'Well,' said Denny diffidently, 'He *did* try to eat me.'

'He didn't know any better.'

'He does now,' said Odin. 'I think perhaps you are right. We will put him outside, with the horses.

'You will not stay for a feast?' he offered graciously.

'Thanks but we ought to be going,' said Tamar firmly. Denny's face fell. He was fond of Vikings who were always unimpressed with him until they discovered that he could eat a whole bull at one sitting, drink a lake-full of ale, had a vast repertoire of dirty songs and, these days at least, could beat up five men at once.

Odin bowed. 'All great men have a strong woman at their back,' he said almost to himself. And it was clear he was not thinking of Denny so much as he was himself.

To Tamar he said. 'A pleasure as always my dear. I knew you would not fail me. I am in your debt for all time. And you may be certain that Loki will get what is coming to him.'

To Denny he said. 'A great warrior should not be judged on the appearance of his strength but by the strength of his deeds. You are a small man by the standards of my people, but you are a great warrior nevertheless. I am humbled by your presence and grateful for my lesson.'

'Peace go with you both,' he called as they turned to leave.

At that moment, however, a loud snarl reverberated through the hall and there appeared in the doorway, blocking their way, the largest wolf either of them had ever seen. Twice as big as Fulk at least and, with its hackles raised, it looked even bigger.

Small beady yellow eyes, filled with hate and frustration, fixed on Tamar and it snarled again in vicious fury. It was Fenrir.

Denny pushed Tamar behind him, back into the hall, and tensed, waiting for the spring. But Fenrir did not spring at Denny. With a howl of triumph, he leapt clean over Denny's head and straight at Tamar. Denny spun, but he was not fast enough. However, Fulk, who had stiffened as soon as Fenrir entered the room, now broke free of his restraint and leapt snarling at Fenrir's throat. He must have taken Fenrir by surprise, because he knocked the much larger wolf sideways as he careered into him and they both went flying into the far wall. They rolled over and over together in a flying ball of fur, teeth and claws, neither getting the upper hand for a moment, and then, miraculously. Fulk was on top, and he had Fenrir by the throat.

'It's not the size of the warrior in the fight, it's the size of the fight in the warrior,' muttered Denny. Which was, more or less, what Odin had been trying to say to him.

Fenrir whined in submission and Fulk looked at Denny, keeping a heavy paw on Fenrir's chest.

'Looks like it's up to you,' said Tamar.

Denny turned away, and Fulk bent his head toward Fenrir and ripped his throat out.

Fulk trotted, jaws still dripping with blood, over to Denny's side and sat down like an obedient dog.

'Oh … Meittlepolyattlepusses!' said Tamar. 'We already have a dragon in the garage.'

'Always wanted a dog,' said Denny absently stroking Fulk's ears. Fulk whined and licked Denny's hand.

'Looks like you've got one then,' said Tamar succumbing to the inevitable for once.

'What do you suppose he eats?' said Denny. 'Apart from other wolves I mean.'

~ Chapter Twenty Two ~

FROM THE MOMENT that Tamar and Denny threw Loki in chains at the feet of Odin, Ragnoroc was officially cancelled – again. Only Hecaté was to remember the battle and the sudden reversal that took place at this moment. For the others, it was as if it had never happened.

And it never happened to Hecaté either, but being a goddess with an unusual memory, she remembered it anyway. The moment when the world around her stuttered and fell away, pin-wheeling into a black hole of emptiness to leave nothing but an empty file, which then became rapidly populated by different events, she remembered being there, although she was never there at all. Not this time. It was happening even now, she understood, while she stood here in the garden watching her husband, who had also been there, but would not remember it.

There was a certain amount of confusion as time spun backwards to the moment where it all changed. Slick had gone with Stiles and Dawber to the empty file, and they had both gone to the wrong file while Stiles interrogated David, whose true identity was revealed. And now they were back arguing with Ray about what to do next since Tamar and Denny had not yet returned, but were clearly heading toward Ragnoroc with no idea of what they were getting themselves into.

The Valkyries were not called in this time (this had originally been Denny's idea) and Ray thought they should go to Asgard through mainframe. 'It's *Ragnoroc*, which means the end of our world too.'

Stiles agreed, but neither Slick nor Dawber wanted to do this. Stiles, who in the absence of Tamar and Denny considered himself in charge, was about to order them to do as they were told, when Hecaté intervened.

'Jack, I need to talk to you,' she said, beckoning him over, away from the others. 'In private please.'

'Is everything all right?' he asked.

'Everything is fine,' she assured him. 'I have not the time to explain everything at this moment. But I promise I will. However, for the moment, let me say that Tamar and Denny are dealing with Ragnoroc and do not need out help. But I need yours my dear. I have had, shall we say, some enlightenment about the nature of the Tuatha and how they might be dealt with. This must be our task now.'

'Ray says they were the Giants in the Norse legends,' said Stiles*

*[He did not bother to ask how she knew what Tamar and Denny were up to. He was used to this sort of thing. If Hecaté said it was okay, then it was okay. She would explain later – when there was time. There was never time for explanations in the middle of things. And he had learned that asking questions wasted valuable time. They needed to trust each other.]

'How very astute of him,' Hecaté said. 'They are indeed. But so much more.'

'Tell me,' he said.

'The most ancient of all the races of gods,' she said, 'were not the products of imagination and belief, as were the later ones. They were a race, like that of humans, similar but with greater powers. They came to this world to rule it. And when they failed, they ascended to a different plane of existence. They became as spirits, harmless, weak and invisible. But now they have descended back into physical bodies. I have discovered their weakness in this form. The manner in which we shall separate them from the bodies they have … have …'

'Hijacked,' said Stiles tersely.

'Yes, but first we need to summon them. And that my dear is why I need you.'

'Okay.' Stiles waited.

'They are waiting to be summoned by Loki. He will summon them to a place of great magic. Their spiritual home you might say. I have seen this place – I flew over it and saw the summoning taking place. I will explain this later. There is a stone, like in nature to the portal stones that guarded the Faerie realm yet not quite the same, there we will summon the Tuatha and undo their spell.'

'You want me to impersonate Loki,' he surmised, 'with the gauntlet.'

'He is Tuatha, as is Leir. In their current form, tied down by the flesh, their consciousness' pulled a million different ways by the demands of their living bodies, buried under layers of human feelings and emotions and distracting thoughts, they will only recognize that a powerful Tuatha is summoning them. They will not be able to make the distinction, not while their minds are thus fogged. This weakness in them, I have now seen for myself. They are expecting Loki's summons. Why should they not respond? They *will* respond.'

'I agree. They probably will. But what are you going to do when they do?'

'I am a goddess, do you doubt me?'

'That's not an answer,' he pointed out.

'I will give them a choice,' she said.

'Oooh, nasty,' said Stiles without a trace of irony.

'So, what are *we* going to do?' asked Ray on behalf of himself, Dawber and Slick when Stiles briefly explained the situation. 'We want to help too.'

'There is one more piece of unfinished business that you are all uniquely qualified to deal with,' said Hecaté smiling.

'The Agency,' said Stiles.

'What do you want us to do?' asked Ray – spokesperson. 'Burn it down?'

'Not at all,' said Hecaté. 'Just the opposite, in fact. Since The Director abandoned it, the Agency has been in disarray. *He* will not be returning. I have a personal guarantee of that. But the Agency itself, although founded on faulty principles, has a place in the work we do. I have no doubt that much good will come of such an institution in the future if it is run well by a good man.' She manifested a broom and handed it to Dawber. 'Go clean house – Mr. Director,' she said.

Dawber looked at the broom in bewilderment. 'Me?' he said incredulously.

'Yes you,' she said firmly. 'You are the one. You have suffered much abuse at the hands of the Agency I know. Who better then, to know what changes must be wrought within its management?'

'I don't think I'm ready for this,' he said.

'No? If you thought you were ready, then you most certainly would not be. You will undoubtedly not make the same mistakes that the last Director made. Mistakes of arrogance and pride.'

'But I *will* make mistakes.' Dawber insisted.

Hecaté laid a hand on his shoulder. 'You have a fortunate habit of making the right decisions, you came here, did you not? Any mistakes you do make will be with the right intentions and, despite what some people think, that counts for a lot. Do not treat people as cattle, as he did, but as equals with more to contribute than their unthinking obedience and you will create a bond of loyalty that will see you through the worst mistakes you could possibly make. For people who love and respect you will forgive you anything and will be there to help you when you stumble. I know you can do that. I see into the very souls of men. You are a good man, with strong principles and a sense of justice. Why do you think Tamar chose you to help her?'

'I've never been in charge, though,' said Dawber. 'I don't know whether I can be a leader. Maybe Ray ...'

'Nothing doing,' said Ray decidedly. 'I'd much rather it was you. I'm happy with my computer. For what it's worth, I reckon you'd make a good leader. You stood up to the Director, didn't you? And people *like* you. *I* don't know you very well, but I've seen you about the place, you always seem to have a little coterie of friends hanging on your every word. Besides, you've got the walk.'

'The walk?' said Dawber puzzled.

'Yeah, you know the long confident stride, head up, shoulders back – the "I can do anything" walk. You get the walk right, and you're halfway there.'

Hecaté laughed. 'Your friend is right,' she said. 'Walk tall and confident – believe in yourself, and you can accomplish miracles.'

'I'll back you up,' said Ray. 'If *she* believes in you, who am I to argue?'

'Good,' said Hecaté. 'Now, we must be off, we have much to do. Jack?'

Stiles gave them the benefit of one of his shark-like grins. 'Wanna see something cool?' he said, slipping on the gauntlet.

The three agency men watched in awe as the gauntlet spread out its glowing tendrils up Stiles's arm and into his nervous system.

'That *is* cool,' gasped Ray. 'Look, his eyes are glowing.'

Dawber nodded. 'Pretty cool,' he agreed distractedly. He was too busy worrying about his new responsibilities.

There was a flash and Stiles and Hecaté vanished. 'Good luck,' the words came sighing over the wind.

'Good luck to you too,' said Dawber to the empty air. He turned to face his new employees. 'Well,' he said, rattling his car keys. 'Let's get on with it then.'

Slick had said nothing throughout the entire exchange; he just stared broodingly into the distance as if he were miles away, in spirit if not in body.

So once again, Finvarra and the boys were left alone in the deserted house.

Time had caught up with itself, and it was as Denny had predicted. Apart from the one file they had altered, it was as if nothing had happened.

* * *

'How, could anyone have missed this thing?' said Stiles in his ordinary voice. The summoning stone was forty feet high and covered in intricate patterns that, according to Hecaté, depicted all the Tuatha, by name and visage. They did not look like anything recognisable to Stiles, but at the back of his mind, Leir knew them all. It was a weird feeling. Whenever he put on the gauntlet, he was, quite literally, in two minds about everything.

He relaxed his own mind and let the consciousness of Leir take over. Stiles would not know a summoning from a stakeout. He supposed, however, that in a way, this was both.

'Who said it had been missed?' said Hecaté.

'Well, it's at least as impressive as Stone-Henge, and *I've* never heard of it.'

'It cannot be seen by mortal eyes.' He answered his own question in a different voice. Then he closed his eyes. 'Enough with the silly questions,' he told himself. 'I must summon my erring brethren. Shall I stand by and allow them to follow evil? They are my people.'

Hecaté faded into the grass.

The stone stood alone on a plain grassy hilltop. Had anyone but the sheep been around to see it, a strange sight would have shortly been witnessed on that exposed spot. First one, then another, then many human figures. Men women, old and young appeared as if from nowhere to gather around the stone. Some appeared in a flash of light, some faded in gently some just appeared to be there, where they had not been a second before.

Witches, wizards, sorcerers, sorceresses, necromancers, spellcasters of all styles and varieties. But all human in origin.

Hecaté stepped into sight. 'Loki is defeated,' she began without preamble. 'I have seen, with my own eyes, him chained hand and foot and thrown down at the feet of Odin in ignoble defeat. Let go your earthly bonds, release these vessels and I will spare you. If not ...' And she seemed to grow, ten, twenty, thirty, forty feet. And a great light shone out from her. Stiles fell backwards and shielded his eyes. He had never seen her do *this* before. 'I will destroy you,' she thundered.

For years, although Stiles had known that technically he was married to a goddess, he had never truly understood what that really meant. Hecaté rarely used her powers even in a small way. She had been diffident and modest. She had shielded the true light of her power, hidden it from the world and him under a skilfully woven cloak of obscurity and shadows.

And, wilfully blind, he had fallen into the trap of regarding her almost as an ordinary woman. He suspected now, that only Tamar had been aware of who and what Hecaté really was.

Knowing something and seeing it – *feeling* it, are quite different things. He realised with a shock that he had never *wanted* to see this. It had always been there had he cared to look. He had accepted the picture of herself that she had shown him and never understood that it was out of her love for him that she had curbed herself. It had been a flawless deception

Now, her power was revealed. Quite literally blazed forth, and he could see it and feel it, he knew he would never see her in quite the same way again.

For one thing, she was utterly terrifying.

The Tuatha clearly thought so too. They quailed and shivered under the blast of her scornful gaze.

'I'll never smoke in the house again,' thought Stiles. A habit that he knew Hecaté deplored, was his fixation on large fragrant cigars. He really wanted one right now – or, failing that, a large scotch.

A collective sigh went up from the assembled Tuatha, and Stiles, with his enhanced sight, could just faintly discern, like faint wisps of smoke, the souls of the Tuatha rising from the bodies of the magical community. They had capitulated.

Hecaté addressed the bewildered former hosts. 'Brothers and sisters,' she said, and as one, they all fell on their knees, not in fear, but in reverence.

'Rise, my beloved ones,' she said, and there was a world of love in her voice, all encompassing and unending love for all her charges, faithful and enduring.

'No wonder they worship her,' Stiles thought. 'They are her children.'

'You have been shamefully abused, my beloved ones,' said Hecaté. 'It shall never happen again.' She pointed to the stone. 'Destroy the stone,' she told them.

She had said she would spare them, but now the Tuatha were betrayed.

The part of Stiles that was Leir knew that the stone was the Tuatha's link to the world, that to destroy it was to destroy them. She had lied to them.

'No, he cried out. 'Have mercy. They are harmless now, mere spirits.'

Hecaté turned cold eyes, not on Stiles, but on Leir, who had been the one to speak. 'No mercy,' she said. 'Did they show mercy to my brothers and sisters?' she asked. 'They will not have the chance to abuse them again.'

And Stiles realised that he was dealing with the goddess not the wife that he knew – *thought* he knew. He looked up into her eyes, cold and unrelenting, yet burning with righteous fury. But they were her eyes, strange and yet familiar. Was this his gentle wife or was it a wrathful goddess? She had shamelessly betrayed her word – had never intended to keep it. It was hard to reconcile this action with the woman he had lived with for – how long now, five years, six? He could not think straight.

She had cleaved to him and lived according to his rules, humanity's rules. But this part of her, the goddess, had no rules. Deities followed no rules. They were supreme, absolute, merciless. He had imposed his values on her, without ever thinking about it, without ever realising that she might have a different set of values. And she had accepted it. But it had never really been who she was.

And he still loved her. Perhaps more than he had ever done. For him, she had done this. Had lived with torn loyalties and a heart divided between her charges and her love for him. Well, no more. If he loved her, and he knew he did, he was going to have to accept her for who she really was. He was not half her equal. He did not deserve her – he never had, and he knew that now.

'But I can try,' he decided.

He fell on his knees before her and bowed his head. Then looked up tentatively into her startled eyes.

'Jack…?' she faltered. And she shrank down to meet him.

'I love you,' he told her. 'Let it be.' And saw her eyes, her familiar eyes, now back on a level with his own, fill with tears.

The stone, under the combined blasts of various magic spells, crumbled and fell with a loud crash, and the witches etc dispersed silently leaving Stiles and Hecaté alone on a barren hilltop among the rubble of a ruined civilisation.

It was, he thought, an appropriate place for a new start.

~ Chapter Twenty Three ~

ALTHOUGH THE defection of Cindy had cast a blight over their victory, Tamar nevertheless decreed that this time, they owed themselves a celebration.

'A party,' she decided. 'A *private* party,' she added. 'You remember what happened last time?'

'But no one knows about it this time anyway,' said Denny.

'Just typical,' she said, 'considering that it was *you* who really saved the day this time.'

'It was *all* of us,' he said. 'Just like always.'

'Still, I reckon you ought to get *something*.'

'I got you didn't I?' what more do I need?'

'Soppy git,' she said.

'And I got a wolf.'

'That thing is not sleeping in the house,' she said. 'I don't care if you *did* save the day,'

'What's up with Jack and Hecaté?' he asked, changing the subject. 'I thought *we* were the newlyweds. They're acting like a couple of teenagers.'

'I think it's cute,' said Tamar. 'I bet I don't moon over *you* like that after six years of marriage.'

'You don't *moon* over me now,' Denny pointed out.

'That's all you know,' she said obscurely.

'Well, you don't.'

'So, a party. What do you think?'

'I think I'll do as I'm told,' said Denny clicking his fingers and sending Fulk obediently into the garden.

* * *

Naturally, Dawber, Slick and Ray were invited back from their restructuring of the Agency for the party.

Ray was his usual loquacious self, but Slick slumped in a corner, drank and drank, and surveyed the room mordantly from under his lids. He never said a word to anyone.

Dawber brought a lovely looking girl who he introduced as Laura. Denny was certain he knew her from somewhere, but he could not quite place her, until she referred to him as the vampire slayer. Then he remembered. She told him that she had been recruited by the agency shortly after he had rescued her. People who had already had a supernatural encounter were prime recruiting material apparently, although it did not always work out.

But how did they know *she had had a supernatural encounter? Unless ...*

But that had been six years ago. It seemed that the Agency had been watching them for a lot longer than they had realised.

'Oh, yeah,' said Dawber through a mouthful of salty cashew nuts, when Denny tasked him about this. 'There are files on you almost from the beginning. But don't worry,' he winked. 'They're "eyes only"' and he pointed to his eyes simultaneously, incidentally, giving himself a distinctly lunatic appearance, in order to illustrate his point. 'Is there any more beer?' he added.

'In the kitchen,' said Denny.

There was a sudden heartrending shriek from the floor above that stopped the party dead. Everyone ran at once to the stairs and were stopped short by Finvarra appearing at the foot of the staircase distraught and shaking, clinging to one of his sons as if he were afraid that someone was about to snatch him away.

'He's gone,' he babbled incoherently. 'Jacky, she must have taken him.'

Tamar's heart sank – *Cindy*. 'When?' she snapped.

'I don't know. He was there last night, but then I went to sleep. I've only just woken. She must have … a spell to make me sleep on, and she took him. I wouldn't leave them but …'

'It's all right. There was nothing you could have done,' Denny soothed him. He turned to Tamar. 'She must have taken him while the house was empty. There was no one here to stop her. We never even thought it was odd that Fin stayed in his room for twenty-four hours. Someone should have checked.'

'Which one did she take?' asked Stiles curiously. 'Her own, or the one she raised in his place?'

'Her own,' said Finvarra.

'Strange,' said Denny. 'Why not just take them both?'

'She always felt closer to the *other* one. She did raise him,' said Tamar in a puzzled tone.

'At least she has left me with *something*,' mourned Finvarra.

'I'm pretty sure that, whatever her reasons were, compassion was not among them,' said Tamar. 'Not now.'

'She didn't *want* the other one,' said Stiles, 'why not?'

'It's cruel to separate them,' wailed Finvarra. 'Why would she do this?'

'*I'm* going to send him to sleep in a minute,' said Tamar callously.

'He's just lost a child,' said Denny. 'Have a heart.'

'We'll get him back for him,' said Tamar. Which was *her* way of showing that she cared.

But the truth was that no one knew how to do this. They had no idea where Cindy was, or how to find out.

'We can put out surveillance for her. We have a good network,' offered Dawber. 'Slick has that department now. Slick …? Hey where is he?'

* * *

Cindy held her son triumphantly. 'We shall change your name,' she told him. 'Something more fitting for the son of an angel. 'From now on, you shall be Ashtoreth. How do you like that?'

'Where's Daddy?' asked Ashtoreth.

'He isn't your *real* daddy,' said Cindy. 'He's just the man who stole you from me. Your real daddy is an angel in heaven. And that other child is not your brother, but an impostor who tried to take your place. But I found you and now we have escaped from these bad people. Oh, I know it's hard to understand, my dear, but I am your mother. You must trust me. I know what's best for you.'

'Yes Mummy,' he said.

There was an ironic slow clapping behind her.

Cindy spun. '*You*?' she said. 'How did you find us?' she pointed an accusatory finger at him.

'Cool your jets,' said Slick holding his hands up as if she had pointed a gun at him. 'I'm alone. The others don't know where you are. And I'm not going to tell them. Nice speech, by the way, the truth?'

'Every word.'

'I thought so. There's an old saying you know. "A truth that's told with bad intent, beats all the lies you can invent".'

Cindy narrowed her eyes. 'What do you want?' she asked.

'Well, it strikes me that we have something in common,' he said.

'I doubt it.'

'Yes we do, I saw it at the wedding. We *both* lost that day.'

Cindy raised an eyebrow. 'That's ancient history,' she said.

'Aw come on. We could play together for a while.' And he made a gesture with his hands that was so like one that Denny made unconsciously all the time that Cindy actually gasped.

She surveyed him for a moment through narrowed eyes. It was remarkable really. With her eyes half closed, he looked just like Denny. The same floppy blond hair, the same slouching stance, the same narrow physique. He was slightly taller but still …

'Don't mind me,' said Slick. 'I'm used to being the substitute.'

'Ashtoreth, run and play, Mummy needs to talk to the man alone,' said Cindy.

Slick smiled.

'What's your real name?' she asked him drawing nearer.

'Why, what does it matter? Would it give you a kick to be the only one I tell?'

'I just want to know.'

'You wouldn't believe me if I told you.'

'I can believe just about anything,' she told him. 'I could *make* you tell me.' She was very close to him now, almost touching.

'It's Denis,'

'Denis? *Denny*? Oh, that's priceless. But I don't believe you.'

'I told you, you wouldn't,' he reminded her.

'Don't talk,' said Cindy. 'Don't talk any more. It's better if you don't talk.' As if to re-enforce her point, she looked at him through half drawn lids

Slick smiled mockingly. Every pleasure must be paid for with an equal amount of pain. Sometimes the pleasure and the pain happen at the same time.

* * *

'Isn't it obvious?' said Hecaté. 'He has gone to her. To Cindy.

'Then, he will bring my son back?' asked Finvarra his voice vibrating with hope.

'I do not think he is coming back,' she said sorrowfully.

'You think she'll kill him?' asked Denny.

'No. I think he has made his choice. Why else would he go to her without telling us first? I only hope he does not live to regret that choice. But I think that he will.'

'We can't be sure that's where he's gone,' said Denny.

'Oh yes we can,' said Tamar. 'Hecaté's right. It *is* obvious.'

'Another one bites the dust,' said Stiles. 'Chalk one up for the bad guys.'

'Cindy's not "bad guys",' objected Denny. 'She's just confused. Although she *is* causing a bit of damage.'

'I think we can count on Cindy doing a lot more damage than this before we catch her,' said Tamar.

* * *

'We *will* find her, won't we?' asked Denny later in their bedroom. The party had broken up, naturally. Dawber and Ray had gone back to the Agency with promises to set a search in motion immediately. Stiles had offered to help. With his police background, he seemed a natural choice to head up the investigation.

'She'll find us first, I think,' said Tamar gloomily.

'Poor Fin,' he said. 'He's really broken up. I think he really loved her too. Some people don't know when they're lucky.'

'Well, I know when *I'm* lucky,' said Tamar bouncing onto the bed beside him.

'Poor Jacky too,' resumed Denny. 'He keeps asking where his brother is. Not that I'm a natural advocate of large families, not after growing up with *my* brother. But some kids need the company. I think it's a shame if he has to grow up on his own.'

Tamar just smiled and stroked her stomach gently. She had a secret.

'Maybe he won't have to,' she said meaningfully.

It took a few moments for this to sink in and then Denny just stared at her in speechless wonder.

'Looks like I've finally shut you up,' she said. 'I mean you're normally such a chatterbox.'

~ Epilogue ~

'PUSH! PUSH!'

'Aaagh!'

'That's it, breathe.'

'Why don't you go and boil something?' Tamar snapped. 'Oh, why does it have to hurt so much?'

'Because you're human now, this is how it happens. I guess there are just some things that no amount of magic can circumvent.'

'Oh, shut up!' Do you have to be so *reasonable*? Would a bit of sympathy kill you? – Ah ah aaagh!'

'Okay, nearly there, and I *do* sympathise, I just don't express it very well. Oh good, Push.'

'I'm not talking to you,' she said. 'Where's Hecaté?'

'She's outside, Jack fainted. Shall I call her?'

'I'm not talking to you,' Tamar repeated petulantly. 'Jack *fainted*? After all the dead bodies *he's* seen. Men!'

Denny was deliberately trying to keep his tone light for her sake, but privately he was in torment. He hated to see her in so much pain. She had not said it, but he had decided – never again.

Hecaté returned to the room. 'Ah, I have not missed it. But ah, I see it. I see the head.'

Tamar screamed.

'Oh, my poor baby,' soothed Hecaté. 'Yes, I remember it does smart a bit, does it not?'

'Just a bit,' said Tamar through gritted teeth.

'Do not worry, after the pain there is the joy. You will see. Very soon if I am not mistaken.'

But for Tamar, a woman who had never suffered real pain in her life, there was joy even in the pain. A new experience, a *real* experience. She felt truly connected to life for the first time.

It did not stop her bitching about it, though.

Hecaté delivered the child while Denny held Tamar's hand tightly.

'A girl,' she said triumphantly. 'A beautiful baby girl.'

'I hope she looks like her mother,' said Denny. 'But of course she will. She can't look like me. Mother Nature wouldn't be that cruel to a girl.'

'She may not look like either of us,' said Tamar. 'This isn't my real face you know.'

'It's been your real face for five thousand years,' said Denny. 'It's your real face all right. And look …' He had taken the baby from Hecaté and was looking at her in wonder. 'She looks just like you.'

Tamar took the baby. 'Apart from her eyes,' she said. 'Those are *your* baby blues. Oh she *is* beautiful.'

'Just like her mother,' said Denny, just about ready to burst with happiness.

'I want to call her Iphigenia,' said Tamar, 'after my mother.'

Denny raised his eyebrows in surprise but said nothing. In all the time he had known her, Tamar had never so much as mentioned that she had ever *had* a mother. Denny had assumed that she had forgotten her long ago. It just went to show, you're never safe from being surprised until you're dead.

'You don't mind do you?' asked Tamar anxiously. 'I know it's unusual and old fashioned but ...'

'I don't mind at all,' Denny assured her. 'I wouldn't mind if you wanted to call her Rocky or Bullwinkle, as long as you're happy.'

'I am,' said Tamar with a sigh.

Denny took his daughter from Tamar's sleepy grasp and went out to the others who were waiting anxiously for news.

In the hall Stiles, now recovered from his faint, was looking sheepish. Finvarra and Jacky, Dawber and Ray were also there, the latter having flown in on a company helicopter. Someone was going to have to fudge the expenses log for that one, but they would not have missed this for a herd of troglodytes.

Denny held up the baby proudly to show them.

'Iphigenia Black, meet the world,' he said.

'World, meet Iphigenia Black.'

THE NEXT TAMAR BLACK BOOK IS...

TAMAR BLACK – Rise of The Nephilim

Tamar and Co. – the Next Generation

Who's that girl?

Meet Iphigenia Black – daughter of Tamar (oh, and er Denny too)

Cindy's back and madder than ever – and she's brought a little surprise with her.
Isn't it amazing how fast they grow up?

Renamed Ashtoreth, son of Cindy has become a powerful threat. Born of a fallen angel and a mortal woman, he is the Nephilim. And Cindy intends to throw him full force at Tamar and Co. – Revenge is sweet.
But Tamar and Denny have a little surprise of their own.

With the power of the Rheingold, Cindy herself has become a formidable enemy. But what will happen when she meets Denny again and realizes that she has not *quite* forsaken love after all?

Also by Nicola Rhodes

SCI 'ON The Shadow Worlds

The first book in the SCI 'ON Trilogy

Whenever a decision is taken that is of significance to the world, the world divides and two alternate futures are created. In the beginning, there was only one world. That world we name SCI 'ON. All other worlds that sprang from it, we name the shadow worlds. Some believe SCI 'ON is the only real world and that all others are mere reflections, hence the name. Others believe that all the alternate worlds are equally real and important – however they may have come into being.

Whatever the case, one thing is certain. If SCI 'ON itself – the cradle of creation– were to be destroyed, all other worlds would cease to exist. For SCI'ON is the mainspring and without it, the shadow worlds would have no point of origin.

Johnny Hammond is not your ordinary computer nerd. He has the makings of a hero. When a mysterious man shows him the way To SCI 'ON, Johnny becomes obsessed. And only he can find a way to get there through the myriad shadow worlds that stand in his way. But someone doesn't want him to get there.

From earliest childhood, Ryan and Kai have been best friends. The fact that they come from separate universes is not allowed to stand in their way.

As they grow up, they realise that this ability to travel between the worlds is no mere coincidence, as their ultimate destiny unfolds.

SCI 'ON II - Legacies

Even his own mother, from the moment he was born, was afraid of Talvas, for she knew whence he had come and wondered what his power would be.

Talvas Firebrand, later known as Talvas de Bellême and "The Destroyer of Worlds" was the son of Toros the fire god. His story and that of the other Undying begins on SCI 'ON back at the beginning.

Watching him from his citadel beyond time is Johnny Hammond, the only man in all creation capable of defeating Talvas and stopping the slaughter of millions.

What will happen when these adversaries finally meet again in a new cycle of time?

About the Author

Nicola Rhodes often can't remember where she lives so she lives inside her own head most of the time, where even if you do get lost, it's still okay.

She has met many interesting people inside her own head and eventually decided to introduce the rest of the world to them, in the hopes that they would stop bothering her and let her sleep.

She has been doing this for ten years now but they still won't leave her alone.

She wrote this book for fun and does not care if you take away a moral lesson from it or not.

You have her full permission to read whatever you wish into this work of fiction. As she says herself:

"Just because I wrote this book, doesn't mean I know anything about it."

www.ingramcontent.com/pod-product-compliance
Lightning Source LLC
Chambersburg PA
CBHW050419260626
47156CB00003B/1080